Praise for
Shelly Fredman's
Brandy Alexander Mysteries

Brandy's self-talk keeps the reader in hysterics, even as she puts it all on the line for people she loves. Her own discomfort with emotional issues promises more Brandy escapades in the future. This reviewer can't wait for the next segment.

--Midwest Book Review

Shelly Fredman's Brandy Alexander Series are fast-paced, gripping mysteries... Thank goodness she's a fictitious character and a tough Philly chick to boot; she'd be dead otherwise. If she were still living in California, she could compare bruises with Sue Grafton's Kinsey Millhone.

--Rambles.NET

Author Shelly Fredman continues her Brandy Alexander series with a topnotch sophomore effort. Fast paced fun, in-your-face Philly attitude and mayhem ensue.

--Mid Columbia Library System

An excellent fast-paced entertaining book you'll find a challenge to stop reading until the last page is finished.

--Skye Lindborg - Mystery Lovers Corner

Other books in the
Brandy Alexander Mystery Series

No Such Thing as a Secret
No Such Thing as a Good Blind Date
No Such Thing as a Free Lunch

No Such Thing As A
Free Ride

A Brandy Alexander
Mystery

Shelly Fredman

Shelly Fredman

AK

Aquinas & Krone Publishing, LLC

First published by Aquinas & Krone Publishing, LLC 2/14/2010

ISBN #: 978-0-9843526-2-3

This book is printed on acid-free paper.

Cover design by Tim Litostansky.

Part of the proceeds from this book will be donated to charity.

Acknowledgments

I would like to express my love and appreciation to the following people:
Corey Fetzer, Dudley Fetzer and Kris Zuercher for their infinite patience, emotional support and creative input; Bill Fordes and Jerry Fest for allowing me to call upon their expertise in matters pertaining to this story and for refocusing me when I saw a squirrel; Audrey Matisa for her generosity in sharing her time and talent and for working so hard to help make my dream a reality; Julie Dolcemaschio for helping me wade through sticky plot points and for being my Saturday morning breakfast buddy; and Franny Fredman for remaining my biggest fan.

Special thanks to:
Tim Litostansky for his fantastic cover design, and to Natasha Adamski, Jill Dearden, Joanna Banks-Morgan, Suzanne Dunham and Jude Brandt (We miss you, Jude) for setting up fan sites and spreading the word about the Brandy Alexander Series.
To Janet Kirer and Anna Harp, I so appreciate all your hard work; Bruce Gram, Marty Schatz and Renee Greidinger, thank you for your unfailing support and friendship. A special shout-out to the wonderful people in our Brandy Alexander Yahoo group. I am so happy to count you among my friends. Thank you all for being Brandy's cheerleader out in the reading community!

To: Judy and Andrew West, the heart and soul of Aquinas & Krone Publishing, I am eternally in your debt.
AND: to author Judith Kristen, your friendship has been a godsend, and your eternal optimism an inspiration.
BEATLES FOREVER, Jude!

For Jerry Fest

The unexamined life is not worth living.—Socrates
Get over yourself.—Brandy Alexander

Prologue

My name is Brandy Alexander and I have just flunked Psychology 101. Not the college course, the *life* course. More specifically, *my* life course. I'd been seeing a therapist once a week for a little over two months (apparently I have "issues" stemming from some scary stuff that's happened to me lately) but it didn't seem to be going anywhere.

Now I'm willing to admit I may have been a tad resistant to the whole idea of talking to a stranger about my deepest fears. Okay, maybe more than a tad. But still, it kind of hurt my feelings when Dr. Sullivan asked me not to come back.

Oh, she was nice about it and all. I mean she didn't exactly ban me from the building. She just suggested that perhaps I wasn't quite ready to commit to digging deep into the bowels of my psyche. Wow, I was just hoping to learn how to sleep without a nightlight.

"But everyone will be so disappointed in me," I told her, thinking of my best friends, Johnny Marchiano and the DiAngelo twins, Fran and Janine. (Just because a couple of people have tried to kill me on three separate occasions within the past few months, they thought I needed professional counseling. Sheesh, what worry

1

warts.) "Can't you give me some sort of Graduation Certificate or at least a note saying I'm not as crazy as they think I am?"

"Brandy," Dr. Sullivan said, as I stared down at her Birkenstock sandals and "ethnic" jewelry, the wearing of which, I'm convinced, are pre-requisites to becoming a certified head shrinker, "therapy isn't for everyone. Granted," she added, "it *is for most peop*le," the implication being that somehow I wasn't normal, which was why I *thought* I was there in the first place.

Dr. Sullivan smiled. "Your anxiety is understandable given the things you've been involved with lately. Having gotten to know you these past few months, I have every faith that you will continue to put yourself in jeopardy without giving it a second thought, if it means helping someone who needs you. I suggest you put therapy on hold and invest in a really good self defense course." She stood, signaling both the end of the session and my foray into self-enlightenment. To tell you the truth, I was relieved.

Chapter One

Contrary to popular belief, the fastest way to a man's heart is not through his stomach or even his genitalia. The way to truly earn a guy's devotion is to buy him a hot new car.

I was standing on the curb outside my brother Paul's South Philly apartment, holding the keys to a fully restored 1972, black Alpha Romeo Spider. I'd bought it off a guy named Ditto, who, miraculously had agreed to an installment plan, as I'm a little short on cash. Ditto even offered to throw in a couple of dates "to sweeten the deal," but I told him he was far too generous as it was and I respectfully declined.

Paul stood beside me now, blindfolded and cranky in the June heat, little beads of sweat dripping off his nose and onto his mustache. My brother's got an 80s' retro look going. *He* thinks his mustache looks cool. *I* think he has a man-crush on Magnum P.I.

"Okay, Paulie, you can take off the blindfold."

Paul whistled. "Nice set of wheels, Sis."

"It's for you."

"What? W-w-what?" Paul is adorable, smart and sweet, but even without the remains of a childhood stutter he's not always the most scintillating conversationalist.

3

"I got it for you," I explained. "Look, I owe you a bar mitzvah present and I did sort of total your Mercedes. Just take it, okay?" I told him, handing him the keys.

"B-but, you can't afford this," he said, climbing into the driver's seat. "And besides, what are you going to drive? You said every time you get behind the wheel of mom's old Le Sabre, it makes you crave Barry Manilow music."

"Nick loaned me his truck while he's away." On Paul's skeptical look I shrugged. "It's a free ride."

Paul dove deep into big brother mode. "There's no such thing as a free ride, Bran. Nicholas Santiago is dangerous. Sooner or later it's gonna cost you."

I would've said, "It already has—my heart," but that was *waaay* too corny. Instead, I said, "You've been talking to DiCarlo, haven't you?"

Robert Anthony DiCarlo, Irish-Italian stud and former boyfriend was currently employed as a plainclothes homicide detective with the Philadelphia Police Department. We didn't see eye to eye on the subject of Nick Santiago, sinner, saint, and all around chick magnet.

Paul did an exasperated sigh. "So how's therapy going?" he asked.

"Great! I passed with flying colors. Doctor Sullivan says I'm her best patient *ever!* I am the poster girl for sane living."

"You quit going, right?"

"Something like that," I said. "Listen, I've got to run. I'm late for class."

Last week I'd signed up for boxing lessons at my Uncle Frankie's gym. I'd told everyone it was in preparation for my upcoming bout with a wallaby at a petting zoo out in Pottstown. (I'm a puff piece reporter for a local news station and this was one of the many truly ridiculous stunts I perform to entertain viewers between "traffic on the Betsy Ross" and "weather on the nines.")

The truth is I'd really taken to heart what Dr. Sullivan said when she gave me my walking papers. I have a slight tendency to act on impulse, which has gotten me in a little over my head with some pretty creepy characters. So far I've managed to survive on luck and instinct, but I figured it wouldn't hurt to add something tangible, like a roundhouse to my repertoire.

My cell phone rang just as I pulled into a staff-only parking spot at the South Street Gym. Being the manager's niece has some perks. I climbed out of the granny-mobile (my pet name for the Le Sabre) and checked caller I.D. It was Franny.

I love Fran to pieces, but frankly, she's been a little scary lately. Fran is eight and a half months pregnant, and her hormonal mood swings could be the subject for the next Stephen King novel. I put on my "happy voice" and said hello.

"Eddie wants to name the baby, 'Caesar'," she said in a tone that told me she didn't exactly embrace the idea.

"And?"

"And I'm not naming my kid after a salad dressing. Besides, I just know I'm having a girl. *A mother knows these things.*"

I gave myself points for not gagging and grunted something non-committal.

"Oh, before I forget," she continued, "My mom wants to talk to you about the baby shower. She figured since you're my best friend you'd want to help her organize it."

The baby shower. Damn, I'd forgotten. An entire afternoon devoted to playing those dopey games like "Find the Dirty Diaper" and "Guess the Baby Mush."

"Um, yeah, about that. I'd love to Franny. I really would. Only wouldn't it be better if she asked Janine instead? Your mom has never exactly been my biggest fan." All through high school Mrs. DiAngelo referred to me as *"the bad influence,"* until, after one particularly unfortunate incident involving the vice principal and a water balloon, when she upgraded me to "that damn Alexander kid."

"If you don't want to, Bran, just say so."

Oh, jeez. This never would have been an issue with the old Franny. The old Franny would have made fun of any attempts to organize such a traditional, sexist party. But impending motherhood does funny things to the female brain. *And not in a good way.*

"I'll call your mom tonight, hon. Man, I am totally looking forward to this."

And on that happy note we hung up. I hiked my gym bag over my shoulder and entered the building.

Uncle Frankie is twelve years my senior and up until I discovered, at the tender of fourteen, the charms of Bobby DiCarlo, I considered him to be the handsomest man on the planet. At forty, Frankie still manages to turn heads, which is why the South Street Boxing Gym is popular with the ladies.

I have always felt that my uncle (who had a few missteps along the way to becoming a productive member of society) and I were kindred spirits. The guy just "gets" me.

I found him at the back of the gym, standing in the doorway that leads to the rear parking lot. The lot was cordoned off. A two-inch thick blue mat covered a twenty by twenty area of the asphalt, where a martial arts class was in progress.

A group of teenage girls, dressed in various forms of workout attire, watched as the instructor, his back to me, demonstrated moves.

One girl, small and blond with multiple piercings hung back against the gate, taking in the instruction with complete focus. She was dressed all in black—not the best choice for a sultry summer afternoon, but who am I to judge people on their fashion sense? My entire off-camera wardrobe consists of jeans and tee shirts.

I walked toward Frankie and waved. He waved back at me and cut across the room to greet me.

"Yo, midget brat," he said, settling his arm across my shoulders. "C'mere for a minute. I want you to meet somebody."

The instructor glanced our way as we approached. I recognized him and my jaw dropped. Tall, dark and muscular, with Chanel 6006 sunglasses resting on top of his head, Alphonso Jackson looked every inch the badass operator he was.

I'd first met Alphonso a few months ago. He rides shotgun for Santiago, and he's bailed me out of a jam or two at Nick's request. Alphonso really likes me. I can tell by the way he pretends I'm a pain in his behind.

He sauntered over to us and grinned, settling his shades over his eyes. "You'd better run while you can, bro," he advised Frankie. "She may not look it, but this one is trouble."

"Tell me something I don't know," Frankie laughed. "She's my niece."

"Ooh, my condolences."

"Uh, fellas, if you can't say something nice…" I interjected, "can you at least wait until I've left the room?"

I was surprised to find Alphonso teaching a class at the gym, especially since Nick owns a martial arts studio on Spring Garden. Turns out my uncle and Alphonso have been friends for years. They met at what my mom used to refer to as a "social club" (when Paul and I were within earshot) but in actuality was "The Clink."

"Your uncle asked me to do him a favor," Alphonso told me. He's one of those civic minded do-gooders."

Well, at least one of them learned the error of his ways. The jury's still out on Alphonso.

Although the gym is technically for boxing, Frankie's "significant other," Carla, talked him into offering a free self defense class geared toward local teenage girls. She said she thought it was important for them to know how to take care of themselves, and, judging by the hormonal gymnastics of local teenage *boys*, it seemed like a good idea.

I went off to spar with a kid from the neighborhood named Jimmy the Rat, an unfortunate moniker he picked up last year after he dropped a doughnut down the sewer, fished it out and ate it. I wasn't really crazy about sparring with Jimmy, but there aren't many boxers out there who're short enough for me to pair up with. I'm five feet two if tip toes count.

Alphonso was just finishing up his class when I got through. I was sweaty, slightly smelly and my hair, mouse brown and poker straight on a good day looked like I'd tangled with an electrical outlet and lost. He took the opportunity to comment on how nice I looked. I just prayed he didn't snap a picture on his cell phone to send to Nick, wherever the hell that was.

Nick took off for parts unknown, about three months ago, under mysterious circumstances. As virtually everything about Nick is a mystery, it shouldn't have come as a surprise. What did surprise me is how much it hurt. How much it still did.

The girl in black was just leaving. I looked over at her and smiled. She slid her eyes downward and took off, a grimy backpack hanging from her shoulder. As she turned, I caught a glimpse of a tattoo nestled under her left ear. I think it was some sort of bird. It was hard to tell, as it looked like it had been drawn by a singularly untalented six-year old.

Frankie came up next to me and caught me staring at her. "She's been to every class," he said, "but she never gets any closer than the gate. I tried to talk to her once and she told me to 'fuck off.' Nice, huh?"

I laughed. "Well, what did you say to her?"

My uncle shrugged. "Oh, I don't know. Something really offensive like, 'The class is free and you're welcome to join in.'"

"Maybe she was just having a bad day." I stared at her retreating back. By the looks of her, I bet she'd had a lot of them.

Alphonso walked me to my car. "How come you're not using Nick's truck?" he asked.

"I told you when you dropped it off, I don't need it. I've got a perfectly good set of wheels right here." I patted the hood for emphasis and the side view mirror fell off. *Crap.*

I caught the mirror before it hit the asphalt and stuffed it into my pocketbook. "So, how is Nick, anyway? Where'd you say he was again?"

"I didn't." Alphonso grinned.

I sighed and he cut me a look that bordered on pity.

"You're jonesin' for him, Alexander."

"I am not!" *Oh god, I so am!*

Alphonso peered at me over the tops of his sunglasses and shook his head. "Whatever you say, chica."

Unhh!

Having worked out at the gym for an hour—okay, technically, it was only forty minutes, the last twenty were spent faking an ankle injury to get out of doing "reps"—I decided I deserved a treat, so I stopped at the Acme on the way home and picked up a couple of pints of Ben & Jerry's Chocolate Fudge Brownie. I guess I could've bought just one, but they were on sale, and I figured it would have been fiscally irresponsible of me not to take advantage of a bargain. As an American, I feel it's my duty to stimulate the economy.

I got home just in time to grab the only available parking space on my street. My house is the last one on a block of rowhomes built in the '50's. I live in a mostly Italian neighborhood where kids grow up being able to spell the word "macaroni" before they can utter "mama."

My mother was born and raised in South Philly in a Roman Catholic household. My Jewish father grew up a few blocks away. They met one Yom Kippur when my dad sneaked out of my Bubbie Heiki's house to stuff his face at a local bakery. My mom was there buying dessert for her family's dinner that evening and they met over the cannoli counter. The rest, as they say, is history.

My octogenarian neighbor, Mrs. Gentile, was waiting for me on the porch as I got out of the car with the ice cream. She had just finished hanging a moth-eaten five-foot wide American flag from her front door. Smaller flags graced either side of her azalea bush. That was going to pose a problem for my dog, Adrian, who liked to pee there when Mrs. Gentile wasn't looking.

Philadelphians are big on ornamental holiday displays. Valentine's Day is greeted with the same fanfare as Christmas or Halloween. My neighbor considers it a mortal sin (or at the very least an affront to the neighborhood) not to participate in the festivities. I felt a fight coming on, as I had not yet decorated my side of the porch with the requisite Fourth of July adornments.

"Hey. Girlie." It's a little game we play. Mrs. Gentile acts like she's forgotten my name and I pretend I don't want to push her down the porch steps.

I sighed deeply and smiled. "Nice to see you, Mrs. Gentile." I held out the ice cream to illustrate the terrible rush I was in to get it into the house before it melted, only Mrs. Gentile thought I was offering it to her and she made a grab for it. I wasn't quick enough and she latched on for dear life.

"I prefer pistachio," she grunted, and before I could think of a snarky response, she turned and walked back into the house taking Ben and Jerry with her. *Unhh!*

I hopped back into the car and drove down to the 7-Eleven. They were out of everything except Drumsticks and, while I'm not all that picky, I do have *some* standards. I ended up driving practically into town before I could find another two for one special.

On the way back to my car, I spied a large group of teenagers hanging out in the parking lot. They ranged in age from about fourteen to twenty, mostly boys, with a smattering of girls, all with enough metal facial piercings to shut down an airport. They all had backpacks, jammed full of unimagined crap. One girl carried a pit bull puppy in her arms. They were loud and obnoxious, hassling people for spare change as they went into the store.

A few people stopped and dug into their pockets for change. Most got that fixed stare in their eyes, acting as if the teens were invisible, and kept on walking.

Pretty soon the store manager came out and yelled at the kids to "get the hell out of there," but I guess they didn't *want* to get the hell out of there, because no one made a move to leave. Well, no one except the manager, who apparently had anger control issues. He disappeared back into the store, returning thirty seconds later with a .38 caliber pistol and a mouthful of curse words that would make a drunken sailor blush.

My first instincts were to "get the hell out of there" myself, reasoning that this was a good time to learn to stop sticking my nose into other people's business. But I seldom listen to reason—one of my many imperfections. I punched in 911 on my cell phone and then headed back toward the manager.

"Hi there," I said, ignoring the gun he held tightly in his hand. "Do you have any TastyKakes? I didn't see any on the shelves."

"I just got a new shipment. Haven't had time to restock yet. Look, I'm a little busy here." He waved the gun in the air in case I missed it the first time around.

I looked over at the teenagers and sighed. "Y'know, guys, this man is just trying to run a business, and I'm sure getting shot wasn't on your agenda today. How about you just…go?"

"This is public property," challenged a tall kid in leather. "We're the public. We have every right to be here. You got any spare change?" he added.

I probably shouldn't have laughed, but it was funny. I slipped my hand in my pocket, extracted a buck and handed it to him. "Listen, the cops will be here any minute. Why not save yourselves some trouble and just leave before someone gets hurt."

A blond haired girl came up behind Leather Boy and began tugging on his sleeve. She looked younger than the others, pale and vulnerable. I knew her. It was the girl from the gym.

"Let's go," she whispered.

A cop car pulled into the parking lot and two officers got out, one in uniform, the other dressed in faded jeans and a tee shirt. The one in full cop attire was Mike Mahoe, a six-foot four-inch transplanted Hawaiian with an easy smile and congenial disposition. He headed toward the manager while the other one hung back, eyeing me and doing a slow shake of his beautiful, Black Irish-Italian head.

"Why am I not surprised to see you here?" he muttered, and since it was rhetorical I didn't bother to explain.

"Yo, nice to see you too, DiCarlo. By the way, I was the one who called 911. I should at least get some credit for that."

Bobby's face broke out in a slow grin. "Well, *that is* an improvement. It's good to hear you're using some common sense for a change."

I smiled back. "I think I've exercised a great deal of common sense lately. I dumped your sorry butt, didn't I?" Well, *technically*, he dumped mine, but that was ages ago.

Recently, we'd had a reunion, of sorts, but we both realized that the timing or whatever wasn't right and we agreed to keep it strictly platonic, at least until the dust settled in our mutually crazy lives. That didn't mean we stopped caring about each other though. I loved Bobby. I always would. And I knew in my heart he felt the same way about me.

"So what started all of this?" DiCarlo asked, jerking his head sideways as the manager handed his gun to Mike. Slowly, the teens began to disperse.

I filled him in, looking over at the small blond girl. She caught me staring at her and quickly moved away.

"Bobby, those kids seem so… I don't know… lost. Are they homeless?" Philly has more than its fair share of runaway youth. Some are locals, but a lot of them end up here from various places like small farm communities in the Midwest. Coming from a loving if somewhat neurotic family, I couldn't conceive of anyone choosing the streets over a home with three square meals a day and a roof over their heads.

Bobby frowned and I could feel his concern. Maybe he was thinking of his own little girl, a sweet little two-year old named Sophia. "I'd say most of them. A few might be weekend warriors—y'know, posers who like to hang with the really hardcore street kids." He rubbed his hands roughly over his face. DiCarlo had seen too many of these kids face down in the gutter, victims of abuse and neglect.

"Well, why don't the cops pick them up and find foster homes for them? Or at least take them to the shelters. Isn't there one on Callowhill Street?"

Bobby grinned again, only this time there was no mirth behind his eyes. "You're asking for simple answers to complicated questions, Sweetheart. I wish it were that easy."

On the ride back to my house I thought about what Bobby had said. *Why wasn't it that easy? Some of those kids were mere babies. Surely, they'd be better off back with their families or in foster care than out on the streets. How bad must their home lives be to choose a dumpster over their own beds? The thought stuck in my brain and wouldn't let go.*

When I got home, I headed into the kitchen to grab something to eat and found my kitten, Rocky, sitting on top of the counter, swiping tomatoes off the window ledge. She looked up when she saw me, gave me the once-over as only a feline can and knocked another tomato onto the floor. It landed with a splat. My dog, Adrian, a twenty-pound furball with a water fountain tail, appeared out of nowhere and began lapping up the tomato goop. I thought about stopping him, but then I'd have to clean it up myself.

Well, now that all the tomatoes were gone, I guessed I didn't have to make a salad with my dinner. I'm trying to eat healthier these days, only all the stuff I really like comes wrapped in foil with the word Hershey imprinted on it. Self-improvement is hard work. It involves a lot of exercise and denial and... leafy greens.

My mother called while I was eating. She and my dad live in Florida, and ever since she discovered the joys of "rollover minutes," she's been burning up the airwaves with free long distance calling.

"I'm worried about you," she announced, my mother's signature way of saying hello.

"Why are you worried? I'm fine." *My* signature way of saying, "Hi back at'cha."

My mother exhaled a long-suffering sigh. "Brandy, it's a Saturday night and most single women your age are out on dates. Doesn't Janine know any nice unattached men she can hook you up with?"

I assumed she meant the 1960's version of the term "hooking up" and not the X-rated one of the new millennium. Either way, Janine didn't know any nice men, *period*.

"Mom, I'd love to talk now, but I'm right in the middle of cooking dinner."

"You're cooking?" she asked, not bothering to hide the skepticism in her voice.

"*Yes, I'm cooking.* As a matter of fact, I made a lovely meal. Roasted chicken, baby new potatoes, steamed asparagus and peach cobbler for dessert." Okay, that was a lie. I nuked a Lean Cuisine.

"Listen, Mom, Paul is thinking about signing up for "J Date." He's dying to talk to you about it. You should give him a call." (I know. I'm a terrible sister. Even buying him a car won't square me away on this one.)

My mother pondered this a moment. Isn't that a Jewish dating service?" Devout Catholic, Lorraine Alexander was nonetheless thrilled to hear that at least one of her children wouldn't die alone. She hung up on me and called Paul.

Fran sat on the floor and leaned forward. Her feet were planted on the ground, legs spread, knees up. I sat behind her, supporting her considerable weight. Swelled beyond all reasonable proportion, Fran's normally slender five-foot nine-inch body looked like she'd swallowed a zeppelin. I held her steady while she exhaled.

The Lamaze instructor, a serene, soft spoken woman in her early thirties walked around the room bestowing smiles of encouragement upon poor, unsuspecting mothers- to-be. I counted the breaths between imagined contractions and sighed. "Are you sure you want to go 'natural,' Fran? My mom tells me it really hurts."

The instructor cut me a dirty look and patted Fran on the shoulder.

Fran grunted as she struggled to turn and look at me. "Brandy, I want my baby to come into this world knowing her mother suffered horribly for her, so that I can throw it back in her face when she's an adolescent and she's going through those obnoxious teen years." The ever-efficient Franny, always planning ahead.

"Do you know what really pisses me off?" she added, and being on a roll she didn't bother to wait for a response. "While I'm here, spending my Sunday afternoon preparing to bring precious life into the world, where's my husband? Off having a great time camping with his buddies!"

"Uh, Fran, Eddie's in the Reserves. I don't think—"

She cut me off. "How much did your mom say it hurts?"

"Well, it's been twenty-eight years and she's still talking about it."

Fran pondered this. "I'm hungry," she said at last. "Let's go get pancakes."

"Fine by me," I shrugged. I stood and helped her to her feet. "Um, we'll be right back," I told the instructor.

"No, we won't." Franny interjected. "I'm getting an epidural and don't anyone try and stop me." We left amid a chorus of "Take me with you's," punctuated by an "Amen to that, sistah!"

I drove us over to the IHOP, but Franny couldn't fit in the booth, so we ordered the breakfast special "to go" and scarfed our food down in the car. In an effort to eat healthy, I'd traded in my hash browns for fruit and then picked the crispy ones out of Franny's container.

"I love breakfast food," Franny announced, stuffing a strip of bacon into her mouth.

"Me too," I agreed. "That's what's so great about being an adult. We can eat pancakes for dinner and our mothers can't tell us not to."

"Bran," Fran said, suddenly, a note of panic in her voice. "What if after the baby comes, I turn into my mother?"

"What do you mean?"

"Don't get me wrong, Bran. I love my mom. But I can't help but think that she was once young and fun, and then she had me and Janine and suddenly she became this thoroughly responsible person who would never dream of allowing her kids to eat pancakes at eight o'clock at night. Is that going to happen to me too?"

"Franny, stop worrying. You're going to make a wonderful mom."

Fran eyed me seriously. Well, as seriously as she could with maple syrup dribbling down her chin. "How do you know, Bran? Eddie and I didn't plan this pregnancy. What if I totally screw it up and my kid ends up hating me?"

"That's never going to happen, Franny." But as the words came out of my mouth I flashed on the teens at the 7-Eleven. Had their parents worried about this too?

I dropped Fran off at Eddie's mom's house and headed over to Carla's beauty salon. I'd gotten gum stuck in my hair earlier in the day, and I was hoping Carla had some magic formula to remove it without taking half my scalp with it.

The salon is located on Ritner, next door to a funeral parlor. Upon occasion, Mr. Kang, the funeral director will ask Carla to pinch hit for their hairdresser. Carla says it always makes her queasy, but just because you're dead doesn't mean you shouldn't still look your best.

Cars were already parked two-deep in front of the salon, so I'd pulled the La Sabre around back and left it alongside a chain link fence. Trash, blown by the wind, clung to the fence like prisoners attempting a jailbreak, reminding me that I wasn't exactly in the classiest part of town.

It was almost closing time. I could see Carla's retro-do beehive silhouetted in the window as she pulled down the shades. I knocked softly and called her name.

"Hey, hon," she called out, opening the door for me. "What brings you here?"

I pointed to the wad of gum. "Can you get it out?"

Carla's magic formula turned out to be an ice cube. She rubbed it on my head and five minutes later I was Juicy Fruit free.

"Oh, thank you, Carla.

"No problem. Listen, hon, I'm glad you stopped by. I heard something the other day I thought you should know." She tapped an inch long hot pink nail against her front tooth and expelled a reluctant breath. "Bobby had a date last night."

"*My* Bobby?" I squeaked. "I mean, *our* Bobby?" Alright, I knew he couldn't stay celibate forever. Just because things didn't work out between us, didn't mean he was through with romance. "So, who is she?" I asked, and hoped those were the words that came out of my mouth instead of, "I hate the bitch, whoever she is."

"Are you sure you want to know?"

I nodded, not sure at all.

"Tina Delvechione."

"I hate that bitch!" *Unhh.* "What I meant was I'm very happy for them."

"Honey, it was only one date, and anyway, John says you've been pining after Nick Santiago for the past three months."

So? I'm an equal opportunity piner.

"I know it doesn't make any sense, Carla."

Carla hugged me to her. "It makes all the sense in the world, Sweetie. Bobby was your first love. The first is pretty special."

Carla was right, I reasoned. It was natural to feel a little bit jealous. Only—Tina Delvechione? Puhleeze! She's been trying to get her meat hooks into DiCarlo since high school. It may have been just one date, like Carla said, but who knew where it could lead? By the time I left Carla's, I had Bobby and Tina married with children. Well, I hope they're not holding their breath for a wedding present.

I walked back to the car armed with a mini flashlight and a can of pepper spray—my constant companions when traveling alone after dark. Following the thin blue light, I groped the chain-link fence as I maneuvered around piles of urban rubble.

I reached my car, put the key in the lock and listened while a cat mewed softly in the distance. A trash can toppled over with a reverberating clang and I jumped a mile. And then the crying grew louder, more guttural, more *human*, and I froze, fear beating a pathway to my heart. I ripped open the car door and locked myself safely inside.

"It's only a cat," I breathed, cursing myself for letting my imagination run wild. I turned on the engine and hit the high beams, squinting as my eyes adjusted to the light. Then I glanced over my shoulder to bust a u-ey, looked back and slammed on the brakes as a young, teenage girl staggered toward the car and collapsed in a crumpled heap on the asphalt.

Chapter Two

It looked like she'd been shot. Blood seeped from her lower extremities, forming a deep red stain on the ground where she fell. A split second passed while I contemplated backing up the car and beating it the hell out of there. *What if she had been shot? What if the shooter was still lurking about? What are the odds of anyone believing me when I tell them I didn't go looking for trouble, but, per usual, it found me?* Whatever, I couldn't turn my back on her. My conscience simply wouldn't allow it. Damn conscience.

I scrambled into the back seat to retrieve the first aid kit my mom bought for the car some eighteen years ago, when the Le Sabre was brand new. Then I grabbed my phone out of my pocketbook and punched in 911 and awaited instructions.

Leaning down next to the girl, I brushed her hair to the side and pressed two fingers against her neck. Her pulse was rapid, but at least she was still alive. Gently, I turned her over. I couldn't see any visible wounds on her abdomen, yet blood continued to leak from her in an ever-widening circle. *Where was the damn ambulance?*

The girl moaned softly and clutched her belly. "I hurt," she whimpered.

I took her hand in mine and, with my other hand, smoothed back the hair from her forehead. She was drenched in sweat and shivering profusely. I was pretty sure she was in shock. As I looked around for something to cover her with, the ambulance pulled up and Tony Blue jumped out. Tony and I went to high school together. He's an EMT now, taking pre-med classes, part time. Tony and his partner pulled the gurney off the truck.

"That you, Alexander?"

"Yeah, Tony," I said, relieved. Now that the professionals were here, I was free to go home and have my own private freak-out. I looked down at the frightened girl, her face pale as the moon. "Tony's a good guy," I said. "You're gonna be just fine."

I began to disengage my hand, but she tightened her grip. "Don't leave me," she cried.

"Don't leave me!" She struggled to rise and a spasm of pain ripped through her.

Tony leaned close to me and spoke softly. "It would help keep her calm if you'd ride in the ambulance with her," he told me.

I nodded and looked down at the girl. "Of course I won't leave you," I told her. I didn't even know her name.

Tony asked me to wait while they ushered the girl into an empty cubicle. I sat sandwiched between a twenty-year-old male who had accidentally shot himself in the foot while chasing down a rival gang member, and an elderly woman whose niece had brought her in after she had mistaken some mini decorative soaps for Petit Fours and ate them. The old lady didn't seem to mind that she was burping up bubbles. She just sat there, smiling serenely through swollen, allergic lips.

While I was waiting I called John and asked him to take Adrian out for a walk. I caught him just as he was leaving "Lucinda's on South," an art gallery that features his portrait photography.

"No problem, Sunshine," he told me. "I'll swing by your place on the way home. Are you still at work?"

"Yes," I said, a little too quickly. I've known John since I was four. He always knows when I'm lying.

"Yeah, sure you are," he said. "Where are you really?"

I heaved a big sigh and told him.

"So, let me get this straight," he said when I finished. "One minute you're a fugitive on the run from Lamaze class and the next you're speeding down Broad Street in the back of an ambulance with a kid you'd never seen before in your life."

"Yeah, pretty much." I figured I'd leave out the part about getting gum stuck in my hair as it was strictly "need to know."

"Listen, do you want me to come down there and keep you company?"

"Thanks for the offer but I'm fine." I glanced up and a large pretty woman in blue rounded the corner and began walking toward me.

"I've gotta go," I told him. "Tell Adrian I'll be home soon." I hung up before he could make fun of me for thinking the dog understands—*which he totally does.* Then I stood and greeted Dr. Martine Sanchez.

Dr. Sanchez and I have gotten to know each other fairly well over the past several months. Seems my penchant for disaster corresponds perfectly with her rotation on the duty roster. She stopped in front of me and shook her head in mock disapproval. I could tell by

24

the dark circles under her eyes that it had been a long night, and it wasn't over yet.

"Do you have stock in this hospital?" she teased. "Is that why you can't stay away?"

"Hey," I joked back, "at least this time I wasn't wheeled in on a gurney."

"Well, I'm glad to see you're staying out of trouble." *(Sheesh, does everybody think I go looking for it?)* "But if you're here to report on the quints that were born tonight, you've got the wrong hospital. They're over at Einstein."

"Actually, I'm here about a teenage girl who was brought in about forty-five minutes ago. She's white, long brown hair, pretty."

"Are you a relative?"

"Um…yes?"

Dr. Sanchez rolled her eyes heavenward. I don't know why I bother lying anymore. I've totally lost my touch.

"Okay," I admitted. "I'm not exactly a relative. But I do feel responsible for her. I was the one who brought her in."

"What can you tell me about her?" she asked.

"Not much. I found her and called 911. She was really scared, so I rode along with her in the ambulance. Who is she?"

"We don't know," Dr. Sanchez told me, her mouth forming a slight frown. "She's running a high fever and drifting in and out of consciousness. She had no I.D. on her. I suspect she's a runaway."

"What makes you think that?"

"All the signs point to it. Even in her weakened condition, she was defiant, giving evasive answers to straightforward questions – we couldn't get her to tell us her real name. Then there's this little homemade tattoo on her ankle. A lot of street kids that wind up here sport those." She sighed.

"What happened to her?" I asked. "Why was she bleeding?"

Dr. Sanchez shook her head. "Miscarriage—or botched abortion. She's developed an infection. It's a blessing you found her when you did."

"Can I see her?"

"May I ask why?"

I didn't know why and for once I was at a loss for words.

"Mija, I've been following your career ever since the first time you ended up in the emergency room, and I know your heart's in the right place. But I'm very protective of my patients. These kids are exploited enough, so if your boss is looking for a quick ratings boost for your station during Sweeps Week—"

When I answered there was a hitch in my voice that I didn't expect. I must've been getting a cold. "I just thought she could use a friend."

"Follow me."

It was after midnight by the time I got home from the hospital. The girl had fallen into a fitful sleep, her slight hands clasped in prayer, an I.V. needle protruding from one thin vein. She was draped in a sheet, her right foot sticking out at an angle, and I caught a glimpse of the amateur etching on her ankle. It took me a moment to realize it was almost an exact replica of the girl's at the gym.

They were waiting to move her, either to I.C.U. or the morgue, depending on how well she responded to the meds. Dr. Sanchez was cautiously optimistic.

I left the cubicle, thought briefly about going home and decided to hang around a little while longer. The guy who'd shot himself in the foot was just leaving, supported by a pair of crutches and two uniformed cops. I didn't see the woman who'd eaten soap. I assumed she'd gotten a *clean* bill of health. (Sometimes I crack myself up.) At 11:00 p.m. a nurse came out to tell me the girl's condition had stabilized. She wasn't out of the woods yet, but it looked promising. I said a silent goodbye to the girl with no name and headed home.

By 7:00 a.m. it was 82 degrees outside with 100% humidity. I woke up swimming in sweat, my air conditioner having given up the ghost in the middle of the night. Even the rain seemed to be suffering from heat exhaustion. It fell in languid plops, steaming up the bedroom windows.

I wasn't scheduled to work today, so I rolled over onto my back and tried to recapture the dream I'd been having—something about a six-foot tall chimpanzee wearing a business suit and smoking a bubble gum cigar. He spoke English with a Brooklyn accent and was just about to ask me out when my phone rang, waking me up and effectively putting the kibosh on my only date in three months.

"Hullo?"

"Brandy, it's Suzanne!" Suzanne is my boss, Eric's, nineteen year old assistant/girlfriend. She's not too bright but she makes up for it with lots of enthusiasm.

"Hey, Suzanne. What's up?"

"It's an emergency! Eric said to get over to 239 Arch Street. Stat! A camera crew will meet you there."

I shoved Rocky off my chest and sat up. "Why? What's going on?"

"He didn't say...or maybe he did. I don't really remember..."

While she pondered this, I hung up.

My mind raced with possibilities. *What could be so urgent? House fire? Bomb scare? Whatever, I'm finally getting a shot at breaking news. Whoo hoo!*

"Mommy's finally going to be taken seriously around here," I told the cat and the dog." I threw on my one nice pair of slacks, gathered my hair into a ponytail and brushed my teeth on the way downstairs. After promising Adrian a long walk when I got back, I made a dash for the car and took off for Center City.

Turning onto Arch Street, I double parked next to a WINN news van and hopped out. The rain had slowed to a fine mist and a crowd had formed on the sidewalk. I looked around. Nothing seemed to be on fire, there was no SWAT team circling the premises, there wasn't even anyone wielding a megaphone trying to talk a depressive off a ledge. *And why was the WINN news van the only one in sight?*

"We must have an exclusive!" I thought, as I made a beeline for Eric.

"What's going on?" I huffed, completely winded.

"Here," he yelled, shoving something into my arms. "Put this on, quick! We're live in two minutes!"

Hmm...What is this? Kevlar? Or maybe something flame-retardant? Or...

I looked down. "A corset?" I said aloud.

"Well, what else would you expect for a segment on Betsy Ross?"

"Betsy Ross?" Behind Eric stood a beautiful colonial structure. It looked like a doll's house, small and narrow and perfect. "Um, is someone being held hostage inside or something?" I asked, hopefully.

Eric gave me a sideways glance. "Real funny, Alexander." He piled a wig and boots on top of an old-timey gown. "Listen up. I know it's short notice, but all your lines are on the teleprompter. All you have to do is read 'em and then toss back to the studio. Now get dressed, we're on in a minute!"

Fuming, I grabbed the garb and entered the van to change. "Stupid Betsy Ross," I muttered, jamming the wig on top of my head. "Stupid Eric, making me wear this stupid get-up," I mumbled as I hopped, first on one foot, then the other, lacing up my boots. "Stupid…" the heel of my boot jammed between two bricks on the cobble stone road. I teetered on the brink as onlookers tried to determine if I'd been dipping into the family spirits, and then I toppled over, landing face first in a fresh puddle of mud.

The wig slipped over my eyes, sparing me the sight of the gawking crowd. In the next instant I felt a hand tug gently at my arm and pull me to my feet. Then the hand moved to my face and nudged the wig off my eyes, and suddenly I found myself staring into twin pools of melted chocolate. I turned three shades of pink and nearly passed out.

"Hello, Angel."

Oh my god.

It had been three months since I'd heard that voice, seen that face, felt that feeling I got in the pit of my stomach whenever I was in the presence of Nicholas Santiago. For three long months I'd dreamed of our next encounter. It didn't look *anything* like the nightmare this was shaping up to be.

I smiled weakly, wiped the mud off my forehead and readjusted the wig. Nick waited patiently while I went through the motions of being very busy—*too* busy for conversation, the show must go on and all that crap. The truth is I had no idea in the world what to say to him that didn't begin with, "Why don't you love me, you heartless bastard?"

Fortunately, Eric showed up at that moment.

"Are you okay?" he asked. At least I think that's what he said. He was laughing so hard he had spit coming out the sides of his mouth.

"I'm fine. I'm sorry I ruined the shoot."

"No worries, kid. Gary caught your swan dive on tape. We'll get tons of mileage out of the replay and feature it on our blooper special." God must stay up nights thinking of fresh ways to humiliate me.

Eric left and it was just Nick and me. He looked magnificent. His hair was slightly longer than the last time I'd seen him, curled at the ends and grazing the top of his shoulders. He had on faded jeans and a long sleeved white dress shirt, rolled at the elbows and open at the neck. His forearms were tan, his almond shaped eyes darker than I'd remembered, with slight shadows underneath, making him appear sexier than I ever thought humanly possible. He even smelled wonderful, which was totally unfair, seeing as I smelled like wet dog.

Well, I would just have to make up for it with witty repartee. "I…uh…um…hi, Nick."

"Listen, Angel, I've got to take off. I've got a meeting a few blocks away and I'm running late. It was good bumping into you." And then he was gone. Just like that.

Well, what the hell was that all about? It was the topic of conversation with myself the entire way home. "Okay," I conceded, the last time I'd seen him, things *had* been left a tad on the awkward side.

I'd been on a mission to tell Nick I loved him. Never mind that I knew more personal info about the UPS delivery guy than I did about him. It wasn't about facts. It was about the way he made me feel. Safe and smart and respected and loved. I mean he just *had* to love me. After all, a guy saves a girl's life a coupla three times, she starts getting ideas that maybe he could return her feelings. Turns out, I was wrong.

I knew I'd made a mistake the minute I'd arrived at Nick's apartment building and found a gorgeous blonde descending the elevator from his floor. She had a sultry, satisfied look on her face that comes from either having really great sex or eating really great chocolate. Ever the optimist, I chose to think it was the latter.

The icing on the cake was when Nick answered the door—*naked*. Clearly, he was happy to see *someone*, but I was quite sure that someone wasn't me.

"Did you forget something?" he asked. *"Oh,"* he said, surprised. *"Hello, Angel. You're up early."*

I'd tried to bow out quickly, but in the end, I'd confessed it all. Seemed pointless not to. The man knew me better than I knew myself. He set me straight on his feelings for me. I was a friend, nothing more.

Nick had the good grace to leave me alone while I pulled myself together. He told me to stay as long as I needed, he had a meeting. And then he left me alone in his apartment, and I did what anyone would have done. I snooped. *Oh, come on, like you wouldn't?*

31

I went into the bedroom in the guise of looking for tissue to absorb the buckets of tears I'd cried. On the nightstand was a pile of books. I thumbed through the *Tibetan Book of the Dead* and decided I should read it. I figured I wouldn't understand one damn thing, but at least when people asked me what I've been reading lately I'd have something to tell them besides Internet Porn and the TV Guide.

And then I opened a drawer and found a photo that John had taken of me. It had been part of a gallery exhibit, but it was never meant to be sold. I'd heard *someone* had paid a boatload of money for it and now I knew who. The question was, "why?"

I never did get to ask Nick that question because he left town the next day. I'm sure I wasn't foremost in his mind while he was gone, seeing as in three months, I never got so much as a postcard from the guy, but still the question of the photo haunted me.

"You shoot like a girl." Bobby took off his goggles and reloaded his pistol and handed it back to me. We were at the shooting range and I had just emptied a clip into the wall next to a paper man-shaped target. Well, that's not entirely true. A few stray bullets hit the ceiling. I don't have the best aim in town.

I made a face and readjusted my ear protectors. "*You* shoot like a girl."

DiCarlo looked at me. "That made no sense at all. And, it's sexist. You should watch statements like that." He grinned and pulled the goggles down over his eyes. Standing behind me he wrapped his arms around me, enclosing my hands in his. "Try it again." I felt his breath, warm on my ear, and it made me forget for a minute that we'd decided to be "just friends." And then I remembered Tina.

It's not that I'm jealous. *I'm not.* It's just that she's stupid and Bobby can do so much better. I wiggled out of his grasp. "Y'know I think I've had enough practice for today."

"I thought you were serious about learning how to shoot." He aimed the pistol and hit the target square in the chest, in rapid succession, emptying the chamber.

"Lucky shots," I shrugged.

"That's not luck, Sweetheart. I'm that good."

I flashed him a major eye roll.

Bobby put down the gun, his face growing serious. "Look, Bran, all kidding aside, I heard about the girl you found last night. She was lucky you were there to help her, but the fact remains that it could've ended up being a dangerous situation for you." I started to protest but he held up the "talk to the hand" sign. "Sweetheart, it's not your fault. You attract danger like flies on shit. I'm just saying as your friend and someone who loves you, I want you to be prepared."

DiCarlo was right. I needed to raise my level of competency instead of relying on luck to keep myself safe. I reloaded and shot round after round until I was finally able to hit the target. Granted, a *moving* target would present more of a challenge, but at least by the end I wasn't aerating the ceiling.

Bobby walked me back to the car. "I've got an hour before I pick Sofia up from her play group. You want to grab a cheesesteak? My treat."

The offer was tempting, seeing as all I had in my refrigerator was a slimy bag of organic lettuce about a week past its expiration date. As John says, it's not enough to buy healthy food, you actually have to eat it, but I had things to do.

"Can I take a rain check? I want to swing by the hospital to check up on that girl. They won't tell me anything over the phone." Plus, I had to walk past Nick's apartment building about a thousand times in the hopes of casually running into him again. My agenda for the afternoon was pretty full.

Bobby leaned against the car, his arms folded across his chest, his expression a cross between amused and aggravated. People look like that quite often around me.

"It's already started," he said.

"I'll bite. What's already started?"

"You're obsessing over that kid. You think you're the only one in the city that can help her."

"Bobby that is so not true. Jeez you make it sound like I go totally overboard. I just want to make sure she's okay is all."

"Did you or did you not call the police station three times last night to see if they've been able to find out who she is?"

"You have no proof that was me. Besides, they wouldn't tell me anything. Could you call for me?"

He cast me another look, this time of pure affection. "I've already checked—because I knew you'd want to know. She finally gave a name to the hospital, but the cops ran a check and it's bogus."

"Listen, there's a girl who's been hanging around Frankie's gym. I think she's homeless. Anyway, she has a homemade tattoo under her ear. It looks really similar to the one the girl in the hospital has. Maybe they're a part of some kind of street club or something. If we could find out where they hang out, maybe we can go down there and they'll I.D. the girl in the hospital."

Bobby shook his head. "No good."

"Why not?"

"The police have already done a sweep of known hangouts. Nobody's talking. Street kids don't give each other up to the cops."

"Unhh! But we're just trying to help!"

"To a youth living on the street, cops are the enemy, Sweetheart."

"Then it makes perfect sense for me to go. These kids just need to know someone cares about them. Once I explain why I'm there, they'll talk to me."

"*And* we're back to square one. Brandy, these kids aren't the innocent little flowers you think they are. They have to be tough to be able to survive on the streets. They're all con artists, most are druggies—and those are some of their better qualities. I know you're on a crusade to save the world, but until you understand certain realities you'd better sit this one out."

"Boy, are you cynical," I sniffed.

The little vein on the side of Bobby's temple began to throb. That was my signal to back off.

"Okay, fine. I'll leave it alone."

"Sure you will. Just be careful and call if you need me."

Bobby told me not to get my hopes up of finding the girl's street family. Homeless kids used to be more visible, hanging out in parks, bus stations, in front of super markets—anywhere there was a possibility of scoring free food or shelter. But business owners began complaining that the kids were desecrating their property and hassling the customers, so the police cracked down and the kids went underground. To the general public, out of sight, out of mind, but they were still out there if you knew where to look.

The problem was I didn't.

I decided to cruise around the 7-Eleven where I'd last seen the girl from Uncle Frankie's gym. The gym, 7-Eleven and a homeless youth center were all located within a two-mile radius of each other. I figured these kids probably wouldn't have their own transportation, so unless they hopped a bus, they'd likely stick within walking distance of their haunts.

After about an hour, I lucked out and found Leather Boy standing on a corner smoking a cigarette next to a dingy, brown brick building. The sign on the door said, "Tarentino's Bar & Grill." By the looks of things it'd been quite some time since Tarentino had done any entertaining. To the right of the door was a large plate glass window, boarded over by mismatched pieces of decaying plywood, sadly, a common sight in this part of town.

I pulled over to the curb and rolled down the window and yelled across the narrow street to him. "Excuse me."

The kid looked up, boredom etched on his face. If he recognized me from the other day he didn't show it.

"Yeah?"

"I'm looking for someone."

His interest piqued, he approached the car, a slow, boozy smile playing about his lips. "Will I do?"

There was a provocativeness to his question that was well beyond his years—or mine for that matter.

"Um, I don't think we're on the same page here. See, I'm trying to locate this girl. She—" My phone rang, interrupting me. "Oh, uh, could you hang on for just a second?"

I looked down to grab my phone out of my bag, and when I looked back up he was nowhere in sight. Note to self: Street kids have short attention spans. Next time, talk faster.

Okay, that didn't go as well as I'd hoped, but if the boy in the leather pants was hanging around here, maybe the blond girl was close by. I traveled east a few more blocks, slowing down to watch a family of rats scurry into a hole in the wall on the side of a condemned building.

The street I'd turned onto was narrow, dirty and smelled like a urinal. I started to roll up the window and blast the air conditioning when I saw her. She was with a guy who looked to be in his late forties. He was white, clean shaven, dressed in nice Khakis and a polo shirt. He could've been a dentist, an accountant, or any number of respectable, white collar professions. Sunglasses shielded his eyes from the afternoon sun.

The girl looked so tiny standing next to him. He angled in close as he spoke, trying to crowd her but she stood her ground, chin stuck out with youthful defiance. From her stance, her body turned slightly, feet poised for action, I could tell she was debating whether to run but trying not to show it.

The guy moved closer still and draped his arm around her shoulder. Pulling her toward him in a rough embrace, he kissed her full on the mouth. The girl wriggled out of his grasp, balled up two small fists and punched him in the gut, knocking his sunglasses off in the process.

A couple of skeevy looking guys stood about fifty yards from them, drinking from a shared flask. They glanced up in mild interest as suddenly, Mr. White Collar

Professional caught her by her ponytail and slapped her hard across the face.

I slammed on the brakes, grabbed my pepper spray and jumped out of the car. By now he was punching her repeatedly over her head and neck. The girl fought back, screaming obscenities and kicking out with her feet, her arms flailing around in his general direction.

He was so busy punching the life out of this kid he never even saw me coming. I jumped onto his back and grabbed him by his hundred dollar haircut. "Let her go, you son of a bitch!" He spun his head to look at me and I caught him full in the face with the pepper spray.

It must've stung like crazy. Screaming, he clutched frantically at his eyes and began running haphazardly down the block. I fell off his back and rolled about three feet, landing on my ankle. Crap! If it wasn't broken it would be a pleasant surprise. As I struggled to stand, I watched the guy stagger blindly around the corner and out of sight.

The girl sat in a heap, holding her head in her hands. Her nose was bleeding and her face was starting to swell. I stood on shaky legs and limped over to her. Quickly she swiped her nose with the back of her hand, leaving streaks of blood across her cheek.

"It's going to be okay," I said, gently. "The cops will catch the bastard. I'm just going to give them a call now."

She gazed up at me, her pale blue eyes wet with unshed tears. "Fuck you bitch! Who the fuck told you to get up in my fuckin' business!"

"Um…you're…welcome?"

Chapter Three

She shot me the same look I gave a cockroach I once found in my breakfast cereal. "You call the cops and I'll find you and fuckin'mess you up."

I totally believed her.

She stood up and shoved past me and I watched her stomp off down the street. Then I got out my cell phone to call the police. *She's just a kid, I reasoned. I can't allow that creep to roam the streets…maybe come after her again or some other unsuspecting girl.* And then I remembered Bobby's words. To a street kid cops are the enemy, so, against my better judgment, I put my phone back in my pocket. I knew I'd catch hell from DiCarlo, but this kid was beaten up once already today. She didn't need me to screw her over too.

My ankle was throbbing and starting to be too tight for my tennis shoe. Not a good sign. I wanted to take my shoe off, but I was afraid I wouldn't be able to get it back on again. I climbed back into my car, rolled up the window and locked it. Now that the adrenalin rush had passed, I was shaking so hard I thought I'd throw up. I waited a minute for the feeling to pass and then I started the engine. I had to go find that kid.

She hadn't gotten far. I found her rooting through a trash bin outside a coffee shop. I parked a few doors down and watched her as she entered the restaurant. I figured she might need a few minutes to cool off, which seemed especially prudent given our recent conversation, so I sat in the car and called John. When he answered, I asked him if his refrigerator was running and then I told him to go catch it and he hung up on me. Then I called to see if he had Prince Albert in a can.

"How did you get to be this old and still manage to retain such an infantile sense of humor?" he asked.

"I'm bored," I whined into the phone.

"Poor baby," he said and hung up again.

I got out of the car and peered through the coffee shop window. The girl was sitting in a booth in the corner, holding a glass of ice water up to her cheek. I entered the building just as the server approached with a cup of coffee, set it on the table in front of her and waited.

The girl glanced up at her. "What the fuck are *you* lookin' at?"

The server was old school and must've been through this scenario a dozen times. She didn't even blink. "Will there be anything else?"

The girl shook her head so the waitress laid a check on the table and walked away.

I blew out a big chicken breath and limped over to the kid, making a conscious effort not to stare at her mottled face. "Okay, before you say anything," I jumped in, "I didn't call the cops, I'm sorry I got all up in your business and could I please buy you a sandwich, it's the least I can do for interfering. Clearly, you can take care of yourself."

She didn't say a word, just stared at me for a tense moment and then she shrugged, too tired to speak.

I took that as a yes.

I sat down opposite her and gave her a quick once-over. Up close she appeared younger than I'd originally thought, maybe 14 or so, with delicate features and small hands, her nails bitten down to the quick. Her eyes were ringed with sleeplessness and she had the gaunt look of someone who was used to going without.

I signaled the waitress and ordered a tuna melt. "Get anything you'd like," I said to the girl.

"Hamburger and a coke," she murmured, not looking up.

"Is that all? Really, order as much as you want."

"I'm not a fucking charity case," she exploded. "You think buying me a hamburger is going to make everything better?"

Wow. It would've been hard to keep up with her mood swings, except that she was in permanent bitch mode. Totally understandable but a little tough to deal with.

"Listen, I'm not all that good in tense social situations, so if you could cut me some slack here, I'd really appreciate it."

She actually cracked a smile at that.

"My name's Brandy Alexander," I said, settling into the booth.

"Yeah, right. You and half my friends."

"No, really. That's my name."

"Oh." She waited a beat before adding, "Your parents must have some weird sense of humor."

My mother is a lovely person, but she's never been accused of having a sense of humor, weird or otherwise.

I picked up my fork and wiped the water spots off with my napkin. "So, do you have a name?" I asked.

"Crystal."

I would've bet money it wasn't her real name, but at least it was a start.

"So, Crystal, where are you from?"

"Around."

Judging by the girl's accent, which was nondescript and the envy of broadcast radio and television students everywhere, I guessed she was from Iowa.

Our sandwiches arrived and she hunched over hers and began eating. It was more inhalation than actual mastication, and I hoped nothing got caught in her throat, because I hadn't paid attention in class when the Red Cross came to work last month and taught us all the Heimlich Maneuver.

It took less than three minutes for Crystal to clean her plate. Sensing she was more receptive now that her stomach was full, I broached the subject of what brought me to her.

"You have a tattoo under your ear," I said.

"So?"

"So I found a girl about your age the other night with a similar tattoo. She was really sick and I took her to Jefferson. I thought you might know her."

"Lots of kids have tattoos like mine," she said, leaning forward almost imperceptibly. "What did she look like?"

"About 5'4" with long brown hair."

"What was wrong with her?"

"She was hemorrhaging. The doctor thinks she may have miscarried. Listen, Crystal, she's all alone and she's not in great shape. If you know anything about this girl…"

"I don't."

"But—"

"I said I don't know her. Thanks for the burger." She stood, abruptly cutting short the conversation.

I picked up the check and stood too. "Listen," I said, handing her my business card, "If you need anything—"

Crystal read the card. "You're a reporter," she said in the same tone of voice one might say, 'You're a Nazi war criminal.' "Well, that fucking figures."

"Hey, what's that supposed to mean?" I asked, but she was already turning toward the door. "Hang on a minute," I told her.

I threw a tip on the table and walked over to the counter to pay the bill. When I got back, the tip was gone and so was the kid.

By the time I got home my ankle was three shades of purple and had swelled to the size of a tennis ball, but at least it wasn't broken. I hobbled into the kitchen and filled a pot with ice water, stopping to throw some fat free popcorn into the microwave. "Needs something," I decided, testing out a piece. I melted a hunk of butter and poured it over the top.

I took the popcorn and the pot of water into the living room and plunked myself down on the couch. Adrian leaped onto the cushion next to me and waited. I tossed him a bit of popcorn and turned on the TV.

Easing off my shoe, I stuck my foot into the ice-cold water. At that precise moment, my cell phone rang. Damnit. I'd left it in the kitchen. I pulled my foot out of the pot and limped, dripping wet, into the other room.

I picked up the phone and checked caller I.D. The number was unfamiliar and it peaked my curiosity. Usually it's Janine asking me if she should go back with Tony Tan, her on-again, mostly off-again no good boyfriend, or John, wanting to know the name of some obscure actress from a short-lived '80's sitcom. My life is *that* exciting.

"Hello?" I said into the phone.

"Is this Brandy Alexander?" asked a female voice.

"Yes?"

"This is Linda Morrison. I'm a nurse at Jefferson Hospital—"

"Oh my God, who's hurt? It isn't my brother, is it? Please tell me it isn't Paul." Okay, so I guess I still have a few minor issues to work out in the "quick to panic" department.

"No, no. I'm sorry to scare you. It's just that we have a small situation here." She dropped her voice and I had to strain to hear it. "A young girl tried to sneak into I.C.U. She became very belligerent when we asked her what she was doing there. Then she pulled out a card with your name on it and tried to pass herself off as you."

"Is she still there?" I asked, instinctively dropping my voice to match her whisper.

"Yes, and she's very agitated. I was going to call security, but she's so young, I thought I'd try you first."

"Do me a favor," I said, scrambling to shove my foot back into my shoe. "Stall as long as you can. I'll be right there."

I arrived in time to see a burly man in uniform with a shaved head escort Crystal down a long hallway. He held her wrist in one of his massive hands, dodging her attempts to projectile spit at him. He was surprisingly agile for a big guy.

44

"Let me go, you fucking asshole." She swung her other arm and he caught it in his free hand, deftly pulling it up behind her back.

A nurse trailed after them, admonishing the guard to be careful, although I wasn't sure who her concern was directed toward. In this round, my money was on Crystal. She was seriously pissed off.

"Linda?" I read off the nurse's nametag.

She cast me a wilted smile. "Sorry, I had to call security. She was becoming abusive to the staff."

I eyed the guard. "Could I talk to her a minute?"

Crystal glared at me, sullen and unrepentant. "I don't need your fucking help," she sneered, the way only an adolescent girl can.

"Um, actually, you sort've do."

The wind went out of her sails and she stopped struggling against the guard's restraints.

"It's okay, Brian, let her go," the nurse said, turning to leave.

The guard cut me a wary look and let go of Crystal's arm. For a moment I thought she was going to run, but she just stood there, unsure of what to do next.

"I want to see that girl," she said, finally. "Only they won't let me in."

I realized she must be in a bad way if she was turning to me for help, so I resisted the urge to blurt out a smart-ass remark about her less than charming behavior. "Let me see what I can do," I whispered.

I walked back the other way with Crystal following close behind, weighed down by her backpack and the enormous chip on her shoulder. The guard trailed after us, in case his services should be needed again which I assured him would not be the case. I hoped I wasn't being overly optimistic.

Linda Morrison had returned to the nurse's station. She raised an eyebrow at the sight of us. "All better?" she asked.

I nodded. "Nurse Morrison, I'm really sorry for the uh-confusion before. This is my sister's kid, Patty. Say hi, Patty."

"Hi," Crystal said, wondering where this was heading. That made two of us.

"So anyway, I told Patty to meet me here. Y'see, I'm doing a story on the girl in ICU—I was the one who brought her in, and uh, since it's um—"Take Your Cousin to Work Day—""

"Don't you mean 'niece'?"

"*Oh*. Yeah. Anyway, I thought we could just take a peek in—y'know say hello, try and cheer her up a little," I finished at record speed. I figure if I tell a lie fast enough folks won't have time to dwell on it.

Linda suppressed a smile. "I see. Well, I think I can arrange a visit, if you only stay a few minutes. The patient hasn't been very responsive. Maybe it will do her some good. They're taking her vitals right now, but have a seat over there and I'll come get you in a few minutes."

We took a seat and waited.

Crystal turned to me. "What a load of bullshit. You're a terrible liar."

"It got us in, didn't it?"

"Only because that nurse is seriously stupid."

"FYI that nurse is your new best friend. *Of course* she didn't believe a word I said, but she knew how important it was to you to see that girl, who, by the way, you said you didn't know—so why *did* you come down here?"

46

"Why did *you*?" she replied, her face suddenly flushed with anger. "Hey! Don't tell me you really *are* going to do a story on her," she fumed.

"Well, why not? There are a lot of kids out there that need help. I wouldn't dream of exploiting them, but maybe—"

"Fuck you, you fucking bitch! I never should have trusted you!"

Oh crap, here we go again. "Listen, do you think you can muster up a few more adjective here, because you're wearing out the 'F Bomb.'"

She leaped to her feet and for a scary minute I thought she was going to punch me. Note to self: When dealing with a young, explosive street kid, sarcasm is *not helpful.*

At least I was beginning to understand how Crystal operated. She had two modes, pissed off and seriously pissed off, and she was gearing up for apoplectic.

"Look," I said, "Believe it or not, I'm not the enemy. All I wanted to do was help this girl get back with her family."

"Yeah? Well, what if her family doesn't want to get back with her? Did you ever think of that?"

Before I could entertain the notion there was a sudden burst of activity down the opposite end of the corridor. Medical personnel converged from every direction as the hospital paging system blared, "Code Blue."

Crystal stared wild-eyed at me. "Code Blue. That's—" she didn't finish her thought. Ashen faced, she bolted down the hall as I limped along behind her on my one good leg.

By the time I caught up to her she was, once again, locked in the security guard's arms. He cleared her out of the way as doctors and nurses crowded into the patient's room, dragging a code cart filled with medical supplies and equipment.

"Let me see her," Crystal screamed. Tears flowed down her swollen cheeks.

"Take her out of here," barked a doctor, as he applied defibrillator paddles to the girl's sunken chest.

The guard took a few cautious steps back with Crystal in tow.

She turned to him, desperation in her voice. "Please. I'll be good. Let me stay."

After what seemed like hours, but was in fact only minutes, the flurry of activity stopped.

"What's happening?" Crystal sobbed, but I could see in her eyes she already knew the answer. "Why aren't you doing something?"

"Honey, I'm so sorry." Nurse Morrison's somber look said it all.

"No!" Crystal tore herself from the guard's grasp and ran straight into the room. She stared down at the bed, at the mass of wires and tubes that hung from the frail body.

"It's—*not*— *her*," she said and promptly passed out.

I had no time to mourn the loss of the tragic stranger lying in the bed. The one on the floor needed me more now. Crystal revived quickly, probably more out of her need to be in control than the smelling salts that were shoved under her nose. She sat up and swore at the nurse, slapping his hand out of her way. With a little orange juice and some admonitions to take it easy she was good to go. The question was "where?"

"Listen, I think we should talk about what happened inside." We were standing on the corner of 11th and Locust. It was late in the day and yet the temperature still hovered in the 90's. It was going to be fun sleeping in my house tonight with no working air conditioner.

Crystal shot me a look that would have been menacing had she not appeared so completely wilted, and I was struck once again, by just how young she was.

"I passed out. It's no big deal. I'm fine."

"That's not what I mean." There was a guy standing next to a kiosk selling water ice and soft pretzels. We walked over and I bought two pretzels and handed one to Crystal. "What kind of water ice do you want?"

"Cherry. Thanks," she added as an afterthought.

We began walking to my car. "I know why you passed out. We witnessed someone die. That *is* a big deal, no matter how tough you are. She was a kid and she was all alone, and it's…" my voice trailed off.

Crystal looked at me. "Are *you* okay?"

"Hunh," I almost laughed. "Not really. But don't tell anyone I said that. I've got a reputation to protect."

I hesitated for a beat and then plunged right in. "Listen, you said something just before you took a header. You said, 'It's not her.' Obviously you were worried that girl was someone you knew. Who were you talking about?"

She didn't answer me right away. She just studied her soft pretzel like it was the most fascinating thing on Earth. When I'd just about given up on her ever answering me she slowed her pace and then stopped altogether. "I want to tell you," she decided.

We sat on a stone bench in one of those little turn of the century parks that are dotted throughout the area. Some pigeons scoped us out to see if we had anything good to offer in the way of dinner. Since it was only 4:00 in the afternoon, I guessed that would qualify as an Early

Bird Special. I tossed a couple of hunks of pretzel over in their direction and watched them devour them.

"Before I tell you anything, I've got to ask you something," Crystal said.

"Okay, shoot."

"Are you really a reporter? Like on TV and all? Because, no offense or anything, but you sure don't look like any news reporter I've ever seen. I mean you look like a kid. You've got stains all over your tee shirt, your hair's all messy—and—"

"Gee, Crystal, no offense taken."

"I just thought you had to be more glamorous if they were gonna put your face on TV."

"I clean up nice. Listen, could you just forget about me being a reporter? I'm not interested in turning your story into some kind of career boost for me. I just think—for whatever reason—we fell into each other's lives and you need some help. I'm asking you to take a risk with me. You can walk away at any time."

Crystal sighed. "My best friend's gone missing. When you told me about that girl in the hospital and the way you described her and all, I thought it might be Star. She'd never just take off without telling me. I think something really bad's happened to her."

"Could she maybe have gone home?"

"What the fuck's with you and home? Some people don't have a home to go *to. Get it?*"

I got it. I just didn't fully understand it.

"When was the last time you saw Star?"

"One night about two weeks ago. We were at our squat and she was heading out to work."

"Star has a job? Where does she work?"

Crystal rolled her eyes at me. "Are you for real?"

"*Ohhh.* You mean—jeez, sorry. Go on."

"Anyway, I told her I didn't think she should go. Kids who hook are always getting the shit beat out of them. Some even get killed. Not that anyone on the outside would notice. Nobody gives a fuck about street kids."

"Are you worried that that's what happened to Star?"

"I don't know," Crystal told me. "Star's smart. She knows how to take care of herself." She stopped for a minute, thinking. "We really hit it off, y'know? Star's a little older than me and she's been out on the streets longer, so she kinda looked out for me."

"In what way?"

"Well, sometimes the newbies get hassled by the old school kids, 'cause they've been out there longer and know the ropes, so they kinda run the show. There's this one girl-she just won't leave me alone. I don't know, she's a real sick bitch and she thinks she owns me or something. Anyway, when Star was around, I didn't have to worry."

"Is that why you were hanging around the gym? So that you could learn to protect yourself?"

"Yeah," Crystal admitted. "But it didn't do me any fucking good. I wasn't gonna join those lame-ass weirdos."

"Um, Crystal, out of family loyalty, I need to point out that one of those lame-ass weirdos is my uncle."

"Oh," she blushed. "I didn't mean—"

"That's okay, don't worry about it. Listen, who have you talked to about Star being gone? Maybe somebody saw something."

"I talked to Little Red—her pimp—but he says he hasn't seen her. He's always trying to get me to be one of his girls but I wouldn't work for that piece of shit. I'd rather starve. Star was talking about quitting him. Too bad she didn't do it sooner. That guy you saw me with today," she added, "was one of Star's regulars…y'know, a john? He was pissed off that he couldn't find her and he'd seen us together, so he thought he'd take the next best thing. I'm not into that scene but he didn't believe me."

I took in all this information, as if I were watching a movie. If I thought about it in any real sense, I would throw up.

"Okay, you said you last saw your friend about a week ago. What day was it?"

Crystal shrugged. "I dunno. Last week sometime."

"Could you be a little more specific?"

"Wait, I'll check my calendar."

"Sarcasm, right?"

Crystal laughed, breaking some of the tension. "Look, I know you're trying to be helpful and all, but things don't work the same way out on the streets as they do in your world."

"Okay, so educate me."

"Why do you care so much?" she asked suddenly. "What's in it for you?"

"Does everybody have to have an ulterior motive for helping someone else?"

"Lesson number one. In my world, yes."

If something bad really did happen to Star, it made an already intolerable situation for this kid that much worse. I wanted to tell Bobby, but my hands were tied. According to Crystal anyone responsible for getting the cops involved in street business was an automatic target for retribution of the worst kind.

I needed someone who understood the code of the streets, someone who could offer real help, without jeopardizing Crystal's street cred in the process. Someone who felt the need to flee the continent after I professed my undying love for him, but was still the only person in the world I'd trust with Crystal's life as well as my own. Swallowing a huge gulp of pride I took out my cell phone and punched in his number. "Nick, it's Brandy. I need your help."

Chapter Four

Nick's Mercedes truck has been parked directly outside my house since Alphonso brought it to me three months ago. I move it once a week for street cleaning and sit in it every night, because it smells like Nick and, yes, I'm *that* pathetic. I don't drive it because I feel like he loaned it to me as a consolation prize for not loving me.

Crystal and I sat in it now, on our way to Nick's studio. We'd made a pit stop at my house so I could feed the dog and grab the truck. Turns out, Adrian had already eaten. I found the chewed up remains of a bag of Nacho Cheese Doritos strewn about the kitchen floor. Adrian sat nearby wagging his overgrown tail, his snout sprinkled with red dye number six. *Great. There goes my dinner.*

I left Crystal in the living room playing with the dog while I ran upstairs to change. Not that I was trying to impress Nick or anything. I just figured with my ankle still being swollen and all, I'd be more comfortable in sandals and, *technically*, strappy stiletto heels qualifies as sandals.

I paused on my way back downstairs, peering over the railing at Crystal and Adrian. The dog was licking her face and she was laughing. It was pure and sweet and very childlike. I fake sneezed to let her know I was coming and the mask went up again.

She glanced over at me as I descended the stairs. "How come you're wearing hooker shoes? You like this guy or something?"

I turned around, walked back upstairs and changed back into my All Stars.

Nick's martial arts studio is a two story red brick building located in a section of the city the verbally indelicate would refer to as "the slums." The accuracy of the label is inarguable, and yet there is a Zen-like quality to the little patch of land the studio sits on that can only be attributed to the man who owns it.

I'd been here on several occasions and had gotten to know some of the locals. I waved hello to Lonnie Juarez as he stepped out of the bail bonds place next door.

"Yo, Brown Eyes. Whaddup?" Lonnie grinned, showing a lot of gold teeth, one of which had a diamond glued to the center of it. Franny's husband, Eddie, is a jeweler and he could tell if it was merely cubic zirconium, but my eye isn't that discerning.

Lonnie runs a lucrative extortion business, but, according to Nick, most of his profits get eaten up by a rather hefty addiction to black tar heroin. Nick says Lonnie's harmless, and maybe to a fifth degree black belt that holds true, but personally, the guy gives me the creeps, and I could tell Crystal wasn't lovin' him either. She slipped her hand into her back pocket and extracted a butterfly knife, palming it discreetly against her leg.

Lonnie hocked a good sized lugie and winked at Crystal.

"*Okay,* then, Lonnie, good to see ya," I said, steering Crystal toward the studio.

As I reached for the door bell my stomach began to tighten. That unfortunate encounter in the Betsy Ross wig not withstanding, I hadn't been face to face with Nick since the morning I'd poured my heart out to him and he'd handed it back to me with a polite "thanks, but no thanks."

Then I got to thinking. *Maybe I'd read the situation all wrong. Maybe he'd been up all night nursing a sick friend,(and it must've worked because she looked like the picture of health to me), so when he answered the door he was delirious from lack of sleep and he didn't know what he was saying. What he meant to say was, "I love you too, Brandy, let's get married and have many beautiful, mysterious little bambinos together, but it came out as "I don't love you" by mistake.*

Then there was the whole "snooping in his bedroom" thing and finding my photo in his nightstand drawer. I wanted to confront him on why he'd spent so much money on a portrait of "just a friend," but I wasn't quite ready to confess I'd been pawing through his personal belongings.

As I'd already polled every friend I had on the subject, including a few I hadn't seen since elementary school, I was about to ask Crystal her take on the matter, when the door opened and out walked Nick.

Crystal's mouth hung slightly ajar as her eyes roved over five feet ten inches of male perfection. His lithe, muscular body was dressed in workout clothes; loose black pants and a tight white tee shirt, damp with sweat. On his wrist he wore his ever-present silver band. His hair was pulled back in a ponytail, revealing a two-inch scar under his left ear that worked its way down along his jaw line. I was the reason Nick sported that scar. I felt guilty and honored at the same time and it only made me love him more.

"Does he always smell this good?" Crystal whispered, forgetting for a moment her "tough girl" persona.

"*Uh huh.*"

If Nick overheard he had the good grace not to show it.

"Hey, Darlin', come on in," he said, and my heart skipped a couple of beats. He held the door open and we stepped inside.

There was a class in session. I recognized Tanya, one of Nick's instructors, as she put a group of Samoan bodyguards through their paces. Tanya is one of those annoyingly beautiful women who thinks she's better than everyone else just because she's drop dead gorgeous, incredibly competent and unfailingly sweet. She looked up when she saw me and smiled in greeting. *Gaah, what a loser!*

"I'm just finishing up here," Nick told us. "You're welcome to stick around for a few minutes or make yourselves comfortable in my office."

"We're okay, here," Crystal said quickly and with uncharacteristic reverence. "I mean if that's alright."

I looked at her and tried hard not to laugh. Even "Ms. In-Your-Face-Tough-Girl" couldn't escape the indescribable quality that was the essence of Nicholas Santiago.

No one volunteered to go mano y mano with Nick so class ended early.

"You need to tone it down a little, Nick," Tanya told him, picking up the mats and stacking them against the wall. "You broke that guy's leg this morning."

"He wasn't paying attention. It's a good way to get himself killed." His voice was hard and dispassionate and was the reminder I needed that you don't want this man as your enemy.

Tanya shrugged. "You're right, she said, smiling. "You always are."

Was she flirting with him? I guessed it wouldn't do to bitch slap her in front of Crystal. Besides, I was way out of my league.

Nick finished helping Tanya stack the mats and then he walked her to the door.

"Nice seeing you again," she called back over her shoulder.

"You bet," I told her. *You bet? Why did I say that? I sound like an idiot.* "I mean nice to see you too," I called out lamely and too late. She was already out the door.

"Now," Nick said, turning his dark liquid eyes on Crystal and me, and I got a rush in parts of my body I'd all but forgotten existed. "What can I do to help you?"

We sat in his office, a cozy sanctuary located in the back of the studio. It's quiet in there and insulated from the worries of the outside world. I'd always felt nurtured and protected curled up in Nick's red velvet armchair, and I hoped it would provide the same comfort now for Crystal.

There was a cigarette butt in a ceramic ashtray on the desk, and I noted with some surprise that he'd started smoking again.

"Just a minor setback, Angel." He smiled, first at me, and then at Crystal. "Don't start if you haven't already. It's a nasty habit and a bitch to kick."

Nick listened intently and without interruption as Crystal filled him in on her missing friend. I was surprised at how freely she spoke to him, as if she sensed a kindred spirit.

"I'm going to run this by a couple of guys who work for me," he told her when she had finished. "They have a lot of contacts on the streets and sometimes they hear things other people aren't privy to. It would help if you had a recent photo of Star," he added.

Crystal visibly stiffened. "Oh great. Some fuckwad walking around with Star's picture asking questions about her. That won't draw *too much* attention."

Oy. I held my breath. This kid had no idea who she was talking to.

Nick, however, didn't appear to take offense. His response was remarkably calm and respectful.

"These people understand how important it is to be discreet, Crystal. They would never do anything to put you or your friend in jeopardy. A photo would just help make identification easier if they do run across her."

Crystal was quiet for a moment. Then, making up her mind she dug deep into her backpack and pulled out a worn strip of photographs, the kind you get in those photo booths at the mall.

"This is me and Star at the arcade on Market Street," she whispered, handing the pictures to Nick. "They were taken a couple of months ago."

Nick held them carefully, giving Crystal a silent nod of understanding. *They were more than just pictures. They were her lifeline.*

He stood and walked over to a small copier and placed the picture on the glass. When he was finished, he gave Crystal back the original. Taking the copy, he carefully tore it in half and handed her the part of the photo with her image on it, keeping only the picture of Star. The gesture spoke volumes. He respected her privacy and was doing his best to preserve what little she had.

"You know, Crystal, there's a chance your friend may not want to be found. If that's the case, she won't be."

Crystal nodded, the possibility obviously having crossed her mind as well.

"We'll take it one step at a time. In the mean time learning self defense was a good idea. I can help with that if you want."

"I can't pay you," she said, regaining a bit of her edge.

"It's on the house."

"What's the catch?"

"No catch. No strings. Just trying to help out one of my own."

My mind had been wandering a bit, thinking about those Doritos the dog ate and wondering what I was going to make for dinner. But at Nick's words, I tuned back in. *"Just trying to help out one of my own"...What the heck does he mean by that?*

Returning Nick's truck left Crystal and me without wheels, so Nick offered to drive us back to my place.

"Could you drop me off at Poplar and Taney?" Crystal asked.

At the mention of the street corner I did one of those cartoon "double takes" where the guy's head swivels around and his eyes almost pop out of his head. Poplar and Taney is one of the worst neighborhoods in the city. Even the vilest criminal offenders won't travel there alone after dark. I opened my mouth to protest, but Nick cut me a subtle warning look and climbed into the truck.

I got in on the other side and Crystal scrambled in next to me, forcing me to scoot in closer to Nick. My leg brushed up against his, and I felt an immediate surge of warmth spread throughout my belly to the region down below. *Oh boy!*

Nick gave my knee a light squeeze. "Everything alright, Darlin'?"

"Great!" I squeaked.

The ride to drop Crystal off was quiet. Nick had the windows up and the air on, drowning out the street sounds of a hostile neighborhood. He seemed preoccupied. Crystal sat slumped against the door, eyes closed, her head nodding slightly forward. I stole a glimpse of her as she dozed off. The bruises on her cheeks and neck had taken on a purplish hue, but at least the swelling had subsided. If anyone had ever dared raise a hand to me, my mom would have ripped his head off. *Didn't Crystal— hell, didn't all kids deserve that kind of love and attention?*

A lump formed in my throat which I quickly squashed down with a handful of Hershey kisses I keep in my bag for emergency situations. Chocolate is a major stress reliever. It's rich in antioxidants, plus it's friggin' delicious!

Crystal woke up when Nick cut the engine in front of an ancient gray brick building. She seemed embarrassed to have fallen asleep.

"Um, thanks for the ride," she mumbled, opening the car door.

Outside it smelled like a frat house after a toga party. The air reeked of stale beer, month old garbage and fresh vomit.

"Are you sure this is where you want to be dropped off?" I asked. "I mean there doesn't seem to be all that much going on here. Maybe—"

I felt Nick's hand on my leg again. If he meant to render me speechless, mission accomplished. "Crystal, come by the studio tomorrow at around three," he cut in. "We'll get you started on some basic training techniques."

Crystal nodded, grabbed her backpack off the seat and hopped out of the truck. I watched as she rounded the corner of the building. As I glanced down at where she'd been sitting I noticed a small, stuffed bear that had fallen out of a rip on the side of her backpack.

"I'll be right back," I said, climbing out of the truck.

I turned the corner and walked down a narrow alley, lined with abandoned tenement housing. The alley dead-ended at the back wall of an old brick building. I found Crystal seated cross-legged on the cement behind a dumpster, inspecting the hole in her backpack. She stood when she saw me, wiping her hands on her jeans. She looked like she'd been crying but I knew better than to mention it.

"You dropped this," I said, showing her the stuffed bear.

"That's not mine," she replied in the belligerent tone I'd come to know and love. "But I guess I could hold onto it for a while," she added, grabbing it from my outstretched hand and stuffing it into her backpack.

"Well, I'll see ya," I told her, having run out of excuses to stick around.

"Yeah. See ya—oh fucking shit!"

"What's wrong?"

I turned in the direction of where Crystal was staring. A tall, chunky girl in her early 20's had appeared out of nowhere and was now heading our way. She was about 5' 8" with wiry, copper colored hair and arms covered in tattoos. She wore a dirty, gray tank top, shorts and army boots and had a bow-legged swagger that made her look like Popeye's twin sister.

"That's the girl I told you about. Her name's Bunny. She's the one who's been after me. Listen, you should go."

"Bunny? Seriously? Boy, is that ever a misnomer."

Crystal heaved a frustrated sigh and explained. "As in 'fucks like one.' Really, just get the hell out of here before there's trouble."

The last thing I wanted was to make Crystal's life harder, so I turned and began walking down the alley, sneaking quick peeks over my shoulder as I moved along.

Crystal didn't wait for Bunny to approach her. She walked over to the older girl with an air of casual confidence I'd bet money she didn't feel. Bunny eyed her, carefully.

"So Crystal, who's the bitch?"

Well, that was uncalled for! I slowed my pace so I could catch Crystal's response, but she was speaking so softly it was impossible. So I retraced my steps a bit and leaned against the wall pretending to tie my shoe. I still couldn't hear anything and when I looked up again, Crystal had disappeared. Street kids seemed to be especially adept at flying under the radar.

Bunny stood at a distance, arms akimbo, glaring at me. She was so mad I could actually feel the heat from her rage wafting toward me. *What the hell did Crystal say to her?*

Before I could ponder that question, Bunny caught up to me and sandwiched me between her and the wall. She got up so close I could feel her hot breath on my face. It smelled like kosher pickles and I wondered if there might be a deli nearby. *Oh crap, Brandy, focus!*

"Have we met?"

63

Apparently, Bunny didn't have an ear for whimsy. I tried to duck out of her grasp, and she grabbed me by the hair, twisting it in her fist.

"Ow. Let go." I tugged at her hands, but Popeye's sister must've been eating her spinach, because she held on with an iron grip.

"Stay the fuck off from my corner and the fuck away from Crystal. You get up in my fucking face again and I'll fucking cut you."

"Wow. Four fucks in one breath. You should really mix it up a little."

Okay, I should've figured Bunny wouldn't be up for a grammar lesson, but it just slipped out.

She raised a meaty hand, all set to rearrange my face, so I jammed an elbow into hers and ran like hell. The one flaw in my plan was that I'd forgotten to retie my shoe.

I got about three feet before I tripped over my shoelace and stumbled head first onto the filthy sidewalk. The palms of my hands stung like crazy, but my chin took the brunt of the fall. Dripping blood, I scrambled to my knees just as Bunny tackled me from behind, sending us both sprawling.

"Are you nuts?" I yelled.

In a split second that felt like an eternity, she set her eyes on me, and I could feel her mood shift from territorial to psychotic. Her pale blue eyes never wavering, she reached into her back pocket and drew out a straight-edged razor.

Oh god, oh god, oh god. What do I do now? I didn't wait for an answer. I launched myself off the ground and took off running down the alley.

With Bunny blocking my exit I was forced to head toward the dead end. Down near the end of the alley, there was a gap between two of the buildings. I tried to squeeze through, but it was too narrow. Wedged between the structures, I spied a dilapidated wooden door that led to the entrance to one of the abandoned apartment houses.

I wriggled out and checked the knob. It was rusted shut so I threw my weight into the door frame. It budged, but just barely. I kicked the bottom panel and the old wood splintered, giving me enough room to crawl through the door.

I waited a beat while my eyes adjusted to the dingy surroundings. There were holes in the ceiling where old plaster had broken away, letting in thin streams of light. Mildew clung to the walls and permeated the air. It was just a matter of time before Bunny found her way in, but if I could just find the front door, I could escape onto the street.

After a frantic search, I located the front entrance, but it was nailed shut. The windows looking out onto the street were boarded up as well, leaving me no way out.

I was about to head back the other way when I heard a loud crash coming from the back door area. I shot up the stairs two at a time and raced down the long hallway, ducking into an open apartment. I opened a closet door and settled in. With any luck, Bunny would get bored looking for me and leave.

Turns out, Bunny had a longer attention span than I gave her credit for. I could hear her creaking around in the apartment next to me, slamming doors and cursing up a blue streak. My heart was pounding so hard I thought she could hear it through the walls.

The next thing I knew, the door to the apartment creaked open and the sounds of footsteps grew louder. I stood stock still. Any moment now this razor-wielding nut case would rip open the door and slice me like a ripe melon. I strained to listen for the slightest movement but—nothing.

After what seemed like forever, I couldn't take it anymore. I had to know what was going on. There was a crack in the door about four inches below eye level. Without a sound, I eased my way down to look though the crack. An unblinking blue eye stared back at me.

Holy shit! I hurled myself against the door with all my might, smashing into Bunny's forehead. The force knocked her off her feet and sent her crashing to the ground. I flew out of the closet and tripped over her army boots. She was out cold.

I stood on wobbly feet, trying to catch my breath. At that moment, Nick appeared in the doorway. He glanced down at Bunny's prone body and then turned an appraising eye on me.

"Thought you were going to be right back, Darlin'."

"Yeah, well, I got a little tied up."

Nick slung his arm around me, smiling. "I see you handled it. That's the important thing."

Less than a moment before, I'd battled a maniac in a life-threatening situation, but now all I could think about was the way my stomach flipped whenever Nick looked at me.

My chin was caked with blood and I had cobwebs clinging to my boobs. Acute embarrassment took over and I raked a hand though my hair, as if *that* would make me look presentable.

"Ready to go?" he asked.

I filled him in as we walked back to his truck. "I don't know where Crystal disappeared to and I'm worried about what's going to happen to her when Bunny wakes up. Maybe I should find her and take her home with me."

"I know you want to protect her, Angel," he said quietly, "but it doesn't work that way out on the streets. "You need to be available, but let her come to you."

Driving around with Nick again seemed the most natural thing in the world. It was almost as if that awkward little scene in his apartment three months prior had never happened, and I was just as happy to pretend that it hadn't. Denying unpleasant memories is an Alexander family tradition…which explains why there are huge gaps in our family tree.

Still, the sting of rejection can make even the most secure individual (for which I don't even remotely qualify) act in regrettable ways. So, when Bobby called me on the way home, I may have led Nick to believe DiCarlo and I were a *bit* more involved than we actually are.

"Oh, hi, Bobby," I breathed in a 'come hither' tone. "It's good to hear from you."

"Brandy, I just saw you yesterday. Why are you talking so weird?"

I made a big show of clearing my throat and asked, "What's up?"

"Well, I was calling to see if you were busy on Saturday night, because the Phils are playing the Red Sox and—"

"Saturday night? Let me think…no, I'm not busy. That sounds *wonderful!* I'd love to—"

"Oh, uh, Bran, I was actually calling to ask if you could watch Sophia for me. See, I've got a date and Eddie's mom usually baby sits, only she's got the flu and—shit. I'm sorry. I just thought since you and I

67

decided to cool it for awhile, that—y'know, I'd—Listen, never mind. I'll ask somebody else."

I sat there feeling like and ass and praying Nick couldn't hear Bobby's end of this ridiculously humiliating conversation.

"No! Hey, Bobby. We are totally *on* for Saturday night. I wouldn't miss it for the world."

"You sure?"

"Absolutely! Ta-ta." *Oh, jeez. Did I really just say "ta-ta"?*

I glanced over at Nick, trying to discern an iota of jealousy. *Nuthin'.* And now I was stuck babysitting Bobby's kid. Well, that's just fabulous.

Nick pulled up in front of my house and cut the engine.

"Thanks for the ride, Nick," I said, looking down at my lap. The adrenalin rush I'd felt when I was fighting for my life had slipped away, and I was left with an indescribable feeling of loss. I hadn't allowed myself to think about the girl in the hospital or Crystal's fate out on the streets or even the circumstances that drove Bunny to the other side of sanity. But it hit me now like a punch in the face and I swallowed hard to keep from crying.

"Okay if I stick around a while?" Nick asked. He opened his car door and hopped out, not waiting for an answer. I hopped out too and felt a searing pain in my ankle as I stepped down.

"Hang on there a second," he told me, and lifted me up in his arms.

"Nick, really, this isn't necessary. I'm fine."

"You're more than fine. Indulge me."

I made an involuntary noise, a cross between a sigh and an orgasmic moan and let him carry me up my steps.

My across the street neighbor, Heather Koslowski was just getting out of her car with Mr. Wiggles. Mr. Wiggles is her dog, but she refers to him as her 'boyfriend.' Swear to God. Ignoring the fact that I was being carried "Windswept" style up to my house, she called over to me.

"Hi Brandy. I haven't seen you for a while. Want to come over and watch *What a Girl Wants,* tonight?" Normally I'd take her up on it, seeing as it's one of my favorite movies, starring perky Amanda Bynes, but I already had what a girl wants, at least for the moment.

"Um, thanks, Heather. Maybe next week."

Nick carried me over the threshold and deposited me on the living room couch. I took a quick look around. I'd left my bra draped over the banister. *Great.* And over in the corner was a box of old Barbie dolls I'd found in my bedroom closet and thought about donating to Good Will, but then Janine came over and we dressed them up and had a fashion show and when I remembered how much fun they were I decided to keep them.

"I've got an Ace Bandage in the truck," Nick told me, heading out the door again. "I'll be right back." He glanced over at the box and grinned. "Barbies. Nice."

"Those are my brother's. He's really into fashion."

"Uh huh," Nick said, and went off to retrieve the bandage.

The instant Nick left tears welled up in me and began spilling haphazardly down my cheeks. *Oh Christ, where's this coming from? Okay, so the day's been a little rough, what with watching a kid die and getting the living crap beat out of me, but things are looking up now. Stop being such a baby.*

I sucked in a deep breath and swiped my eyes with the back of my hand. Nick came in at that moment and sat down next to me on the couch. He was holding a small first aid kit and some bandages.

"You okay, Angel?"

"What? Me? Pfft. I'm fine." *That's the Alexander spirit.* I flashed him a big old smile and split my chin open again. "Ow."

Nick carefully lifted my chin and inspected the damage. "You could use some stitches." He opened the kit and extracted an antiseptic wipe and dabbed at the cut, covering it afterward with a butterfly bandage. Then he reached down and pulled my legs up onto his lap. Easing off my shoe he began cuffing my pants.

Oh shit! How long has it been since I shaved my legs?

Thank God he stopped at the ankle. Nick slowly rotated my foot. "There's some swelling, but nothing's broken," he decided, only I wasn't really paying attention. His touch was sending electric currents straight to my crotch.

Too soon my ankle was wrapped and my legs back on solid ground.

"You're going to be feeling those bumps and bruises, if you haven't started already," Nick told me. "Where do you keep your aspirin?"

"In the kitchen, above the microwave, only I really think I could use some chocolate. Studies have shown it helps in the healing process."

While Nick was getting the medicinal Hershey's I put in a call to the hospital. Nurse Morrison was still on duty. "It's Brandy Alexander," I said, when she got on the line. "Listen, I know you've got rules against giving out patient information and I totally respect that. It's just that I can't stop thinking about the girl who—" I stopped, choking up.

"Who died," Nurse Morrison supplied. "Dr. Sanchez vouched for you. She says you're one of the good guys. What do you want to know?"

"It's just that I thought she was going to be okay. What happened?"

"Miscarriage, in all likelihood caused by the drugs we found in her system. She developed an infection and it attacked her heart." She let out a weary sigh. "And as sad as it is, it's a common story. My friend works in the coroners' office in Camden. Called me up about a year ago in tears. Said this pretty little white girl had come in— she was a runaway and she'd O.D.'d. She'd just given birth. God only knows what happened to her baby." Another sigh, then, "Well, I'd better go tend to the living. Brandy," she added, "Dr. Sanchez was right. You *are* one of the good guys. If more people cared about these kids, there would be far fewer that end up like this one."

After we said our goodbyes, I reached for the Homer Simpson Pez dispenser I keep on my coffee table, for moments like these when I need some quick cheering up. Homer is hilarious, especially when he's dispensing pure sugar pellets from his neck. Only the Pez dispenser wasn't there.

I crawled around on the floor, checking under the couch, but it was nowhere in sight. The last time I'd seen it, Crystal was helping herself to some candy.

"Weird," I mused aloud, plunking myself back on the couch.

"What is?" Nick came into the living room and handed me a chocolate bar and some aspirin and sat down next to me again.

71

"I'm pretty sure Crystal stole my Pez dispenser. I had a twenty dollar bill sitting right next to it, and that's still here."

"Not so weird, Darlin'. She wasn't trying to rip you off, she just wanted something of yours to take with her. This may be hard to believe, but it's actually a compliment. It shows that she trusts you."

I sandwiched the aspirin between two bits of chocolate and popped it into my mouth.

"How do you know so much about this kid, Nick? You just met her but you seem to understand her better than I ever will."

Nick's normally placid face showed the slightest bit of distress, but it was enough to send a pang through my heart. "Why is that?" I pressed. "Why did you guys connect the way you did?"

He cut me a lopsided smile and my heart officially broke. "The reason I understand Crystal is because when I was a kid I lived on the streets too."

Woah! I did not see that one coming…although, now that he'd told me, it made all the sense in the world.

"I've been on my own since I was twelve," he continued, quietly. "Luckily, I had some help along the way."

My eyes got all teary again. "Nick, I'm so sorry."

"It's okay, Angel. I got through it," he said, pulling me to him. I rested my head against his shoulder and prayed to the universe I'd never have to move again.

"But how?" I nearly sobbed. "How do you 'get through' something like that?"

Nick stroked my hair, comforting me. "My maternal grandfather was Cherokee. He died when I was just a little boy, but he taught me a very wise Cherokee saying. 'Don't

let yesterday take up too much of today.' I try to live by
that."

"Nick," I said, turning to face him. "I asked you
something a while ago, but you never gave me an answer.
Tell me about your childhood. Please."

"Someday," he said, returning my gaze.

"But—"

"Shhh," he whispered, and cupped my face in his
hands. "I've missed you, Brandy Alexander." And then
he kissed me.

Chapter Five

"…and then he kissed me."

"Tongue?" Janine asked.

"Janine! Please. I'm trying to eat, here," John grumbled.

I gave a silent nod to Janine, and smiled, remembering.

We were crammed into a booth at DiVinci's Pizza; Carla, Janine, Johnny and me, AKA "The Party Planning Committee." Mrs. DiAngelo couldn't make it. She was having a gnocchi crisis. Janine said her mother, famous for her Italian dumplings and the undisputed neighborhood champ, was recently usurped by Eddie's mother, who, according to a reliable source, had been perfecting a new recipe for months in an effort to capture the coveted title.

Carla, her foot-high beehive shrinking in the heat, cast me a big-sisterly look, mixed with a slight tinge of envy. "Be careful, hon. I know that man has charm. And he gets points for being honest with you. But knowing the score and following your heart don't always take you to the same place."

Carla was right, of course. Only, when it came to Santiago I was willing to risk a train wreck. I'd been touched by his willingness to open up to me about his past, however small the revelations. It meant he trusted me, and that in itself was huge. Nick was a man who did not trust easily. So maybe the kiss was meant to shut me up, keep me from pressing him about places he didn't want to revisit. But there was genuine affection in that kiss that slowly turned to passion.

His mouth was warm and I melted into him, my breasts, twin heat-seeking missiles, happily brushing up against him. He'd started out gently, placing soft, full lips on mine, but I'd been deprived of his touch for far too long and this was not going to cut it. I opened my mouth and let him taste me, and soon he was returning the heat, his tongue playing tag with mine.

We sat on my couch, entwined in each other's arms, exchanging steaming hot kisses, when suddenly, for a brief, painful moment I remembered he doesn't love me. I pulled back for a beat, but then I figured, "what the heck," he'll never know what he's missing if he doesn't have a point of reference, and I slid my tongue back into his mouth, making sure I gave him something to remember me by.

Nick moved on top of me, pressing me backwards and I could feel his desire for me grow in quite the literal sense of the word. I wanted this man so bad my hormones were about to spring a leak. I opened my legs and he settled in between them and then—the doorbell rang. *Oh, fuck-a-roo!*

"Aren't you going to answer it?" Nick asked, smiling down at me.

"I wasn't planning to, no." My breath came in short spurts as I struggled to ignore the activity outside.

The doorbell rang again, followed by the grating sound of my neighbor's voice. "Yoo hoo, Girlie." I sighed and opened the door, almost ripping the knob off in the process.

"Mrs. Gentile," I said, through barely gritted teeth. "What a nice surprise." She was wearing an old lady flowered housedress that made her look like a giant, wrinkled petunia. It got me wondering at what age you begin thinking floral mu mu's are the height of fashion.

"Your television is up too loud," Mrs. Gentile complained. "It's interrupting my afternoon nap."

"I'll turn it down, Mrs. Gentile," I told her, figuring it was easier than trying to convince her that my set wasn't even on.

"See that you do." She turned and stomped back inside her house.

Nick was sitting upright on the couch. He stood now and walked toward me, signaling the end of our make-out session. Disappointment and a sudden urge to knock Mrs. Gentile clear to Jersey threatened to consume me.

Tilting my chin upward, Nick gave it a quick inspection and then kissed the tip of my nose. "Be sure to keep that wound covered. You don't want it to get infected."

I nodded, but I wasn't thinking about my chin. All's I really wanted was for Nick to kiss me again.

Nick crossed the threshold and turned back to me. "You know, Angel, Crystal's lucky to have you in her corner."

I shook my head. "I haven't done anything. She's lucky to have *you* in her corner."

"Hopefully I'll have some information on her friend soon. I'm putting Raoul's little brother on it. He knows just about everything that happens on the streets."

Raoul works for Nick, but I'm not sure in what capacity. Since rumor has it that Raoul killed a couple of guys who looked at him cross-eyed, I thought it best not to ask.

"If you're in the neighborhood tomorrow, stop by the studio. I know you're perfectly capable of taking care of yourself, but it never hurts to learn something new." He flashed me another smile, not quite his old familiar one. This one had a touch of sadness. And with that he was gone.

I saved all the really juicy details for a private girl-chat with Janine, and even then, I'd only tell the parts that were relevant to me. It never occurred to me to talk about Nick's private business.

"Can we get back to the subject at hand?" John asked, dabbing grease off his chin. "This pizza has heart attack written all over it," he added, blotting a slice with a paper napkin. I guess he pressed too hard because when he lifted the napkin all the cheese went with it.

"Stop playing with your food, John," Carla told him, sliding another slice onto his plate. "And if you can't take the 'girl-talk,' stay out of the hen house."

"And just where would that leave you guys? I'm the only one with good taste around here. This baby shower had tacky written all over it until I offered my services."

I looked at Carla, decked out in her "Kiss me, I'm Italian" tee shirt, then at Janine, wearing a faux-jeweled sun visor. Wiping some pizza sauce from my hand onto the leg of my torn jeans, I decided that John had a point.

"Okay, ladies," John said. "We need a theme."

"Uh, John, did you miss the part where Fran's having a baby? I thought we'd go with *that* theme."

"Shut –uh-up. I mean something like—" he closed his eyes, pausing for effect— "famous babies throughout history or—"

"Rosemary's Baby!" Janine chimed in all excited.

"Neenie, have you ever seen *Rosemary's Baby*?" I asked her.

"No."

"Do you even know what it's about?"

"Some chick named Rosemary has a baby. Duh."

John opened his eyes. "Maybe we don't need a theme."

Carla leaned forward, squinching up her eyes and staring at the front entrance. "Is Bobby part of the planning committee?" she asked as DiCarlo appeared in the doorway.

Janine waved and called out to him. "Yo, Bobby. Over here."

My hand touched my chin, reflexively. "Listen, you guys, don't mention anything about what happened to me. If DiCarlo finds out about Bunny he'll have her arrested, and that could spell disaster for Crystal."

I wouldn't recommend you telling your Uncle Frankie about it either," Carla advised, "because if he knew he'd beat the living hell out of that Bunny person. Girl or no girl."

I guess I shouldn't have gotten such a kick out of the idea, but I did.

Bobby reached the table and slid in next to me in the already crowded booth. His eyes roved over my face, settling on my chin. "I heard you've been sparring with Jimmy the Rat," he said, gracing me with a dimpled smile. "I should've warned you he's been working on his left

78

hook." He rubbed his thumb lightly over my cheek. "Man, you look like you got hit by a ton of bricks."

Well, I suppose *technically* that was true. Bunny was built like a brick shit house.

"Lucky punch," I shrugged, happy not to have to make up a lie of my own.

Bobby raised an arm and flagged down our server, Lindsay Sargenti. "Tuna melt to go, Linz." He turned back to us, absently drumming his fingers on the scarred wooden table top. He was brimming with cat-like energy, a sure sign that something was up.

"So, what's going on, Bobby?" I asked.

John noticed it too. "Yeah," he said. "You've got the *shpilkas*," a term he picked up when he was a kid living next door to my Jewish grandmother.

"Aah, it's this case I'm working on. It's been a real nightmare. This woman bought it down near 10th & Oregon. No sign of sexual assault, no personal effects were taken, her money and credit cards were still in her wallet. According to friends and family she didn't have an enemy in the world." He let out a frustrated sigh. "Well, obviously she had one."

"I'm sorry," I said, placing a hand on his. "I guess being a homicide cop isn't all fun and games."

DiCarlo smiled again, locking his fingers with mine. "Yeah, it pretty much sucks. By the time I'm called in you know there's not going to be a happy ending."

"Any leads?" Carla asked, rooting in her pocketbook for her lipstick. She pulled it out and heaped a generous portion of Fuchsia Delight onto her lips.

"None that I can talk about. Her family—" he shook his head. "Well, they're completely broken up. She was a case worker for homeless youth, out to save the world."

79

"You say that like it's a bad thing."

Bobby disengaged his hand from mine and rubbed his fingertips against his temples, a gesture he reverted to whenever he was on overload. "I'm just tired of seeing good people get hurt. Well, I can't pick and choose who the homicide victims are. Listen," he said, abruptly changing the subject, "thanks again for agreeing to watch Sophia on Saturday night."

Janine perked her head up. Until now she had been chowing down the pizza at a yeoman's pace. *"You're babysitting? A real live kid?"*

"Jeez, Janine. Have a little faith. I'm perfectly capable of taking care of a toddler for a few hours. I've babysat before." Okay, so maybe she was remembering the time when we were fourteen and we'd started a babysitting service, and we accidentally left six-year-old Benjy Shapiro at the mall. It could happen to anyone. And it's not like we didn't find him again.

"Should I be worried?" Bobby asked me.

This was my chance to get out of watching Bobby's kid while he went off on a date with someone who wasn't—*well*—*me*. But pride goeth before a fall and all that.

"Of course you shouldn't be worried. What could go wrong?"

Janine, Carla and Johnny all exchanged glances. "I'm not busy Saturday night," John lied. "Maybe I'll come by and keep you company."

"Count me in," said Janine. "Bobby, didn't you say last week that Sophia got a new tea set? I totally want to check it out."

"Frankie and I were going to go to the Springsteen concert," Carla added, putting her lipstick back in her purse. "But this sounds like a lot more fun."

"Maybe I should just cancel my plans," Bobby said.

Lindsay arrived with the tuna melt wrapped and ready to go.

Bobby slid out of the booth. "Thanks, Linz. Listen, I'll catch you guys later."

He wasn't three feet away from the table when Janine turned to me. "You volunteered to babysit? What were you thinking?"

That I thought he was asking me out on a date and I wanted to make Nick jealous.

"Oh, y'know, Bobby and I are so over each other. I just want him to be happy. And if he has an opportunity to socialize with someone of the opposite sex, I will do whatever a good friend does and support him however I can."

"You didn't know what you were agreeing to when he called, did you?" John said.

"Not a clue."

John was off to a photo shoot, Janine had a one o'clock appointment with a temp agency and Carla had to get back to the salon.

I had to go too. Eric had called earlier in the day to ask me to fill in for Godfrey, the Traffic Dog. Kevin Sanders, the actor that plays Godfrey, was ordered by the court to pick up trash on I-95 as a community service for some undisclosed, but, my guess is, highly embarrassing indiscretion, which left a hole in the mid day traffic report. Playing a safety-tip- dispensing St. Bernard wasn't part of my contractual agreement, but Eric offered me an extra fifty bucks and I could really use the money.

81

On the way back from the studio, I cruised by Poplar and Taney. I didn't know what I was looking for. I just had a vague feeling of unease. Nick said I should let Crystal come to me, but I couldn't help but worry about her. What if Bunny took it out on Crystal because she couldn't take it out on me?

The afternoon heat must've driven everyone indoors. The streets were empty. I pulled over and parked, careful to lock myself inside the car. Then I took out my cell phone and called Nick.

I got his voicemail, which in itself gave me a little thrill. I didn't leave a message, but a moment later my phone rang.

"Hello, Angel. I was on the other line when you called. What's up?"

"I was just wondering if you saw Crystal today. You'd told her to come by at around three."

"She hasn't been here."

Panic rose up in me. I couldn't believe how invested I was in this kid. "It's after four, Nick. She said she'd be there. Something must've happened to her."

I could hear the smile in Nick's voice, calm and reassuring. "Street kids have their own concept of time, Darlin'. She may show up later on or even tomorrow. Try not to worry about it."

"I'm not worried."

"Of course not." I could picture that gently mocking smile.

"Okay, maybe just mildly concerned. Call me if you see her."

I hung up and started the car. Radio station WMGK was having a David Bowie retrospective and I tried to immerse myself in it, but my thoughts kept returning to Crystal and Star. Crystal was convinced that Star wouldn't have just split on her own. Assuming that were true, the alternatives weren't pretty.

Maybe Star had gotten arrested. If she was into prostitution, chances were good she'd end up in jail sooner or later. *But they wouldn't hold her for a week. She'd be out on the street in a matter of hours.* I made a mental note to have Bobby run a check.

Alright, what else…Crystal said Star had a pimp. What was his name again? *Little Red.* Maybe he got pissed off at her for not bringing in enough money, or whatever pimps get upset with their ho's for. He might've beaten her and she was lying low, trying to get her strength back. He'd told Crystal he hadn't seen Star, but how trustworthy is a guy who sells fifteen-year-olds for a living.

Then there was Bunny. Could she have had something to do with Star's disappearance? I knew first-hand that Bunny was the jealous type. She went ballistic after seeing me just talking to Crystal. She probably had it out for Star because Star was Crystal's protector. *Oh God, what if Bunny decided to get rid of her competition permanently?* The thought made my stomach turn.

I stopped off at Sam's Deli on the way home to get a hoagie for dinner. Out of deference to my "new and improved" eating regimen, I asked Sam to hold the mayo.

"Brandy, I've been making hoagies for you since you were a little girl. You've never asked for mayo on a hoagie in your life. And besides that, I'd never *make* a hoagie with mayo. It's just not right."

"Then it shouldn't be a problem to hold it," I told him.

Sam laughed and put down the lit cigar he'd been chewing on. The health department has rules against smoking in public places, but Sam considers his deli an "extension of his home."

"So how's your father?" he asked me, grabbing a roll from beneath the counter. "Are he and your mother ready to move back from Florida?"

"Nah. I think they're pretty happy there," I told him and prayed it was the truth. I love my parents very much, and eleven hundred miles seems just the right amount of distance to keep it that way.

While I was waiting around for my sandwich, I checked out the dessert case. Sacrificing the mayonnaise left room in my almost cholesterol-free diet for a cannoli. I got one for myself and then I realized that Rocky and Adrian would probably like some too, so I bought a couple more. I figured I'd keep them in my refrigerator and they could help themselves. And if not, I'm sure *someone* would eat them.

"Here ya go, doll." Sam handed me a paper bag. Grease stains had already begun to form on the bottom, assuring me it was going to be an excellent dinner.

Paul was waiting for me when I got home. He was standing on the curb outside of the Koslowski's house, talking to Heather. I got a nervous pang that he was going to be hungry and I'd have to offer him some of my hoagie. I waved at them and walked into the house heading straight for the kitchen.

Paul trailed in after me. "Did you tell Mom I signed up for J Date?"

"Try some of this hoagie. It's delicious!"

My brother knows it bugs me to have to share my food. He sighed and took a spite bite.

"I'm sorry, Paulie." I cut the hoagie in half and stuck it on a napkin in front of him as a peace offering. "It's just that she was on a roll about me not going out with anyone. I had to throw her a bone."

"It's okay. I'd have done the same thing." Eyeing the sandwich he added, "You sure?"

"Yeah, go for it. And just to show you how much I love you, I bought a canoli and I'm willing to split it with you."

"Wow. You do love me. So," Paul continued, with a mouthful of food, "Heather s-says you had some c-company yesterday. Some really good looking g-guy was carrying you up the steps." He tried to keep his voice casual, but the stutter was a dead give away.

"Well, Heather's a regular little Chatty Cathy, now isn't she?"

"Bran, is there any-th-thing I should know about?"

"Nope. Not a thing."

"It was Nick, wasn't it?"

I sighed. "Paulie, there's nothing to tell. I ran across him while I was out jogging and I'd sprained my ankle so he was helping me home. End of story."

"*You? Out jogging?* Now I *know* something's up."

"Oh, fine. Don't believe me!" It's amazing how self-righteous I get when I'm telling a big fat lie.

Paul left at around eight. His bartender called in sick and he had to get back to the club. I'd offered to fill in for him, but he said he'd be okay. Ever since I worked for Paul a couple of months back, he always turns me down whenever I volunteer my services. I think he feels like he'd be taking advantage of me, but I like helping him out. Besides, I have excellent people skills. My customers were always asking to see the manager, telling him they couldn't *believe* the kind of service they were getting.

The house felt really empty after Paul left. I'd been so busy running around all day it was easy to block unpleasant thoughts from my head. But now, they were all consuming. *Where was Crystal? Was she curled up asleep under a bridge somewhere? Had she eaten dinner? Was she safe? Was she scared?*

And what about the girl from the hospital? She died a "Jane Doe." Was someone grieving for her tonight? The thought ate away at me. I had to know. I picked up the phone and called the police station.

I asked for Mike Mahoe. It took a while but he finally got on the line. I sensed he was reluctant to talk to me. I'm pretty in tune with these types of things...Plus, I overheard him whisper, "Christ, what does she want from me now? Tell her I'm not here."

Mike and I used to be an "item." Well, not exactly an item. More like a "passing thought." That is until he realized I had some unresolved issues with Bobby. And by the time we'd gotten past that hurdle, he'd decided I was way too high maintenance to pursue in the romantic sense of the word. But I know he considers me a friend...if the phrase "relentless pest" can be considered a term of endearment.

Mike is my "go to" guy when I need information and *don't* want to "go to" Bobby.

"It's not my department," Mike said, getting on the line.

"But you don't even know what I'm going to ask yet. How are you, anyway, Mike? It's been ages."

That got a laugh out of him. "I'm fine and I want to stay that way. If you need anything that could get me into trouble with DiCarlo I'm hanging up."

Okay, so I may have asked Mike a time or two about things Bobby considered strictly police business, but this wasn't one of them. The reason I didn't go to Bobby about the girl who died is I didn't feel like hearing a lecture about the pitfalls of becoming emotionally involved in the lives of strangers. *As if I do that. Sheesh.*

"Look, a kid was brought into the E.R. the other night. She didn't make it. She was a runaway and the hospital couldn't I.D. her. I just wondered if anybody—y'know—claimed her, is all." I tried to keep the hitch out of my voice, but it was a fruitless effort.

Mike softened. "I'll see what I can find out and get back to you."

"Thanks, Mike. I really appreciate it."

It was after midnight but I just couldn't fall asleep. I tried to conjure up sleep-inducing thoughts, like Bergman films or my mother's story about the time she ran into a Dolly Parton look-alike at the airport in Des Moines, but nothing worked. It didn't help that it was about 110 degrees in my bedroom. I really had to get that air conditioner fixed.

I finally gave up trying to sleep and went downstairs. First, I surfed the net looking for information on homeless youth and then I took a quiz. *"What kind of dog are you?"* I took it three times, but it kept coming up Daschund. I was sorta hoping for something a little less sausage-like.

Adrian sat beside me on the couch. Now, he sat up, his head tilted toward the front door. A slow growl grew in his throat and became full-fledged bark. Someone was right outside the door.

It has been my experience lately that midnight callers almost never turn out well.

I scanned the room for some form of protection but all I could come up with was the TV remote. I crept over to the door and put my ear against it and listened.

There was some muted shuffling and then the doorbell rang. I let out a surprised squeak. "Who is it?" I asked.

"Crystal."

Sighing with relief, I opened the door and stared directly into the barrel of a gun.

Oh, shit.

Chapter Six

She pushed her skinny frame through the crack in the open door. Her eyes were practically bulging out of her head and her hands were shaking so hard I thought the gun would go off from motion sickness. For a minute I figured she might be tweaking, but, no, this was rage, pure and simple.

"Come on in," I said, acting like it was my idea and as if I had a choice.

"Fuck you!"

I tried to remain calm but it was impossible, what with a .22 staring me in the face and Adrian bouncing around at my feet like he was on puppy uppers.

Suddenly I found it very difficult to breathe. I steadied myself against the arm of the couch forcing myself to focus. "Okay, Crystal, you're obviously really mad at me, only I don't know what I did. Could you put the gun down so we can talk about it?"

"Why?" she screamed, waving the friggin' thing in my face. "So you can lie to me again? I *never* should have trusted you." She glared at me with utter loathing. "You've fucked up everything. I should blow your goddamn head off."

"I really wish you wouldn't. Look," I said, trying to appeal to her animal lovin' side. "You're scaring the dog. How about I sit down on the couch, and you put the gun right next to you on top of the television set. If I move, shoot me."

I sincerely hoped she knew that was just a figure of speech.

Adrian began to whimper. He curled up against Crystal's leg, pleading for his mommy's life. Well, in all honesty, he was probably reminiscing about the swell time he had the last time she was here and he just wanted to play some more. Whatever, the momentary distraction seemed to break the mood. Her eyes never leaving mine, she slid the .22 on top of the TV set. Maybe it was wishful thinking on my part, but she actually seemed relieved.

"If you call the cops I'll fucking kill you."

Staring back at her, I eased myself onto the couch. "Understood. But why would I call the cops on you? And what is it you think I've done?"

"Oh, don't act like you don't know. They raided our squat because of you. Tore the place apart—"

"Crystal, back up. Look, I swear to you, I haven't talked to the police. I know you don't know me very well, but I would hope I've built up a little credit with you. What's going on?"

Crystal quieted down a notch. "You mean you really don't know? It was all over the news tonight. I don't even own a TV and I saw it!"

"The news is depressing. I was watching High School Musical on the Disney Channel."

She gave me the biggest eyeball roll in recorded history and turned on my computer.

A minute later a clip from tonight's WINN broadcast popped up on the screen.

It was Art Metropolis, news anchor and colossal pinhead. "Police are searching tonight for a person of interest in the murder of thirty-nine-year-old Olivia Bowen, a case worker for homeless youth in Philadelphia. Bowen was spotted earlier on the evening of the murder, speaking with an unidentified person in the parking lot of Kenny's Steak House. Bowen's body was discovered late last night by dock workers, in the Delaware River marshes, just north of the airport."

"Why would Crystal want me to see this?" I thought. A split second later I had my answer.

"If anyone has information on the identity or whereabouts of this person, please contact the police department at the number on the screen below."

I automatically glanced down at the number and when I looked up again a graphic of the "person of interest" appeared on the screen. She was big as life and twice as ugly.

"Holy Cow, it's Bunny!"

Crystal clicked off the computer screen. "Don't act so surprised. If you didn't tell the police where to look for her who did?"

"Crystal," I said, trying to choose my words carefully. "I honestly don't know. I gave you my word that I wouldn't involve the police and I didn't. But I think you're missing the big picture here. The cops probably think Bunny killed that woman. 'Person of interest' is usually just a euphemism for 'We know you did it but we can't prove anything yet.' If you know where Bunny's hiding, then—"

"Then *what?*" Crystal exploded. "Turn her in? You think it's that easy? You have no fucking idea what my life would be like if word got out that I snitched. I'd be dead inside of a week."

Uttering those words seemed to unleash a torrent of pent up emotion in the poor kid. She paced around the room, talking non-stop for the next thirty minutes, describing, in sometimes horrifying detail, what it was like for kids living on the streets. I sat cross-legged on the couch, silent, listening and fighting my impulse to fling my arms around her and tell her it would be alright. Because the truth was, I had no idea in the world if things would ever turn out okay for her, and the last thing she needed was one more lying adult in her life.

When she was finished she stopped pacing and sat down, the wind finally out of her sails. I got up and went into the kitchen, returning a minute later with a package of Tastykakes and two glasses of milk. I set them on the table.

"Help yourself."

"I haven't had one of these since I was little," she said quietly. "My grandma used to send them to me every year on my birthday." She picked up a cupcake and took a big hungry bite.

"So, you didn't grow up around here?"

Crystal shook her head. *A regular fountain of information, that one.*

"Is your grandma still alive?"

"I haven't seen her in a long time. After—" She shrugged. "We don't keep in touch."

Crystal finished her cupcake and downed the rest of her milk. "Thanks." She gestured toward the empty glass. "Look, for the record, I don't know where Bunny is. I

92

haven't seen her since yesterday afternoon. You don't have to believe me but that's the truth."

"I believe you. But if you *did* know—well, just do what you have to do to keep yourself safe."

She gave me a look that was borderline sheepish. "Um, there *is* something I should maybe mention to you."

Uh oh. I've said those very words to people just before I tell them something they really don't want to hear…Okay, stay calm. She won't confide in you if you overreact.

"Yeah? What's that?"

"Bunny knows who you are and probably where to find you."

Shit! Fuck! Damn! Piss! "Oh?"

"Man, you're taking this a lot better than I thought you would. I thought you'd be mad at me."

"No, I'm not mad." *I'm freakin' petrified!* "I'm glad you told me. So, just out of curiosity, how did she find out?"

"Remember when she saw us together? Well, I've got this little tear in my backpack, and your card fell out. I didn't tell her on purpose, I swear it."

My guess was she did, but felt bad about it.

"So, did you tell her I'm helping you look for Star?"

Crystal shook her head. "Not at first. I just told her you were lost and needed directions. But…"

She stopped and I waited. "But then she started hassling me about wanting to be my street mom and I thought—I thought if she knew Star was coming back she'd leave me alone."

Crystal's shoulders slumped, the magnitude of her situation finally catching up with her. "I fucked up so bad. I should've kept my mouth shut. But it just came out. And now it's not just Bunny I have to worry about. She's going to tell everyone I was the one who got you involved in street business."

The news report said the woman who was murdered was a case worker for homeless youth. Did Bunny thinks Olivia Bowen had somehow gotten all up in her business too? Wow. If she did kill Bowen, I got off lucky. If I hadn't knocked Bunny out, I could've been the warm-up act.

"Crystal, did Bunny and Olivia Bowen know each other?"

"I don't know. I stayed away from Bunny as much as possible. Why?"

"I was just wondering what their connection might be. If she is involved in this woman's death, what would be her motivation?"

"Maybe she got pissed off because of Star."

"What do you mean?"

"That Bowen lady was Star's case worker."

I tried to keep the "Why *the hell* didn't you tell me" tone out of my voice and said calmly, "Crystal, that's the kind of information that could be very helpful. I'm wondering why you didn't mention it sooner."

She shrugged. "You didn't ask."

I opened my mouth and closed it again. I had to remember I was dealing with a teenager trapped in an alternate universe. What was obvious to me wasn't always the case with Crystal.

I needed time to sort all this out, but right now, there was a more pressing problem.

While Crystal helped herself to another cupcake I got off the couch and sauntered over to the television, and casually deposited the gun in the plastic palm tree my parents sent me from Florida. The thing is hideous, and I suspect the cat has used it as a litter box on more than one occasion, but I can't throw it out. That would hurt its feelings.

Now that the lethal weapon was out of plain sight, I turned back to Crystal.

"Listen, kiddo, I don't know how to say this except to just, well, say it. I think we should tell the police about Star going missing. Her disappearance may be tied in somehow to Olivia Bowen's murder."

Crystal's delicate blond eyebrows arched and I could feel the heat rise from her body.

"Now before you get all bent out of shape, just hear me out. You said it yourself that everyone was going to blame you anyway for the police showing up, so it's not safe for you to go back there. And what if by withholding information from the cops we end up endangering Star's life? Look, Bowen was Star's case worker. Star's missing and Bowen's dead, and Bunny was involved with them both."

"But what if I'm wrong about Star? What if she's fine and she doesn't want to be found?"

"You don't really believe that, do you?"

Her silence spoke volumes.

"Listen, the important thing right now is getting you to a safe place. I can arrange for that if you'll let me."

"I can take care of myself."

"I know you can take care of yourself. But for once you don't have to."

It was after two and Crystal reluctantly agreed to stay here overnight. As she so graciously put it, she couldn't go back to her squat and all the good outdoor crash spots were taken, so she might as well hang out with me. She fell asleep immediately, curled up in a fetal position on the couch with Adrian sacked out beside her. She didn't seem to be concerned about the whereabouts of her gun. I think she was just as happy to be rid of the damn thing.

After Crystal had gone to bed I went around and checked doors and windows. A couple of months ago I'd had an alarm system installed, but for some reason it kept going off every time Mrs. Gentile used her microwave. I never got around to getting it fixed, but I turned it on now and prayed Mrs. Gentile didn't get an urge for popcorn at three in the morning.

I'd talked a good game about finding Cyrstal a safe place to stay, but I had no idea where to start. If retribution on the streets was as harsh as she'd described it I couldn't put my friends in jeopardy by having her stay with them. Besides, Crystal wasn't exactly what you'd call easy to be around. Bunny knew where I lived, so that ruled out my place …which left me with one choice and I'd already imposed on him enough…so, what's one more favor, right? I'd make the call in the morning.

As it turned out it wasn't necessary. Nick called at 7:00 a.m.

"Did I wake you?"

Well, speak of the devil. I was just lying here making passionate love with you in my head. "No, you didn't wake me. What's up?"

"I got a call from Raoul's brother, Octavio. He has a friend who recognized Star from her photo, and she agreed to talk to you for a little monetary compensation."

"How does she know Star?"

"Seems they shared the same employer."

"She works for Little Red?"

"Unfortunately. The guys a real sweetheart. A couple of months ago he thought she was holding back some of her night's profits so he threw acid on her leg. Told her

96

next time it would be her face. Scarred her up pretty good. And scared her enough to want to get out of town. She'll talk to you for the price of a ticket back to Georgia."

The mental image that accompanied Nick's words seared my insides.

Crystal had said Little Red was mad that Star had disappeared on him. Could that have been just an act to cover up the fact that he'd done something to her?

"This young woman mentioned seeing Star get into a silver van a while back," Nick continued, "and she hasn't seen her since."

"When was this?"

"It could've been last week, it could've been last month. Street time is hard to pin down."

"So did Octavio say how I can get in touch with his friend?"

"You got a pen?"

I grabbed a pen and a pad of paper off the nightstand.

"Her name is Harmony Valentine."

"For real?" *Like I have room to talk with a name like Brandy Alexander.*

"As real as it gets on the streets, Darlin'."

I thought for a minute. "When Harmony saw Star climb into the van, was she close enough to I.D. the driver?"

Nick laughed. "In a manner of speaking. She said, and I quote, 'All those white assholes look alike'."

"Then I guess it's too much to hope for a license plate, huh?"

"Normally, yes. But this was a vanity plate so it stuck in her head. SLIMEY 1."

Wow. How appropo was *that?!*

97

He recited Harmony's phone number for me along with the obligatory reminder to be careful.

"Um, Nick, there's just one more thing. There was something on the news last night about Bunny."

"I've already heard, Angel. Looks like Crystal's going to need a safe house for a while. I'll put in a call to Sal. I'm sure he'd be willing to take her." Sal, AKA Father Salvador Domingo is Nick's childhood friend, the yin to his yang and the head honcho at a parish in the badlands.

"I really owe you, Nick."

"You don't owe me a thing, Darlin'. Glad to help."

I hung up and jumped in the shower. I was exhausted, having slept a total of about four minutes. I hadn't dared open my bedroom window last night on the off chance that Bunny decided to hop on by (I make God-awful puns when I'm stressed) and my bedroom was like a sauna.

Rocky was sitting in the bathroom sink waiting for me when I got out of the shower. I've tried to teach her about personal space, but she's not too good with the concept, so I brushed my teeth and spit in the toilet so's not to disturb her.

Since I wasn't scheduled to work today, I pulled on a pink wife-beater undershirt and some ripped jeans, ignored the dark circles under my eyes and headed downstairs. Crystal was awake and playing with the dog. They both stopped when they saw me and followed me into the kitchen. She sat down at the table and began fiddling with a bowl of wax fruit my mother bought for me the last time she came to visit. My mother is big on things that don't spoil, need watering or have to be replaced.

I took a box of Cheerios out of the cupboard and set it on the table. Then I filled her in on my conversation with Nick.

Crystal absently rubbed her teeth against her tongue stud. "Look, if you want to tell the cops about Bowen being Star's case worker, fine. And you can tell them that Bunny had it in for Star. That's common knowledge on the street anyway. But don't go shooting your mouth off to them about anything that Harmony Valentine bitch says about Little Red. Because if it turns out that Star is really okay and the cops start hassling her pimp, he'll kill her."

"But if she knows something and Star's in trouble, then what?"

"Can't you check it out? I mean isn't that your job?"

My job is to dress up like cauliflower and host the Lehigh Valley Summer Veggie Festival. But somehow that didn't seem quite as professional.

"Okay," I told her. "I'll see what I can do. But if I find out anything that would indicate this guy is involved in Star's disappearance, I'm going straight to the cops."

She didn't argue the point, which relieved me no end. Teenagers are hard work.

"Your mom called while you were in the shower."

"Um, you answered the phone?" I pulled out a bag of dog food from under the sink and began to fill Adrian's bowl.

"Yeah. She asked to speak to you but I told her you were busy turning tricks and you'd get back to her."

"You what?" I spun hard and kibble flew out of the bowl rolling in every direction on the kitchen floor. Rocky appeared out of nowhere and began pouncing on them like tiny round mice.

Crystal laughed. *"I'm kidding.* I didn't even pick up the phone. She left a message. I didn't know you had a brother. She wants you to call him...What's a 'J Date'?"

I dropped Crystal off at Frankie's gym on the pretext of him needing help cleaning out a storeroom. I figured it would be tough for anyone to get to her in a gym full of sweaty, iron-pumping boxers, and my uncle would make sure she stayed out of trouble. To insure that she wouldn't balk at the idea, I told her he'd pay her ten bucks an hour.

"Ten bucks? Really?" Frankie said. "That's a hell of a lot more than I used to pay you to keep *you* out of trouble."

"That's okay, Uncle Frankie, mom made up for it by slipping me an extra fiver to keep *my* eye on you."

I swung by the police station on the way back from the gym. Bobby was at his desk talking to someone on the phone. I could tell by the relaxed way he was smiling and nodding that it was a personal call.

I stood by the door but he didn't invite me in. Instead, he held up his index finger in the universal sign for "hang on a minute" and kinda hunched over his desk, his voice dropping to a whisper.

I'll bet he's talking to a girl! Oh, fine. He's entitled. After all, he's a free agent...is it my imagination, or do his eyes seem bluer, his dimples more pronounced, the muscles beneath his Oxford shirt with the rolled up sleeves more...more...muscley?

There must've been something wrong with those Cheerios I ate for breakfast, because I got a sudden sick feeling in my stomach and I didn't feel much like talking to Bobby anymore. In fact, for some inexplicable reason, I felt like strangling him. I turned to leave.

"Yo, Brandy, wait up. I've got to go," he said into the phone. I'll catch you later."

He hung up and motioned me forward.

"Are you sure?" I asked, and if looks could kill I'd be talking to a corpse. "I mean I wouldn't want my police business to interfere with your personal phone call."

"What crawled up your butt this morning?" He was smiling, which made it worse.

"Bite me."

DiCarlo leaned back in his chair, his smile widening. "Think I'll leave that to your new boyfriend. I heard he's back in town."

"FYI Nick's not my boyfriend, although I do find it interesting that you bother to keep tabs on him. Jealous?"

"Strictly professional curiosity, Sweetheart. It's my job to know what the criminal element is up to." Before I could get in a good one about his current dating status, he called a truce.

"Brandy, let's just admit it's weird for us to think of each other going out with someone else. Okay? I'll start. I hate it. Especially knowing you have real feelings for this guy. And if he hurts you I'll kill him. But I respect your right to move on in your life. Now, is there anything you want to say to me?"

"Your fly is open."

Bobby automatically glanced down.

"Made you look."

He straightened up, blushing. "You're a piece of work, y'know that?"

"So I've been told. Listen, Bobby, I really did come here for a reason. I have some information you may find helpful in the Olivia Bowen case."

"Yeah?" He was all business now. As much as DiCarlo had always tried to discourage me from getting involved in police matters, he trusted my instincts and recognized my ability to get the job done—no matter how ineptly I went about it.

He opened his desk drawer and extracted a notebook and pen. "What have you got?"

I started at the beginning, leaving out only the part about Little Red, because I'd promised Crystal I'd check that out myself.

"So where is this girl, Crystal, now?" Bobby asked when I was finished. "I'm going to need to talk to her."

"She's—unavailable."

The pulse in Bobby's temple flared and throbbed and I knew I was skating on thin ice.

"Look, Bobby, you've said it yourself. To kids in Crystal's position, cops are the enemy. I've told you everything she's told me. If you try to talk to her she'll run or stonewall you, and what good will come of that? Just give me a few days to try and convince her you can be trusted. Okay?"

"Do I have a choice?" By the resigned way he tossed his pen onto the desk, I knew it was strictly a rhetorical question.

I got up and walked around to his side of the desk and laid a kiss on his cheek. "Thanks."

"Piece of work," he muttered, shaking his head.

Harmony Valentine was all of twenty years old, but she looked like she was pushing forty. Freebase cocaine had taken its toll on both her youthful appearance and her attention span. She sat across the table from me, now, tapping out an erratic rhythm with dirty, chipped nails, her eyes darting back and forth, her foot swinging in perpetual motion, interrupted only by the occasional, unintentional kick to my shin.

We were seated in a back booth at Mondo's, an airless, roach-infested eatery that was, apparently, invisible to health inspectors. There was a slightly used napkin sitting on the table when we sat down. The server glanced at the napkin and threw a fork on top of it, handing me a greasy menu. It was filled with color photos of plastic-looking food that looked about as appetizing as fake dog poop.

"Um," I said, looking first at the napkin, then back at the server. He stared at me, daring me to complain. "Gee, everything looks so delicious I hardly know what to order." I put down the menu and flicked a roach off the table while Harmony decided between the egg salad on rye and chicken fried steak.

She settled on the steak and then with sudden ferocity reached under the table and yanked up her pant leg, demanding I take a look at Little Red's handiwork. "Sonuvacocksuckingbitch put me in the hospital. Said I hadn't shown him the proper respect. My leg got infected so bad they thought they was gonna have to cut it off."

She sneezed and wiped her nose with the back of her hand, leaving some goop on the tip of one nostril. I stifled the urge to heave and slid a napkin across the table, hoping she'd take the hint. She didn't.

"So, Harmony, Octavio said you had some information about Star."

"Who?"

Unh! This was not going well. "Star," I repeated, trying to keep the irritation out of my voice. "Remember, that's why we're here. You're going to tell me what you know."

"You gonna pay me?"

"Yes. I'm going to pay you. But first you have to give me some information."

"It's like I told Octavio. I saw her last week or somethin' gettin' in a van with a funny license plate, and I ain't seen her since."

"Why'd you think the license plate was funny?"

"Cuz it spelled out SLIMEY 1. Now why would anyone want to brag about that?"

"Do you remember the date or what day of the week it was?"

"Now how would I know that? Do I look like I carry around a calendar with me? All I know is all the nuts were out that night. Must've been the full moon." She leaned across the table, dropping her voice to a whisper. "That Star ho was Little Red's favorite. But she start talking like she gonna quit him and he say he gonna take her outta the box."

"Outta the box?" I asked, hoping it was just a colorful way of saying he accepted her resignation.

To illustrate her meaning she sliced her index finger across her throat. "I'm gettin' out of this muthafuckin' town soon as I get enough money to get on a airplane." Her eyes strayed to the dessert case. "I want some pie," she announced, as if we'd been discussing dessert all along. "They got any blueberry?"

I tried to keep her focused but it was like trying to catch bits of Styrofoam in a strong wind. "Listen," I said, motioning the server over. "Did you personally ever see Little Red get rough with Star? Or threaten to kill her?"

Harmony thought for a minute. "I don't remember. Like I said, she was his favorite, so maybe she got away with shit none of the other girls could get away with. But Star brought in a lot of money, and he told everybody that she'd be needing a lesson in loyalty if she even thought about leaving."

She grabbed a menu off the table next to us and read aloud. "Says here they got babble pie. What the fuck kind of pie is that?"

"Um, I think they meant 'apple'."

She shrugged and ordered a slice.

Harmony's revelation put Little Red at the top of my "to do" list. The thing is I didn't know what that list entailed. Did I go to the cops with this alleged threat on Star's life—a girl who hasn't even been officially declared missing? I could try the direct approach—find the guy and ask him myself, but that didn't seem the most prudent choice.

Hey, maybe I could pretend to interview him for a segment on Pimp Fashion Wear. "My, what a lovely fedora, and by the way, did you happen to axe your employee, in the most literal sense of the word?"

"Harmony," I began, but her attention was elsewhere. She probably saw a squirrel.

Abruptly, she stood and slid out of the booth. "I got to get back to work," she announced and stumbled toward the door. The server brought the pie and set it down in front of me. It didn't look half bad so I ate it.

I was parked halfway down the block in a *No Parking* zone. I figured in a town where "double parking" is a celebrated local custom, the sign was more of a suggestion rather than a hard and fast rule.

I left the restaurant and spotted Harmony standing on the sidewalk next to my car, talking to a tall, slender white guy. With his baby face, perma-press jeans and western hat he looked like something straight out of *Midnight Cowboy*.

I didn't want to interfere in case Harmony was conducting business, so I tried to sidestep around them. Immediately, a muscled arm shot out and grabbed me hard by the wrist.

"Yo, jerk-off, let go." I reached over with my other hand, grabbed his pinky and bent it back until he howled like a stuck pig. Cowboy Bob let go of my wrist and I yanked my arm away.

Ignoring me for the moment, he turned to Harmony. His voice was perfectly controlled, but it couldn't have been more frightening if he'd come right out and smacked her one.

"I thought you said she was looking for a job. Were you lying to me, bitch?"

"I ain't lyin' to you, Little Red. She's new here. Tha's why I was talkin' to her."

Little Red? Acid-pouring, throat-slicing Little Red?

Harmony stared at me, sweat pouring off her brow. "Ain't that right, Honey? Didn't you say you was lookin' for work?"

I cast my eyes around the deserted street and calculated how many steps to the driver's side of my car. Too many. I decided to play along.

"Yeah, that's right. I'm new here and I need a job. Guess I'd better start pounding the ol' pavement." I smiled and inched my way out onto the street, but the scuzzball planted himself in front of me, blocking my way.

He eyed me up and down, his gaze lingering between my thighs. "I could use some young white chicken," he mused aloud. "You're in luck, bitch, because I'm hiring. Only I'm gonna need a little demonstration of your talent first." He gave a sharp nod to Harmony and she took off

106

running down the block. I tried to run too, but he caught me around the waist and dragged me into the alleyway.

Holy shit!

"Listen, Mr. Red, I would love to audition for you, only I'm late for band practice. I'm—a Mummer. The parade doesn't get put on by itself, you know."

He shoved me up against the side of the building and began unbuckling his pants. "You're going to love working for me, baby. All my girls do."

"Yeah, only I don't think I'm cut out for streetwalking. I don't even own a pair of 'Fuck Me Pumps.' Listen," I told him, reaching into my jeans. "I've got some money that's just burning a hole in my pocket. How about I give it to you and we call it a day?"

I pulled out the wad of cash that had been Harmony's ticket home. My legs were beginning to buckle and I couldn't catch my breath. And then my ears started ringing and I knew I was going to pass out. The ringing got louder, only it sounded more like a siren, and then a male voice shouted, "Put your hands up and turn and face the wall."

Little Red shoved the money back into my hands and turned toward the wall, his pants slowly slipping down around his knees.

A uniformed officer approached us. "You too, little girl. Up against the wall."

"Me? What did *I* do?" I asked, holding a fistful of cash.

"The cop looked at me. "Last time I checked, prostitution was illegal in this state. You have the right to remain silent."

107

Chapter Seven

It took two hours and a phone call to my friend, Vince Giancola, in the D.A.'s office to get me sprung. I cried all the way to the precinct. Between the heat and the tears, my face blew up to unnatural proportions. As if being booked on prostitution charges wasn't humiliating enough, my mug shot looked like the Sta Puff Marshmallow Man.

"Don't even tell me. I don't want to know," Vince said when I tried to explain the series of unfortunate events that led up to my arrest. "I've made it go away, but I couldn't do anything about your car being impounded. Those signs are there for a reason, Brandy. You've got to stop acting like the rules don't apply to you."

I knew he was scared which is why he was yelling at me about the parking violation. The truth is I was scared too. I'd thought I'd played it smart this time. I'd had no intention of tracking down Little Red on my own (whose nickname became apparent the moment he'd dropped his drawers). But things just happen sometimes, and it reminded me that I needed to be better prepared.

I'd managed to keep my identity safe from the person who counted the most. As far as Little Red knew, I was just some middle class suburban, college student looking for a walk on the wild side. But that still didn't solve my problem. I was no closer to finding out what happened to Star than I was when I started out in the morning.

"I think this kid could be in real trouble, Vince. Nobody's seen her in weeks."

"I understand that, kiddo. Believe me, there isn't a day that goes by that I'm not plagued by shit like this. We've got a city full of throwaway kids. Their parents don't want them, the authorities don't know what the hell to do with them, and then the dregs of society prey on them. But my hands are tied. Unless someone files a Missing Persons Report, we can't spend the funds to go looking for her. Life sucks, sometimes, don't it?"

Vince dropped me off at the impound lot. "Uh, listen," I said, climbing out of the car, "Let's just keep this between the two of us, okay? I mean there's no reason to mention anything to DiCarlo or Frankie, right?" Some things are just better left unsaid.

Just as I pulled into the South Street Boxing Gym's parking lot, my cell phone rang. I'd forgotten my Bluetooth, so I'd stuck the phone in between my legs for easy access while driving. It was set on vibrate, which gave me a little thrill, all the more appropriate because the caller was Nick.

"I just got off the phone with Sal," he began. "He said he's got a spot for Crystal at one of his safe houses. She can come and go as she pleases, but I think she's going to like it there."

"Hard to tell what she'll like. She's a *little* on the moody side."

Nick laughed softly and another thrill went through me. "Sal's coming by my apartment in a bit. Why don't you drop by with Crystal? It will give them a chance to meet. If she's comfortable with him, he can take her back with him. If not, we'll move on to Plan B."

"There's a Plan B?"

"There's always a Plan B, Darlin'."

Uncle Frankie was in his office, talking to a guy in grey sweats. Crystal was slumped in a chair, tension crawling out of her pores.

"She *bit* me, man!" he growled at Frankie. "I didn't say nuthin' to her and she bit me." He rolled up his sleeve, shoving a massive arm in front of my uncle's face. There was a definite bruise, but it didn't look like it broke skin, so I really couldn't see what all the fuss was about.

"I need a Tetanus shot!"

Crystal stood, glaring at the guy and I scrambled to wedge myself between them. "Oh, come on, man. She's just a kid. Quit being such a baby."

Frankie shot me a look and turned to the guy, giving him a friendly slap on the back. "Listen, Ray, it's just a little misunderstanding. "*You* said hello to her and *she* thought you'd dissed her. It was a natural mistake. How about we just let it go and I throw in free workouts for the next month?"

Ray nodded a begrudging assent. "Yeah, awright."

"So we're cool?" Uncle Frankie asked, guiding him out the door. "Great."

He turned back to Crystal and me and sighed deeply.

"So," I said, brightly. "If you can just pay Crystal for helping you out today, we'll be on our way."

With a "fighter's" nose and muscular frame, Father Sal appeared more at home in a boxing ring than behind a pulpit. In fact, Nick once told me that when Sal was a kid he had trained to become a professional boxer, until one day he "got religion" and never looked back. He sat, now, on Nick's couch, patiently fielding questions from Crystal.

"So if I hate it there, I don't have to stay?"

Sal gave a nod toward Nick. "Nicky says you're smart and capable of taking care of yourself. He also told me you need to lay low for a while, so my offer is good for however long you want it. You're free to stay or go. It's entirely up to you."

Nick handed her a cell phone. "Just say the word and I'll come and get you."

Crystal turned to me. "What do you think?" I was touched by the show of vulnerability in her question.

"I would trust these guys with my life," I said. "*Have* trusted them," I amended quietly.

She gave a short shrug. "Okay. I'll go." That settled, she added, "Can I use the bathroom?"

"Down the hall, first door on your left," Nick directed her.

While she was gone I filled Nick in on my encounter with Little Red. "All I can say is, thank God for overzealous meter maids. If the cops hadn't come along and seen my car parked illegally, I'd be part of his street harem by now."

Nick was quiet for a moment. "Where did you say this low-life hangs out?"

"As of this afternoon the city jail. Look, Nick, I appreciate you wanting to avenge my honor and all, but really, I'm fine. What I need to do now is to construct some sort of plausible timeline to pinpoint just when Star disappeared. Only everyone's recollections as to the last time they saw her are so vague. And who are my sources anyway? A kid who doesn't know where her next meal's coming from, let alone what day it is and a drug-addicted prostitute named Harmony Valentine."

I was trying to stay calm, but from everything I've seen on Law and Order, Criminal Intent, the longer someone goes missing, the less chance for a happy ending. "Oh, and did I mention that Bunny practically has the key to my house?"

Crystal walked back into the living room, holding one half of a pair of diamond earrings. It was distinctly feminine and mega expensive. I was torn between hoping they were Nick's, (which would make him a cross-dresser) or left behind by one of his many female admirers. Both alternatives left me wanting to throw up.

"I found this on top of the counter in the bathroom. It's pretty," she said. "Can I have it?"

Nick gently took it from her outstretched hand. "I'm afraid the young lady who left it here may want it back."

She left it here on purpose, just for an excuse to come back, the slut! I would never use such a corny excuse...except for the time I left my Game Boy over at Danny Pelosi's house—and he wrapped it up and gave it to Tina Delvecchione for her birthday!"

Sal cut me a look.

He couldn't possibly know my feelings for Nick. My face is the picture of nonchalance.

"Well," he said, rising off the couch, "I think we'd better head out now if we're going to beat cross-town traffic."

I walked Crystal to the front door. "I'll let you know the minute I hear anything. And you can call me whenever you want...not that you'd need me or anything—"

She cut me off with a brief, embarrassed hug, surprising the heck out of me. Then she opened the door and walked out without a backward glance.

Nick was still on the couch, but he rose as Sal approached. "Mi hermano, gracias por tu ayuda," I didn't understand the words, but there was no mistaking the sentiment.

Father Sal grinned. "It's what I signed up for."

The two friends clasped hands, ending in a familial embrace. Then Sal walked over to where I was standing at the door. He wrapped his arm around my shoulder and leaned in close to my ear.

"Hang in there, Little One. He needs you."

The air in the room suddenly ceased to exist as the weight of Sal's words sunk in.

Nick needs me? How could that be? Nick is an island, beautiful and self contained. He doesn't need anyone, least of all me.

By the time I got my breath back, Sal had left. I returned to the living room feeling confused and not a little pissed off. How long had Nick been back from his trip before the parade of bimbos had begun forming a line at his door? And yet, the person who knew him more intimately than anyone else in the world said he needed *me*. It just didn't make sense.

Nick had settled on the couch again, a glass of single malt nestled in his hand. His look was pensive, and for a moment I got the feeling he'd forgotten I was still in the room.

I coughed to let him know I was there. He looked up from his drink and smiled, the mood broken.

"Well, I guess I'd better head out too," I told him, hoping he'd beg me to stay.

He gazed at me with smoldering eyes. "There is no other woman, Brandy. I bought those earrings for you. They're yours if you want them…as am I."

"It was good seeing you, Angel. Keep in touch."

Keep in touch? What the fuck?

"Why do you have that photo of me in your nightstand drawer?" *Oops!* "I mean thanks for helping Crystal out. I'll see you around." I bolted toward the door and I almost made it when a strong hand landed on my shoulder, stopping me dead in my tracks.

"Nice try, Darlin'."

"Nick, I'd love to stay and chat, but John and I have tickets to the uh… The Jackson Family Reunion concert…minus Michael, so it's not technically the *whole* family…"

"Do you want to tell me how you knew about the photograph?"

"Um, not really."

He put both arms on my shoulders now and sat me down on the couch. "Didn't anyone ever teach you it's not polite to snoop in other people's belongings?"

I couldn't tell by his expression if he was amused or mad at me, but I'd had a good three months to sit on this question and I wanted an answer.

"Yeah, okay, the secret's out. I'm a compulsive drawer opener. But that photo cost $1200 bucks. Why did you buy it, Nick?"

Nick let out a soft sigh. "I saw the photo in the art gallery window and I thought it would embarrass you to have it on display, so I bought it. My intention was to give you the photo but I left town before I had a chance to deliver it. Brandy, I'm sorry if you read more into it than there was."

114

"Don't be silly. I'm fine. It was really thoughtful of you and—*oh hell, Nick! I'm in love with you!*"

Shit! Well, 'in for a penny, in for a pound.' "I'm in love with you," I repeated, not bothering to hide the tears that welled up in me. "Look, I know I'm not telling you anything you haven't already figured out on your own. I'm just tired of pretending, y'know?" I sat back on the couch, emotionally drained and yet, somehow, relieved. Tossing pride out the window was oddly freeing.

Nick slid over and wrapped himself around me, tucking me into the crook of his arm. "I wish I could give you what you want, Angel. What you deserve. But it's just not in me."

I leaned into him, resting my head on his shoulder. "You don't owe me a thing, Nick. You've been there for me since the moment I met you, and I couldn't ask for a better friend. You can't help how you feel any more than I can. So, if all you have to offer is a friendship with benefits, I'm willing to take it."

He hugged me closer, his voice filled with extraordinary tenderness. "Do you have any idea how dear you are to me?"

"I'm beginning to." I sat up, facing him. "And just so's you know," I added, wrapping my arms around his neck, "I don't plan on giving up." And then I kissed him.

Wow. Who knew that honesty could be so empowering?

I tasted the single malt on his lips as I pressed my mouth against his. He was surprised, but his response was immediate. He groaned and fisted his hands in my hair. Rubbing my lips seductively against his, I delivered the kiss of a lifetime and then I pulled back suddenly and slipped out of his arms. "Gotta go," I told him, smiling down at the bulge I'd created in the front of his jeans.

Shelly Fredman

"Brandy Alexander, you do not play fair," he sighed, but he was smiling too.

Nick walked me to the elevator and pressed the button. "So now that Crystal's safe, what's next on your agenda?"

I shrugged. "Check the local hospitals and city morgue to see if Star's turned up there, check out that license plate, find Bunny before she finds me...enroll in Clown College."

He thought I was joking. Unfortunately, I wasn't. Eric thought it would be "hilarious" and a real ratings booster.

The elevator doors opened, revealing a fairly hefty, uniformed delivery guy. He was wrestling with an enormous crate that was balanced precariously on a dolly.

"Sorry," he said, trying to swing past us. "The service elevator is broken."

As I scooted out of the way, my eyes settled on the top of the box. "Oh, Nick, it's for you."

"Nicholas Santiago?" the guy asked.

Nick gave a curt nod, his eyes roving over the crate. His mood, which a moment ago had been light and playful, darkened.

The return address said Bogotá Columbia. My imagination leaped into overdrive. *What could be in the crate? Guns? Well, that didn't make any sense. Wouldn't he be sending them to third world countries instead of the other way around? Drugs? No, Nick didn't seem the type to mess with that. And anyway, I'm sure if he was transporting illegal drugs he wouldn't use Fed Ex... Eighty pounds of coffee?*

"Sign here, please," the man said. "And I'm going to need some I.D." He shrugged apologetically. "Special orders."

116

"No problem," Nick said, and took out his wallet.

"That's a really big box, Nick. I wonder what's in it."

Okay, so it wasn't the most subtle hint in the world, but at least I wasn't jumping up and down yelling, "Open it, open it," like I wanted to.

The elevator door began to close. Nick reached out and forced it back open, ushering me inside. "Don't want you to be late for Clown College, Darlin'."

"But —"

The elevator door closed. *Crap.*

Glenda Maroni is my mother's third cousin and a forty-year employee of the Department of Motor Vehicles. Cousin Glenda has a voice like a chainsaw. She smells like Johnny Walker Red and Dentine Gum and she once set fire to the tip of her nose in an ill-fated attempt to re-enact a classic *I love Lucy* episode. Growing up, I didn't see much of Cousin Glenda. My mother thought I had enough crazy ideas of my own without adding Glenda's to the mix.

I found her the next day at her cubicle typing up a report, a lit Marlboro balanced on the edge of an ashtray that sat atop a pile of papers on her desk. She was about to pick it up as I walked over to her, automatically checking to see where the fire extinguisher was located.

"Cousin Glenda, it's Brandy."

Glenda looked up. "Brandy? *Get out!* Come here! Give me a hug! Look at you! You're all grown up. I heard you bought your parents' place. Are you still going out with the cop? What's on your face, Honey? Is that a pimple?" Before I could squirm out of her grasp, she gave me a "wet thumb cheek rub." Eewww.

117

After the preliminary familial catching up, I finally got to the reason for my visit. "Listen, Cousin Glenda." I shot a discreet look around, lowering my voice to a mere whisper. "I have a huge favor to ask you."

She compensated for my whisper with a full-on shout. "Anything for you, Sweetie. You were always my favorite."

I tried again, edging closer. "This is kind of a personal matter—"

"Oh my Lord, you're pregnant! Does your mother know? Don't worry, Honey, in this day and age it's not the worst thing that could happen."

"Glenda," I all but screamed, "I'm not pregnant."

"You're not?"

I shook my head. "No."

"Oh, thank God. A kid would make your life miserable. Now, take my Bernardo. Sweetest baby you could imagine, but—"

"Um, Cousin Glenda, I need you to find out who owns a vehicle with a vanity license plate that reads 'SLIMEY 1'."

"No problem, hon. I'll just be a sec."

The legality of dispensing with private information to anyone that walked through the DMV doors never seemed to cross her mind. And being the nonjudgmental type, I figured it would be rude to mention it.

Through the magic of technology, Glenda got the information in a matter of minutes. She was frowning.

"What's wrong?"

"That license plate doesn't exist, Honey. Are you sure you got it right?"

I rooted through my bag and found my notebook. "SLIMEY 1," I read aloud.

118

"No good," she said, looking again.

Oh double crap! Harmony gave me the wrong license plate number. Well, that's just great. I now have exactly zero leads. "Listen, thanks for trying, Cousin Glenda."

"I'm sorry I couldn't help you, hon. Tell your mother to give me a call."

After leaving the DMV, I swung by the firing range. I still wasn't loving it, but, basically, I'm a very competitive person, and I kinda dug giving those paper perps "what for!" I could tell I was getting better, too, because this time the guy behind the counter didn't duck when I handed him back my gun.

Shooting people in their vital organs really worked up an appetite, so I stopped by the Barnes and Noble across from Rittenhouse Square and took the escalator up to the café. Settling in with some decaf and a low fat muffin, I sat at a table near the window and got out my notebook. I took a few sips of decaf and a bite of the muffin and congratulated myself on making such a sensible choice. Then I tossed them both in the trash and got some regular coffee and a pack of chocolate grams instead.

I was feeling frustrated. It had been days and I still wasn't any closer to finding Star. If I could just pinpoint when she disappeared, maybe I'd have a place to start. *What was it Harmony had said about the night she saw Star getting into the van? It was a full moon.* I gulped down my coffee and headed for the reference section.

Flipping through the Farmers' Almanac, I found what I'd been looking for. The date of the last full moon was June 15th. That was about two weeks ago, which fell within the time frame of everyone's vague recollections of the last time they'd seen Star.

I called Crystal on the cell phone Nick had provided her. She sounded almost happy to hear from me.

"How's it going?" I asked.

"Okay. The people who run this place are pretty cool. Have you found out anything about Star yet?"

"I'm working on it. Crystal, I know you don't remember the date of the last time you saw Star, but do you happen to recall if the night she left there was a full moon?"

"I can't remember. Why?"

"I'm just trying to establish a time line for when she disappeared."

"Oh," Crystal said, thinking. "Y'know, on the morning of the night when she didn't come back, Star left the squat early. I think she told me she had an appointment with her caseworker...I'm not really sure though. I was half asleep when she left. I might've just dreamed it. Does that help?" she asked. The little girl quality of her voice gave me a pang.

"Yeah, actually, it does. Oh, and one more thing. Do you know if Little Red drives a silver van?"

"Definitely not his style," Crystal snorted. "He's a throwback. Drives a black Cadillac El Dorado. He must watch a lot of bad '70's TV."

"Okay, Crystal, thanks." I told her I'd keep her posted and hung up.

So Star had an appointment with Olivia Bowen the day she disappeared, and then two weeks later, Olivia turns up dead.

I called DiCarlo and left a message for him to call me back. The cops had to have gone through Olivia's appointment book. If she'd had a meeting with Star the morning of Star's disappearance, Bobby would be able to confirm it.

Franny called me on the way out of the bookstore. "You're not driving, are you?"

"No. What's up?"

"Bran, I wanted you to hear this from a friend. You know that date Bobby has on Saturday night?"

"Really, Fran, I have more on my mind than Bobby's love life."

"Uh huh. Just thought you should know it's with Tina."

"Get out! I was stopped in the middle of the doorway and looked up to see a little old lady scurrying away. She looked terrified.

"Are you okay?"

"No, I'm not okay! Eddie is Bobby's best friend. Before you know it, you guys will start double dating and I'll be weird, old Aunt Brandy, the babysitter, who can't get a date but is great with kids, watching Barney videos with them and teaching them how to knit!"

"That's not going to happen, Bran," Franny reassured me. "You don't know how to knit."

"Fran, if I wanted sarcasm, I would have spilled my guts to John."

"Sorry, hon. Really, I am." She didn't sound sorry. In fact, she sounded like she was stifling a laugh. My suspicion was confirmed a moment later.

"Oh, by the way, weird, old Aunt Brandy, don't forget we have La Maze class on Thursday night."

"Fran?"

"Yeah?"

"Bite me."

I stopped by the Farmers' Market on the way home to pick up some fresh fruits and vegetables for dinner. My mother doesn't believe in fresh vegetables. She figured if God had meant for green beans to be eaten straight out of the ground, He never would have invented cans to put them in.

It had started raining, one of those east coast summer downpours that are over in a minute but leave you soaking wet and wreak havoc on your hair. I really should keep an umbrella in my car, but I always thought it was sort of wimpy. However, the sprint from the curb to my front door left me looking like a contestant in a wet tee shirt contest.

Adrian came bounding to the door to greet me, knocking the bags out of my hands and onto the floor. The vegetables spilled out and he immediately pounced on them, grabbing the "bunch carrots" and running around in circles playing "keep away." I let him keep them, figuring he could use a little roughage in his diet.

I was starving, so I threw a potato into the microwave and was on my way upstairs to change when the doorbell rang. I peered through the spy hole. It was DiCarlo. *Shit*.

"Just a minute," I yelled, figuring I could be upstairs, showered, changed, hair blown dry and maybe a touch of make up in about fifteen.

"Come on, Alexander, let me in. I'm getting drenched out here."

I sighed and let him in, figuring we were both caught in the same downpour, how good could he look?

Unfortunately, he looked damn good.

Bobby crossed into the living room, droplets of water hanging from his dark curls. He shook them loose and peeled off his long sleeved, over-shirt, settling down on my couch. From out of nowhere Rocky appeared and began purring at his feet, welcoming him like some long lost paramour. It really ticked me off.

"She acts this way with all the guys," I told him, as he bent to scratch behind her ear. Rocky rolled over and stretched out on her back so that he could rub her tummy. "See? She's a total slut."

Bobby eyed me, a smile playing at the corners of his mouth. "Is that so?"

"That cat will roll over for just about anyone. I don't want you thinking you're something special."

Now, he full-on grinned. "You're not talking about the cat, are you?"

"Of course I am. Who else would I be talking about? And stop grinning."

"Are you mad at me?"

"No…yes."

"Why?"

"I don't know." I sat down next to him and scooped the cat into my lap.

"It's just that—well, *I'm* supposed to be moving on in my love life and you're supposed to be sad about it. Only *you're* the one moving on."

"So, you want me to pine after you for the rest of my life?"

"No, not necessarily. Just let me get a head start."

"Oh, so in other words, this is just a competition to you."

"God, when you put it that way, I sound like such a brat."

"I love the brat. And I'd be perfectly willing to pine if I knew it would eventually lead somewhere. But I've got to move on too, whether you're ready to accept it or not."

"Yeah," I said, "only, jeez, Bobby, why'd it have to be Tina?"

The timer went off on the microwave, giving him a temporary reprieve. He followed me into the kitchen.

"So why are you here, anyway?" I asked, taking an oven mitt out of the drawer.

"I passed by your house on the way to Sofia's daycare. You'd called so I figured I'd just stop in. Yo, are you actually cooking something?"

"Don't act so surprised. I can cook."

"Since when?"

I tossed him a look. "I never thought I'd hear myself say this, but you sound just like my mother."

He smiled and helped himself to a TastyKake while I reached into the microwave with a gloved hand and extracted the potato. It had been in there for fifteen minutes but it still felt rock hard.

I checked to see if the power level was on high. It was. I picked up the potato with my bare hand and began to squeeze it, trying to decide if I should pop it back into the microwave.

The skin was crisp and unyielding so I squeezed a little harder. Suddenly my thumb poked a hole straight into the core of the potato, releasing a whoosh of steaming hot air. Intense pain shot through me as the potato clamped its jaws around my thumb.

Holy Mother of God! It must've been a thousand degrees in that sucker! I tried to yank it off with my gloved hand, but the mitt was huge and awkward and I couldn't get a grip on it. My eyes started to water as part of my anatomy baked inside the potato shell.

Frantically, I began shaking my hand, trying to dislodge my thumb before Bobby noticed what was

124

happening.   He turned to me and I slipped my hand behind my back.

"What are you hiding back there?" he asked.

"Nothing."

"Then you won't mind if I take a look."

He reached around my waist and caught hold of my wrist, drawing my hand out in front of me, the spud still attached to my digit.

"Don't!" I yelled and pulled hard against his hand. The potato flew off and sailed across the room, landing in Adrian's water bowl.

Bobby stood there, dumbfounded as I held out my hand to inspect the damage. My thumb looked like a cartoon special effect, all blistery red and bulging with steam wafting off it.

"That's gotta hurt," DiCarlo sympathized, only he was struggling to keep a straight face.

"Don't you dare laugh. And if you tell a soul about this, you are so dead."

"Sorry, Sweetheart," he said, losing the battle. This is too good to keep to myself. Only you would get your thumb stuck inside a baked potato."

"Oh, fine," I told him. "Go ahead and laugh."

I hated to admit it, since it hurt like hell, but it really *was* funny.

Bobby fished the potato out of the dog bowl while I slathered antibiotic ointment on my rapidly swelling thumb. I guess he felt sorry for me, because he offered to take me out to dinner. Well, sort've. He and Sofia were going to Chuck E. Cheese's and I was welcome to tag along. It wouldn't have been my first choice, but it would give me an opportunity to pump him for information in the Olivia Bowen case. I knew it would be a battle to get him to tell me anything, but at least he wouldn't yell at me in front of his kid.

"Hi Bandy," Sofia called, climbing into her car seat. "I learned a new song. It's called *Now I Know My ABC's Next Time Won't You Sing With Bees.* Do you know that song, Bandy? I could teach it to you."

I turned in my seat to face her. "That is very nice of you, Sofia. Maybe your daddy would like to learn it too."

"Okay," she giggled, "it goes like this. Now I know my abc's next time won't you sing with bees. Daddy, I didn't know bees singed. I thought they just buzzed."

"Sofia, Sweetheart," Bobby said. "Daddy's got a little headache."

"I'm sorry, Daddy. I will sing you a song and help you feel better."

"Could you sing it in your mind, Honey? That will help me feel a lot better."

"Okay dokey."

I had to wait until Sofia was safely ensconced in the play area of the restaurant before I broached the subject of the dead caseworker.

"Come on, Brandy, you know I can't divulge anything that could compromise the case."

"But I'm not asking you to. All I want to know is if she'd had an appointment scheduled with that girl, Star, on June 15th. How does that compromise anything?"

"It doesn't," he conceded. "I just know you. It may start out with you wanting to find this girl, Star, but before you know it you'll be knee deep into investigating Olivia Bowen's murder."

"Well, you've got to admit, it's a little suspicious. Do you think there's a tie-in?" I asked, all excited.

DiCarlo sat down on the edge of the ball pit, eyes closed, rubbing his temples and muttering softly to himself. Sofia climbed out and put her little arms around his neck, pressing her cheek against his. "Did your headache go away, Daddy?"

He opened his eyes. "Not yet, Honey."

I'm sure it was just a co-incidence that he was looking directly at me.

It was almost midnight by the time I got home. Janine had called while we were scarfing down rubbery pizza. It seemed her mother was having a nervous breakdown over the guest list for Franny's shower. Fran wanted to keep it small—ten to twelve of her closest friends and relatives, while Mrs. DiAngelo thought it would be impolite to exclude anyone within a fifty-mile radius. After all, she reasoned, who wouldn't want to be included in the festivities for the birth of her first grandchild. I told Janine I'd meet her at her mom's and talk her through the crisis.

Janine drove me home. She pulled up in front of my house and cut the engine. "Do you want me to walk you in, Bran?"

"Janine, I appreciate the thought, but I am *so over* being scared. Honestly, I'm fine…" *That's weird, I was sure I'd turned a light on when I left the house.* "Um…y'know, Neenie, you haven't seen the dog in ages. I taught him to beg. It's the cutest thing ever."

"Well, I can't just take your word for it," Janine said, climbing out of the driver's side. "I'll have to come in and see for myself."

When we got to the front door I checked the deadbolt. It was still in locked position. I breathed a little easier, inserted the key and pushed open the door.

Adrian ran to greet us. He was making little gagging noises, the way he did one time when he mistook my mom's meatballs for something edible. *Oh jeez, what did he eat now?* As I kneeled down to take whatever it was out of his mouth, Janine flipped on the light. An unnatural silence hung in the air. I looked up.

"Oh, Holy Shit!" Janine whispered. "Is she dead?"

Chapter Eight

Heather Koslowski sat motionless in the middle of my living room. She was tied to a dining room chair that had been dragged over the rug, the track marks still visible. Heather's head lolled forward on her chest, revealing a walnut sized lump behind her left ear. Her hair was matted and caked with blood.

Every nerve ending stood on guard as I listened for signs that the intruder could still be in the house. "Call 911," I told Janine quietly, while I knelt beside Heather to feel for a pulse.

Gently, I lifted her head and almost dropped it back down again. A message had been scrawled on her forehead in permanent marker. "I'm coming 4 u". There was no signature, but there was no need for one. Over her eyebrows, someone had drawn two perfect bunny ears. Sick and highly effective.

I felt for a pulse and Heather stirred. I began untying the ropes. They were just tight enough to make sure Heather was still there, front and center, when I came home.

Janine walked in from the kitchen, the phone still in her hand. "The cops are on their way." She stared down at Heather's tattooed face. "Bran, you know who did this, don't you?"

"I have a pretty good idea. Heather, it's Brandy," I said, gently shaking her shoulder. "Can you open your eyes?"

With great effort, Heather slowly opened her eyes. "What happened?" she moaned, holding the back of her head.

"We were hoping you could tell us."

"I don't know. I-I think I'm going to be sick."

I ran for a wastebasket while Janine helped Heather untangle herself from her constraints. Obviously, Bunny had come looking for me and had stumbled across Heather instead. It made me dizzy with fear and guilt and outrage that someone would take out their hatred of me on an innocent victim. I wanted to find Bunny and beat the living shit out of her.

Mike Mahoe had been patrolling the area when the call came in. He arrived two beats ahead of the paramedics. More cops appeared out of nowhere and, guns drawn, they searched the house and yard, in the unlikely event that the perps were still there.

Satisfied that they were long gone, Mike came back into the living room to check on Heather. An EMT was bent over her, taking vital signs and asking her to look into the beam of his flashlight. As horrible as her ordeal had been, she seemed to be enjoying the attention.

According to Heather, she had come by at around 9:30 p.m. to see if I wanted to watch a movie with her. When she got to the front door she heard voices coming from the back yard.

"It sounded like you were having a party, so I went around the side of the house to see. Your back door was

130

open and it looked like the glass had been shattered. I was just about to call your name when I heard someone coming up behind me. And then I felt this really sharp pain in the back of my head." She touched her skull and winced.

The EMT's insisted on taking Heather to the hospital. Before she agreed, she made me swear I'd take Mr. Wiggles over to my house for the night. Her parents were out of town and he didn't like to sleep alone. I knew just how he felt, only Mr. Wiggles wasn't exactly my first choice for a bed buddy. That's okay, I probably wasn't his first choice, either.

We watched Heather get loaded into the ambulance and then Mike walked Janine and me back into the house.

"You've been uncharacteristically quiet, Neenie. What's up?"

She gave me a long look. "I just keep thinking, what if you'd been home alone tonight?"

"The trick is not to think about it."

Mike turned to me. "Do you have any idea what the message on Heather's forehead meant?"

"Long story."

"I've got time."

I filled him in on my first encounter with Bunny and her belief that I was the one who ratted her out to the cops after Olivia Bowen was killed.

"We found fresh footprints around the side of the house," Mike told me. "Looks like there was more than one person here tonight. Possibly two males and a female. My guess is that Heather showed up and one of the guys confused you with her, so he knocked her out and dragged her into the house. When Bunny saw that it wasn't you,

131

she decided to leave her calling card on your neighbor's face."

"Well, if her point was to scare me, mission accomplished."

"This was more than your average blowhard threat, Brandy. I've seen her kind of rage before and this psycho means business. Oh," he added, "and don't even think about asking me not to tell DiCarlo. I really like you, but I want to live to see another day."

The events of late felt overwhelming, so I did what I always do when I'm stressed to the limit. I scrounged around in the kitchen for dessert.

After stuffing myself sick with Oreos (while sugar doesn't take away the pain, it does a hell of a job masking it) I was ready to tackle the world again. Mike helped me board up the broken window while Janine reconnected the alarm system. From now on, Mrs. Gentile would just have to do without her midnight popcorn runs.

Mike walked me over to Heather's to pick up the dog. She had laid out little doggie pajamas for Mr. Wiggles, but had never made it back home to put them on him. The thought made me sad. Well, I decided, after all that Heather had been through tonight, the least I could do was change her dog into his p.j.s. It took me fifteen minutes and the little pisher bit me.

Janine insisted that she stay over and I wasn't about to argue with her. She went upstairs to get ready for bed while I walked Mike to the door.

"Uh, Brandy, can I ask you something?" He stood there looking embarrassed, not quite making eye contact, nervously clenching and unclenching his hands, his weight shifting from side to side.

Uh oh. I know that look. Mike still has a "thing" for me. He tried to fight it, but after seeing me in danger tonight, he just can't contain himself any longer. Oh jeez, Mike's a great guy, but my heart belongs to Nick. It wouldn't be fair. Only—look at him. He's going to be crushed. I need to let him down gently.

"Mike, I'm really flattered—"

"Do you think Janine would go out with me?"

"—that you want to ask my friend out. I'll put in a good word for you."

"Thanks, Brandy."

"Sure, no problem."

My life sucks.

I woke up in the morning with a dog on my face and a colossal headache. Mr Wiggles stretched and yawned and climbed out of the bed, with Adrian following suit. I was drenched in sweat but preferred that to leaving my window open. Janine had opted to sleep downstairs with the only working air conditioner.

I went downstairs and found her sitting in the kitchen with three bowls of Cheerios. She stuck two on the floor and Mr. Wiggles pounced on one of them. Adrian sat beside the other bowl, waiting.

"I think your dog is sick," Janine said, through a mouthful of cereal. "He's not eating his breakfast."

"That's because you forgot the sliced banana."

"Really?" Janine asked.

I picked up the bowl and set it on the table and added some fresh fruit. "He's very finicky that way."

"So what do you think of Mike?" I asked, changing the subject.

"What do you mean, what do I think of Mike? He's a nice guy." She waited a beat, then said all excitedly, "Omigod, he finally asked you out. That's it, isn't it?"

"Not exactly. He's sort've, um, interested in you."

"Seriously?"

"Yeah, well, he almost swallowed his tongue trying to ask me if you'd go out with him."

"You sound mad."

"Me? That's ridiculous...okay, maybe a little ego-impaired. But now that I think about it, Neenie, he's really a sweetheart and I think you should give him a chance."

"But what about Tony?"

I gave her a look. "Tony is—how can I say this politely—scum."

"Yeah," she agreed, good-naturedly. "But he's my scum. Still, it would be nice to go out with someone who didn't revolt virtually all of my friends."

"Yeah, well there *is that*. So, can I tell him it's a go?"

Janine nodded, smiling. "It's a go."

After Janine left I called the hospital to check on Heather. She answered on the first ring and sounded none the worse for wear. I offered to pick her up, but she told me that wouldn't be necessary. Seems Heather and the EMT had hit it off last night, and he stuck around after his shift to take her home. As my Bubbie Heiki used to say, "Sometimes good comes from bad." I was hoping this was one of those times. Plus, even if I did almost get her killed, it was nice being a part of a budding romance.

DiCarlo called me when I got to work. He didn't sound too happy.

"I heard about what happened to Heather last night."

"Yeah? Well, I just spoke to her and she's totally fine. Plus she got a date out of it, so 'all's well that ends well'."

"Damnit, Brandy. They could've killed her. Or you."

I sighed. "Look, Bobby, it's not like I don't know that. And for once I didn't invite this trouble. So could you please put a lid on the lecture for a minute? My day is hard enough. We're shooting our winter promo. It's 100 degrees out here and I'm standing on the sidewalk dressed in a parka and ski boots."

Bobby emitted a small grunt. "Alright, I was going to give you hell, but I guess you're already in it."

"Listen, as long as you're in a forgiving mood, can you please just tell me if Star had an appointment with Olivia Bowen on the 15th? I can get the information myself, but it would be so much easier if you just told me."

"Christ, you're relentless. Okay, yes. She did. Happy now?"

"I won't be happy until I find that kid." *Alive.*

After the shoot I stopped by Eric's office to talk to him. He was very busy playing pinball on his computer, but he waved me in and offered me a seat.

"I can see how busy you are, Eric," I said, without a hint of sarcasm, "so I'll get right to the point. "I'm looking for a runaway. She's been living on the streets and she disappeared about two weeks ago. Her caseworker was that woman, Olivia Bowen, who was found dead a couple of days ago. I have reason to believe this girl's disappearance may be tied in to Bowen's death. I want to look into it, but I need you to back me up if anyone questions my legitimacy as a reporter."

"That's never stopped you before."

"Yeah, well, I'm trying to do things a little differently these days. So what do you say?"

He gave me a long look followed by a heavy sigh. "I say go for it."

"Really? I mean you're not even going to try and get me to go out with you first, like you usually do?"

Alexander, I am so over that. You are entirely too much work."

That seemed to be everyone's consensus these days.

"Look, you're a good employee and the public loves you. And if I'm lucky I'll get a decent news story out of it. So go on, knock yourself out."

"Thanks, Eric," I said, and headed out the door before he decided to change his mind.

"Yo, Alexander," he called after me.

"Hmm?"

"So, uh, if I *were* to ask you out again—"

I turned back to look at him. "To tell you the truth, Eric, that would be the best offer I've gotten in a long time."

"No kiddin'?" he wolf-grinned.

"No kiddin'. But the answer would still be no."

The building that housed New Beginnings Homeless Youth Services was located on Patterson Avenue, approximately eight blocks from the squat where Crystal had been residing. The building was old and tired, but the people that worked there more than made up for it. A tangible quality of limitless positive energy permeated the atmosphere.

I sat opposite Cynthia Mott, the agency's director, in her windowless office, a no-frills, yet cheerful environment. Pictures of "her" kids as she called the countless runaways that had availed themselves of the services dominated the walls. On her desk sat a basket of trinkets. I picked up a miniature troll doll, the kind one would see on the tip of a pencil, and rolled it in my hand.

"When kids come to my office, they generally like to leave with something. They would feel guilty taking anything of real value, so I keep little things around. They're insignificant to me, but to them it's a lifeline." I remembered what Nick had told me about Crystal taking my Pez dispenser and nodded.

"So, Ms. Alexander, you'd said on the phone that you wanted to do a story on homeless youth facilities."

I nodded, feeling like a rat for lying to this woman. I wondered if she knew what kind of power she wielded, with her stupid unconditional love and acceptance.

"I'm curious as to why you chose our agency," she continued.

"Oh. That's a good question. You see—well, actually, you were mentioned in the papers the other day, in connection with one of your case workers who had an — uh— an unfortunate accident—"

"You mean Olivia Bowen. I'm still reeling from her death. The police have been here and questioned the entire staff. Ms. Alexander, why don't you just tell me what this is really about? I can see that you want to, and it will save us both a lot of time."

I breathed an embarrassed sigh of relief. "It's not that I don't *want* to do a story about your agency, it's just that—well, right now I'm looking for something specific." I dug in my purse and retrieved a copy of the photo of Star.

"Do you recognize this girl?"

Cynthia Mott picked up the photo and studied it. "Yes, her street name is Star. She was one of Olivia's clients. She would have been reassigned to a new case worker by now, although, come to think of it, I haven't seen her around in a while."

"According to Star's best friend, she left their squat about two weeks ago and she hasn't heard from her since. Somebody spotted her getting into a car that same night, but I don't know if she went voluntarily or not. I was hoping someone here would have some information on her."

"What makes you so sure she didn't disappear of her own free will?"

"I'm not sure," I admitted. "But she was very protective of her friend. It would seem out of character that she'd leave without at least telling this kid that she was going. And now her case worker turns up dead."

"And you think there's a correlation?"

"I'm asking if *you* think there's one." I leaned forward in my seat. "There's a young woman on the streets that goes by the name 'Bunny.' She had it in for Star. Co-incidentally, she was seen talking to Olivia Bowen the evening she was killed. Trust me when I tell you this Bunny person is dangerous. I need to find Star before Bunny does, that is if she hasn't found her already."

"This sounds like a police matter."

"Look, you more than anyone should know how sensitive this stuff is. What if I'm wrong and Star is fine. If I get the police involved without just cause, she's as good as dead on the streets."

Cynthia nodded in silent agreement. "The sad thing is we know so little about these kids. All we really know is that they're in pain and they need our help, but most of them slip through the cracks."

She waved her hand toward the photos on the wall, beautiful faces drawn from every ethnic group, varying in age from pre-teens to early twenties.

"These are all kids I've worked with. Some have gone on to lead happy productive lives. Others, you think you're helping and then one day they're just—gone."

She picked out a photo of a young Caucasian girl. "This kid was a twelve-year-old street walker when we connected with her through an outreach program, three years ago. Her friends called her Sunny because she always had a smile on her face. I worked with her for almost a year and I really thought we were making some progress. Then one day she didn't show up for an appointment. I scoured the streets for days. But no one seemed to know what happened to her.

"One day, about a year and a half ago, a police officer came to the agency and showed me a photo of a young girl. *This* girl. He asked me if I recognized her. I did, but just barely. The cops had found her dead in an alley, a needle sticking out of her veins. She was all of thirteen years old." Mott smiled grimly. "I keep this picture up there as a reminder of how fragile their lives are."

There was a tentative knock at the door and a woman who looked to be in her middle 40's poked her head into the room. "Sorry to interrupt, Cynthia. I just need you to sign off on these so I can get them out in the mail." Her eyes flickered toward the photo still in Cynthia Mott's hand and then settled on me.

Mrs. Mott waved her in. "Ellen, this is Brandy Alexander. She's a reporter, and she's interested in learning more about homeless youth agencies for a possible story."

I was surprised that she hadn't divulged the real nature of my visit, but I appreciated her discretion.

"Ellen is one of our tireless case workers. If you decide to go ahead with your story, she's the person you need to talk to. Before she came to us Ellen worked in New Jersey, and if my memory serves me correctly, you also put in some time in Chicago and New York, didn't you, Ellen?"

Ellen leaned in to shake my hand. "Well, there is certainly no shortage of homeless kids, and their needs are the same no matter what city they come from or run to."

Mrs. Mott returned the picture of Sunny to the bulletin board. "I was just telling Ms. Alexander that as much as we'd like to claim success on every kid that walks through our doors, more often than not, it's not the case. Do you remember Sunny?"

Ellen studied the picture a moment. "Vaguely...I think she must have left the agency around the same time I'd started. I remember something tragic happened to her." She shook her head. "Sometimes this job is heartbreaking."

Ellen slipped a pile of papers on Mrs. Mott's desk and turned to leave. "It was nice meeting you, Brandy."

"You too."

Mrs. Mott called to her as she reached the door. "Ellen, have you by any chance seen Star around recently?"

"Star? Which one is she? I'm sorry, my goal is to know all the kids that come through here, but I've got enough trouble keeping track of my own cases." She emitted a small, embarrassed laugh. "Well, it's been a long day," she ended, opening the door. "I'm heading out, Cynthia. Bye, Brandy. Good luck with your story."

140

I waited for the door to close behind her.

"Do you think it's possible that Star went home?" I asked.

Cynthia shook her head. "Possible? Yes. But not probable. Well," she said, standing up, "I'm sorry I couldn't be more help. The police took everything they thought was relevant, and Olivia's office has already been cleaned out, but I'll let you know if I hear anything."

"Thanks. I'd appreciate it."

Ellen was in the hallway as I emerged from Mrs. Mott's office. Nodding another goodbye, I felt her eyes on my back as I walked down the hallway and out the door.

I was seriously low on dog food, so I swung by the 7-Eleven to pick up some beef jerky for Adrian. He absolutely loves the stuff and I thought he deserved a treat. While I was there, I grabbed a word puzzler magazine off the rack at the counter. My mother insists it wards off senility. "A puzzle a day keeps the Alheimers' away," she always says and it must be true because she heard it on "Oprah."

When I got to the car I realized I hadn't eaten in hours, so I took out one of the sticks of beef jerky, figuring my dog wouldn't mind sharing. Then I thumbed through the magazine, zipping past the anagrams because they're way too hard until I found a word jumble and kicked back for a few minutes, enjoying my lunch.

As I sat staring at a group of mixed up letters that would eventually, if I was skilled enough, turn into a word, I began to wonder if dyslexic people automatically saw the letters in the "correct" position. I mean, if they normally scrambled up words in their own brains, then if the letters were *already* mixed up, wouldn't the opposite be true?

And as I pondered this, something began to nag at the back of my brain, until it shoved its way to the forefront and smacked me upside the head.

"Harmony Valentine is dyslexic! That's why she had such a hard time reading the word 'apple.' Granted, lots of people function quite well with dyslexia, but maybe she was never diagnosed as a kid and didn't get the academic help she needed.

Okay, Brandy, stop analyzing the state of public school education and think! Maybe Harmony got the letters right, but she somehow rearranged the order in her mind.

I took a pen and pad of paper out of my bag and wrote "SLIMEY 1." Then I tried several different combinations until I hit on one that made an actual word. "SMILEY 1."

I punched in the number for the DMV. "Yo, Cousin Glenda. It's Brandy. Listen, I have a favor to ask you."

Ten minutes later, Glenda called me back. "You were right on the money, doll. "SMILEY 1" is a silver Dodge minivan, belonging to a James Garner. "Ha! Ha!" She let out a big belly laugh. "I wonder if it's James Garner the actor. I loved him in The Rockford Files."

"I'm willing to bet it isn't. Can I get an address?"

If I've learned nothing else over the course of the last several months, I've *have* learned that no man is an island and if I need help I shouldn't be too proud to ask for it. I was about to embark on what could turn out to be a dangerous mission and I needed someone I could trust, someone to watch my back, someone I could count on to go to the mat for me. Barring that, I'd settle for someone who wouldn't try to talk me out of it and would actually enjoy a little adventure. I called Janine.

"Sure, Bran, I'll go with you. "It's not like I have a job or anything, and it sounds like fun. So, what does one wear on a recon mission anyway? Do I like dress up or can I go in flip flops and shorts?"

I wasn't really sure, seeing as I no idea what our jaunt to the Greater Northeast would entail. "You can never go wrong with 'Business Casual,'" I decided. "See you in about twenty minutes."

There was something I'd forgotten to ask DiCarlo, so when I got to Janine's I parked in front of her walk-up and punched in his number. He was still at the precinct.

"How did the cops know where to look for Bunny if they didn't even know who they were looking for?"

DiCarlo let out a longsuffering sigh. "You know I can't discuss details of a case with you."

"Yeah, I know…so just give me a hint. Who was it?"

"Brandy," he said through gritted teeth, "I mean it. I'm not going to have this conversation."

"*Ohhh, I get it.* There's someone there with you. That's cool. Just give me the first and last initials…Bobby? Hellooo…" *He hung up on me! Oh, fine.*

I rolled down the tinted windows and honked, and a few minutes later Janine appeared decked out in a cammo mini-skirt and high heel sandals. She made a face at the Le Sabre and climbed in.

"What's with the face?" I waited while she buckled up and then I put the car in gear.

"I thought we'd be taking Nick's truck. You know, drive around in style for a change."

"I gave the truck back."

143

"Oh." Janine contemplated this for a minute. "You wanna talk about it?"

I shook my head. "Nah. I'm good."

Janine glanced around. "This is way better than Nick's truck anyway. I mean we don't have to worry if we spill something on the seats, and if somebody's stomach gets upset, nobody will notice cause of the—y'know—mildew smell."

"Yeah, it's way better."

"So what's the game plan?" she asked, settling into my, apparently, unbearably gross car.

"Game plan? Oh my God, Neenie. I was so bent on finding out who owns the silver van, I totally spaced on what I'm going to say when I meet him. Jeez, I can't exactly go up to him and say, 'Yo, buddy, did you happen to pick up a fifteen year old hooker in your travels, and if so, do you remember where you put her when you were through?'"

Janine took out her make up bag and extracted her eyeliner. "Where are we going, anyway?" She pulled down the mirrored sun visor and glopped some on her eyelids.

"Welsh Road…*are you dressing up for this guy?*"

"You catch more flies with Honey," Janine said. "You might want to freshen up too."

Call me old fashioned, but I really didn't feel like gussying up for a creep who spends his lunch break trolling for underage prostitutes.

Following the directions that Glenda had printed out for me, we found ourselves cruising around a middle class housing development built in the late '70's. Well-kept single-family homes dotted manicured streets with names like Lindy Lane and Bethany Drive, homage, no doubt, to the developer's daughters.

144

We parked across the street from a white, two story wood and brick house. Mini American flags lined the walkway leading up to the front door. A couple of cars were parked out on the street; a dark green Saturn and a Toyota Camry. A silver van was parked in the driveway, the back end visible from the street. I scrunched up my eyes and read aloud, "SMILEY 1."

Bingo!

Janine unhitched her seat belt, her hand on the door. "Let's roll."

"Um, Janine, *I'm* gonna roll. You stay here and if you hear me scream call 911."

"That's it?" She sat back, folding her arms across her chest. "I thought you brought me along to help you kick this guy's ass."

"That's really nice of you to offer, Neenie and if it comes to that, feel free to jump right in. But for now I thought I'd just pretend I'm a realtor in case there's a Mrs. James Garner." I reached into my bag and produced a calling card. It was from Ricco Realty and had a picture of an Asian woman with long dark hair. Close enough.

Janine dug into her bag and produced a card of her own. She had actually spent about a day and a half working at Tony Tan's realty office and considered herself quite the housing expert. "Come on, Brandy. I won't say a word. I'll just be there to add a little authenticity."

"Okay. But promise me you'll let me do all the talking."

"My lips are sealed."

We opened the doors and climbed out. As we walked across the street I started to panic. I mean what if it's all a giant misunderstanding and here's this poor innocent guy who was—for all I knew—giving young girls rides to church services or something. The last thing I wanted to do was jump to any wrong conclusions. I'd just put it out there in a careful and non-accusatory manner.

One half of a double garage door was open and a man was working inside. His back toward us, he was bent over, sorting nails in a box. The room was filled with art canvases, some very large, stacked neatly against the wall. I glimpsed one of the paintings; an "abstract" that looked like it was created by a three-year old, but would probably sell for about a million dollars if you told people it was painted by someone famous. I guess I'm not highbrow enough to appreciate shit like this. It just looked like bad art to me.

The guy must have been expecting someone else, because he stood up now and turned toward us, smiling. "You're home early, Honey," he said.

Gazing at the two strangers standing before him, confusion registered in his eyes. At that exact moment, recognition registered in mine.

"So, you're James Garner, you son of a bitch."

Chapter Nine

Janine snapped to attention. "Um, excuse my partner. She's got allergies. We're realtors and we're just canvassing the neighborhood—"

"Forget it Janine. I know this scumbag."

Garner paled. "Look, I don't know who you are, but you'd better get the hell off my property before I call the police." He took a step back and stumbled, and for the first time I noticed his foot was in a cast. Good. It must've happened when he was running blindly down the alley after beating Crystal to a bloody pulp.

"I don't think you're going to want to do that. You don't recognize me, do you? Maybe this will jog your memory." I pulled out my can of pepper spray. He recoiled, and for a minute I thought he was going to pass out from shock.

"How did you find me? Are you the police?"

"You're not in any position to ask questions, Mr. Garner." (*Impersonating a police officer is a federal crime, but I think it's okay if you just allude to it.*) "What you need to understand is we know who you are and we could make life very unpleasant for you unless you cooperate with us."

I didn't know where I was getting this. It's like I was channeling some B-movie thug, circa 1940.

Garner dropped his voice to a dead whisper. "Hey, I know who you are. You're a reporter, aren't you? What? Are you in a ratings slump or something? Looking for a juicy story?" He gave a hard nod in Janine's direction. "Well, whatever this street tramp told you is a lie. I've never seen her in my life."

It took me a beat to realize the impression he was under, and then another to swallow my surprised laughter. Janine, however, was *not amused.*

"I ought to pop you one, you little weasel." Her fist tightened and for a minute I thought she'd make good on her threat.

"Janine, please. Look," I said, turning back to Garner, "I'll make this real easy to understand. I've got proof that you were a *client* of a young kid that goes by the name of Star. So, what are we looking at...statutory rape? But I digress," I noted, pleased beyond belief that the bastard was sweating bullets. "Now, Star's gone missing, and the last time anyone saw her, she was climbing into your car. Would you care to elaborate on that?"

"I swear to God I didn't hurt her. We went to a motel, she—did her thing and I dropped her off on a corner somewhere. I haven't seen her since. I—I was looking for her the day you saw me—"

"Saw you beating the shit out of another little girl?" I supplied, anger turning my voice hoarse.

Suddenly he jerked his head up, straining to see over our shoulders. I didn't think it possible for a person to turn any whiter, but the last ounce of blood drained from his face as we followed his gaze down the street. A couple of teenagers were walking toward the house. The girl looked to be about sixteen, slim, pretty and petite, the boy, a year or two older and a head taller and built like a fullback.

"Please," he begged. "It's my daughter and her boyfriend. You have to go."

My stomach churned. *This sicko has a daughter?*

They turned onto the walkway and stopped at the garage entrance.

"Hi Dad." The girl stood on tiptoe to kiss Garner's cheek before casting a puzzled glance in our direction. "Oh, I'm sorry. We're interrupting."

"Not at all," I said, extending my hand to her. "My name's Kim and this is my partner, Mary Beth. We're realtors and we wanted to introduce ourselves to the neighborhood."

"I'm Caitlin," she told me, her eyes glued to Janine, "and this is my boyfriend, Ben."

Ben gave a quick nod in our direction and began thumbing through the paintings. "Mr. Garner, I'll get these out of your way soon. I had them stored in my dad's sound studio out back, but I've been using that space while they're away. I'm working on cleaning it out, though. Even though he doesn't record music anymore, he still likes to go in there, y'know to get away from my mom sometimes."

Garner forced a laugh. "No rush, Ben. When will your folks be back from Europe?"

"Another week."

"Honey," Garner said, "I'm just finishing up with these ladies. Why don't you go inside? I'll be there in a few minutes and I can help you guys put together that slide show you were working on."

"We could just wait for you," she said. "Hey, you're not thinking of selling the house, are you, Dad? We haven't even unpacked all of our boxes yet."

"Caitlin, Sweetheart, I assure you we're not moving. You guys go inside and I'll be there in a minute. Your mother will be home soon and we can all go to that new restaurant you've been talking about for dinner."

My head reeled. Who *was* this guy? Loving dad or sexual predator? Clearly, the answer was *both*.

Caitlin shot one last glance at Janine and dragged herself into the house.

"Let's get this over with," he whispered. "What do you want from me? Money? Just name your price."

"You really don't get it, do you? My concern right now, besides for that sweet kid who has the misfortune of being your daughter, is finding Star. So, for starters, I need you to tell me exactly when was the last time you saw her. Time and date."

"Look," he said, "Do we have to do this now? Caitlin's waiting for me."

"She's going to have to wait a hell of a lot longer if your ass ends up in jail."

Garner leaned up against the van, shifting his weight to his good foot. His polo shirt was soaked with perspiration. The creep was trapped between a rock and two very pissed off South Philly girls and he didn't much like it.

"Okay," he said finally. "It was the afternoon of the 15th. I had an appointment down town—"

"Where did you take her?"

"I don't remember."

"Let me explain how this works, Garner. We're going to find out one way or another, and I guarantee you that if we have to work for this information we're going to make sure it's real embarrassing for you."

"Oh, Christ. I swear to God I don't remember the name of the motel. We used to get together maybe twice a week at some dump near the corner she worked. We didn't go to the usual place that day. She was acting kind of funny, and she finally told me she was afraid of running into her pimp. I didn't ask questions. We just drove around until we found another motel. Look, I know what you must think of me, but I treated that kid right."

"Did you now? She's fifteen years old. If it were your kid out there, would you still feel like she was being treated *right?"* I let the thought sink in for a minute, then, "What time did you drop her back off?"

"I don't know. Maybe three p.m.?"

"Hmm. My witness says it was at night."

"That's impossible. I left town early that evening. I was gone for over a week. I just got back a few days ago."

"Where did you go?"

He looked like he wanted to rip me a new one, but he answered my question. "L.A. I had business there. I can prove it."

"Who else has access to driving your car?"

"My wife. But you can't possibly imagine…look," he said, "I'm trying to cooperate, but if my wife finds out about this, it will kill her. My wife and daughter mean the world to me," he continued, choking up. "They're the innocent victims here. Please don't involve them in this. I don't know who took my car. Maybe someone from the repair shop I take it to. It's in there all the time. Damn air conditioning. Somebody could've made an extra set of keys and taken it joyriding while my wife was out that night."

"And just coincidentally picked up the exact same girl you've been having sex with? Listen carefully you freakin' perv. I'm watching you. And I have friends in the mafia in case you were thinking of leaving town. And they're watching you too...not to mention the police—and the FBI." I would have added the Boy Scouts of America, but that would have been overkill. "I'm planning on checking out your story, so I'm going to need your flight info, the name of the hotel you stayed at in L.A. and a contact number...unless you want me calling your home phone."

"I'll give you whatever you want."

"Great," I said, cheerfully. "Oh, there *is* one more thing."

"I've told you everything. What else could you possibly want?"

"Just this." I raised my leg and stomped on his bum foot with every ounce of strength I had.

Garner doubled over and Janine lunged at him. "And this is for calling me a hooker," she growled, hammering her spiked heel deep into his other foot.

The pain must have been excruciating, made worse by the fact that he had to suffer in silence or explain to his daughter why the nice lady realtors went wack-o.

"Take care," I told him. "We'll be in touch."

Janine and I high-fived it all the way back to the car.

"Man," Janine said, buckling herself into her seat. "We should've cut off his nuts while we had the chance. Think we should we go back and finish the job?"

"Don't think I didn't consider it." I buckled up, too, and started the engine.

"Brandy, you're talking about a child molester. As far as I'm concerned, that's all the permission we need to beat the living shit out of him. And, oh yeah, did you notice how his kid kept staring at me? That was a little weird."

"Eh. She's probably just never seen a realtor that was so fashionably dressed. Hey, thanks for coming with me, Neenie. Sometimes I get tired of facing the dregs of the earth alone."

"I spent five minutes with the guy and I feel like I have to take a shower. I am used to bottom dwellers— I've dated more than my fair share. But that guy really takes the cake. And the worst part is he looked so normal."

No, the worst part is if he wasn't going after someone else's kid, he'd be doing it to his own.

"And then he basically shoved me into the elevator and that was that. I'm telling you, John, there was something about that box that really upset him."

I'd gone directly from the Garners to meet John at *Party On*, a local party-planning store. We were joint-heads of the shower decoration committee; John, because he had more taste than the rest of us put together and me, because, well, nobody else would partner up with me. (They say I'm too "controlling." Well, *somebody* has to take charge.)

John picked up a gigantic inflatable baby bottle and inspected it. "$19.95. Who buys this crap?"

"We do." I took the bottle out of his hands and threw it in the cart. "So what do you think, John?" I asked, heading down the invitation aisle.

"I think this place is tacky. We should start Eddie and Fran's kid off right with something elegant. Let's head over to Tiffany's and pick up some silver baby spoons."

I gave him a major eye roll. "I meant what do you think about Nick?"

"I know what you meant, but I was hoping to change the subject. Okay, since you asked, and you know I won't mince words with you, I think you're looking for things that just aren't there. You need some mysterious reason for Nick to keep his distance from you, because you've never been able to accept 'no' for an answer. He flat out told you he doesn't love you, Sunshine. You want my advice? Cut your losses and move on."

"Jeez, John, it wouldn't kill you to mince them a *little* bit."

"Sorry, Sweetie, that's not what we're about."

I started to give him an argument but was interrupted by a high-pitched squeal loud enough to shatter glass.

"Omigod, Bran-deeee!"

The greeting emanated from Monica Winiki, formerly, Monica Sargenti, our old high school classmate. She made her way toward us, pushing a doublewide stroller down the length of the aisle. Inside the stroller sat an infant and a disgruntled looking toddler, sucking on a lollipop.

"Brandy," Monica yelled again, stopping to retrieve the items her two-year old had grabbed off the racks along the way. "Stop that, Billy, or Mommy's not going to get you ice cream."

"Oh no," John groaned. "The last time I ran into Monica she gave me a blow by blow description of her C-section. Then she went and showed me the scar." He shuddered. "Come on, let's act like we didn't see her and sneak out the back entrance."

"No, this will be fun," I told him, still a little ticked off from his remarks about Nick. "Hey, Monica, I heard you had a C-section."

Monica reached us and smothered John in her oversized, milk-producing breasts. "John, it's so good to see you!" Then, she threw her arms around me and repeated the process. "Brandy, I am so happy for you!"

Why? Did she think being on the shower decoration committee was such an honor she had to offer congratulations?

"When are you due?" She beamed and gave me a little pat on my stomach.

"Do what?" I asked, backing away slightly. I should've listened to John and bolted while we had the chance.

John broke out in a grin. "Are you holding out on me, Sunshine? Is there a baby Alexander on the way?"

"What? Oh my God, Monica, you think I'm pregnant?" I knew I'd been hitting the Tastykakes a little hard, lately, but did I really look like I was about to give birth?

"Oh," Monica whispered, sagely. "It's still early. I understand. I didn't want to tell anyone either until I was past my first trimester."

I had to shout to be heard over John's convulsive laughter. "I am *not* pregnant! Where did you get an idea like that?"

Monica's face fell. "You're not?"

I shook my head emphatically. "No."

John was still busy chuckling at my expense, so I didn't bother to tell him that the toddler had taken the lollipop out of his mouth and was now rubbing it against the side of John's pant leg.

"I was at the Ac-a-me," Monica explained, adding an extra syllable, South Philly style, "and I ran across Mindy Rebowitz. She said she was at the DMV and she overheard your cousin talking about it." She lowered her voice, and added, "It's Bobby's, isn't it? I always knew you two would get back together."

John giggled and I thumped him on the arm.

It took me twenty minutes to finally convince Monica that there were no babies on the way, Bobby's or otherwise. Thank God I nipped it in the bud before any real damage was done.

My phone rang at that precise moment.

"Brandy?"

"Oh, hi, Mom. What's—"

"I'm going to be a *nonna*!"

I couldn't tell if she was laughing or crying. Oy.

It took another twenty minutes to convince my mother that there were no babies and, therefore, no "shotgun" wedding in my near future. But by that time, the store had closed so we decided to call it a day.

"I'm making stroganoff tonight," John informed me, as he walked me to my car. "You want to come over?"

The offer was tempting, but I just wanted to get home. Ever since leaving Cynthia Mott's office, I'd had a weird feeling that I was missing something, only I couldn't quite put my finger on it.

"I've hit a wall trying to find that missing girl, John. I've got to work tonight."

"I don't get it," John said, shaking his head. "Eric's been offering to give you real assignments and you've turned them down. You said you needed time to recuperate from everything that's happened to you lately, maybe get some skills under your belt. Why the sudden change of heart?"

I thought about it for a minute. "I guess that's your answer right there. For all of her foulmouthed attitude,

Crystal got to my heart. She trusts me and I'm not going to let her down."

John hugged me to him. "Did I ever tell you you're my hero?"

"Oh man, you're not going to start singing *Wind Beneath My Wings*, are you?" I said, turning beet red.

"You never could take a compliment, Sunshine."

As I pulled onto my street, I spied Mrs. Gentile out on our shared porch. She was standing on a stepladder running a hand vac over her screen door. I figured I should offer to help her, although I couldn't see a speck of dirt and anyway she doesn't like me. Still, it was the neighborly thing to do.

I climbed out of the car, calling to her from the sidewalk. "I'd be very happy to vacuum your screen door for you, Mrs. Gentile," I offered, mustering up my somewhat meager enthusiasm.

She glared down at me from her stepladder. "I don't thinks so, Missy," she said all huffy. "You do a piddley little favor for me and the next thing you know you'll be expecting me to babysit while you go out on the town."

"Um, did I miss something here? Babysit who?"

"You and Bobby DiCarlo's "*love child*," she said, making a face and the universal sign for quotation marks.

I sighed. Neighborly or not, I wanted to push her down.

Rocky, Adrian and I sat on the couch watching television. Well, technically, only the cat and the dog were watching. I was reading over my notes and checking for stray sounds in the house. Even with the alarm system reactivated and the extra patrol cars circling the neighborhood, I couldn't shake the feeling that any moment now Bunny would come bursting into the house wielding a six-inch blade and skin me alive.

I tried concentrating on Star, resolving to check out Garner's story in the morning, but my thoughts kept drifting back to the girl in the photograph on the bulletin board at New Beginnings. What had Cynthia Mott told me? *She had been found with a hypodermic needle sticking out of her vein.* Suddenly I knew why it sounded so familiar. Nurse Morrison had told me a similar story about a girl who had O.D.'d in Camden. That girl had been pregnant...like the girl I'd found in the alley. I picked up my pen and started writing.

Girl #1 (Sunny) was found approximately a year and a half ago. She was young, white, made her living by hooking and died of what appeared to be a self-inflicted overdose.

Girl #2, according to Nurse Morrison, was found dead about a year ago. She was also young, white, had also overdosed and had recently given birth.

I sat back and strained my brain for another memory. Something to do with DiCarlo. In a moment I had it. I picked up the phone, disregarding the fact that it was after midnight and he was an early riser.

"Yeah?" he said into the phone, his voice groggy with sleep.

"Bobby, remember about three months ago when my parents were in town and my mom had everyone over for dinner?"

"I remember. In fact, I'm still trying to digest the meal. But why are you calling me about this now?"

I ignored the slur on my mother's sub par culinary skills. "You had to leave early that night. Someone found a body in a dumpster. You told me later it was a teenage hooker and that she'd O.D.'d. Do you remember?"

"Yeah, I remember. Why?"

"Was she a white girl?"

"Brandy, what's this all about?"

"The sooner you answer me the sooner you can go back to sleep."

"Or, I've got an idea. I could just hang up."

"Bobby, please."

"Okay, yeah. She was white."

"One more thing…could you tell if she'd recently given birth?"

I waited a beat but he didn't answer. "Bobby?"

I could hear the rustling of sheets as he sat up in bed, the sleep gone from his voice. "What are you? Psychic?"

"So that's a yes?" My mind scrambled to understand the possible implications of this news.

"Autopsy revealed she had recently given birth."

"So what happened to the baby?"

"That's the million dollar question. But you still haven't answered mine. How did you know this girl had been pregnant? I never discussed that with you."

"Believe it or not, it was a lucky guess. What was the official ruling on cause of death?"

"Drug overdose. Listen, you're obviously onto something. What is it?"

"I'm not sure yet. Let me work it out a little more and I'll call you tomorrow."

"It is tomorrow."

"Good point." I hung up and went back to my notes.

Okay, so what do I have here? Four dead, white, teenage prostitutes, all within a span of approximately a year and a half. Three died of what was assumed to be self inflicted overdose. Two had recently given birth before their demise. One died of complications of a miscarriage, in which drugs were thought to be involved. All Jane Doe's.

What was the common link in their lives...the something or someone that tied them together? They weren't even all found in the same city. And even if they were, it's a big city, and with the thousands of kids that run away each year, there's bound to be some overlap in their personal stories.

I vowed to turn my notes over to Bobby and let him decide if I was on the right track or just making a mountain out of a molehill. In the mean time, my first priority was finding Star, and as much as I hated the thought, I had some unfinished business with an urban cowboy named Little Red.

I woke up on the couch at 6:00 a.m., soaked in sweat, despite the living room air conditioner running full blast. My dreams were disjointed and frightening, filled with mixed metaphors; Bunny, wearing a cowboy hat and a red bandana, chasing me with a saber. Then Little Red appeared in Dr. Denton's carrying a bucket of lye.

I called Fran as soon as it was reasonable. "Do you still have that dream interpretation book?" I asked.

"Yeah, why?"

"What does it mean if you dream about pimps wearing footie pajamas?"

"It means you're seriously disturbed. And speaking of disturbing things, it's my last La Maze class tonight. Are you available?"

"Absolutely."

"Damn."

"Franny, I said I'm totally available. What's wrong?"

"I don't want to go," she whined.

"Why not?" I entered the bathroom and begin squirting toothpaste on my brush.

Fran heaved a gigantic sigh. "I have to do *everything*. I've been carting this baby around for almost nine months and do you think anyone's offered to take her off my hands? Frankly, I'm sick of it. Can't you just go *for* me tonight?"

"You do know you're making absolutely no sense at all, right?"

"Humor me. I'm really scared, Bran."

"I know you are, Sweetie. I'll pick you up at 7:00."

I was supposed to do a live spot at the zoo, but just as we set up, three orangutans escaped their habitat and one ran off with the camera, so that left me free for the rest of the day. Heading back to the car I crossed off "go to work" on my "to do" list and moved on to item number two. "Check up on Little Red." Oy.

Some of that checking up entailed actual contact with the man. I skipped over that happy thought for the moment and concentrated on what I could do from a safe distance.

I sat in the car and punched in Mike's number. For some reason, he didn't sound that happy to hear from me.

"Do you think we'll ever have a conversation that doesn't begin with, 'Yo, Mike, can you do me a favor?'" he grumbled.

"You're right. I'm sorry. But as a matter of fact, I have two reasons for calling. Okay, so one *is* to ask you a favor, but the other is to tell you that I spoke to Janine, and she'd be happy to go out with you."

"She would? Really?"

"Really. Do you have a pen? I'll give you her number."

"Wow. That's great. So, what kind of stuff does she like to do?"

"Well, she's into pole dancing and—"

"You're kidding me," he said, all excited.

"Yeah, I am. Sorry to disappoint you. Listen, Janine's terrific. All you have to remember is she used to wait tables so she hates cheap tippers and you're good to go. Now, about that other reason I called. There's a pimp who goes by the name of Little Red. He got arrested the other day and taken to the South Street station."

"I'm not even gonna touch how you know about this character," Mike said. "What do you need?"

"Whatever you can tell me. His real name, for starters, any prior arrests, home address if you've got it."

"You're not planning on paying this guy a visit, are you?"

"Don't be ridiculous," my stock phrase meaning 'you're right on target.'

"And before you ask me if DiCarlo knows, I don't need his permission to do my job…but it's probably best not to mention it."

I could tell he was grinning. Mike's got the best smile around. "You are something else. I'll call you as soon as I know anything."

"Thanks, Mike."

Okay, then. Next stop South Street Gym.

As I pulled into the lot I spied DiCarlo's Mustang parked under the shade of an ancient Maple tree. *What's he doing here in the middle of a work day? He must be buffing up for his big date on Saturday night.* The thought depressed me. Then the guilt set in. *Why am I acting like this? I should be*

162

happy for Bobby. He deserves some fun in his life. I am a terrible person.

I was really getting down on myself. I needed some unconditional mother's love. I fished out my phone and called Carla.

"I'm a jealous, bratty bitch," I announced, hoping she would contradict me.

"Eh, it's part of your charm."

Total acceptance. Even better. "Love you, Carla."

"Love you too, hon."

It was hotter inside the gym than it was outside. Massive fans blew the fetid air around but did nothing to cool things off. Bobby sat shirtless in the corner of a ring, sweat glistening off his perfect abs. I recognized his sparring partner, Gordie Hankins. Gordie's a cop who used to work out of the same precinct as Bobby, until he was transferred out. He was at the South Street police station the day I got hauled in.

I made a u-turn a hair too late. "Yo, Brandy," DiCarlo yelled. "Wait up. I want to talk to you."

"Forgot my gym bag in the car," I mumbled, not looking up.

"It's in your hand. C'mere."

Gordie climbed out of the ring and approached me. "You look familiar. Have we met?"

"I'm very famous. You've seen me on TV." Head bent, I started to walk toward Bobby. Gordie put out a hand to stop me.

"Nah, that's not it. I mean I've seen you in person. Recently." Suddenly, recognition lit up his eyes and he grinned like he'd just won the Lottery.

"Long story," I told him. "I was working undercover that day. I'm a reporter. Honest!"

163

Thankfully, Gordie got a call which saved me from further explanation.

Jimmy the Rat was nowhere in sight so Bobby offered to spar with me. We worked out mostly in silence, with Bobby giving me the occasional tip. I was serious about learning how to defend myself and according to DiCarlo it showed.

"You've improved," he said, afterwards. "You're anticipating moves and you're packing some real muscle with your punches now."

"Thanks. Listen, Bobby. I have a favor to ask you."

"Yeah? What's that?"

"I need to find out if someone got on a flight from Philly to L.A. and if they caught the return flight as well. I'm following a lead on that girl, Star and, well, it would really help me out if you could do this for me."

"Sure."

"Just like that? No lecture? No argument?"

"Look, Bran, I know I haven't said it, but I think what you're doing for this kid is pretty terrific. So I'll do what I can to help you out."

"Wow. Thanks." I said, handing him the flight information.

I waited while he showered and changed, emerging from the lockers ten minutes later, wearing ragged jeans and an old beat up tee shirt, but still managing to appear like he'd just stepped off a Gucci billboard.

"Bran, I want to finish our conversation, but I just got a call from Sofia's daycare and I've got to go pick her up. Seems she ate some crayons and the burnt orange didn't agree with her."

"That's okay. I'll catch you later." I watched him as he swung his gym bag over this shoulder.

"You're staring at me, Sweetheart. How come?"

"You're a *dad*, Bobby. Does that ever like totally freak you out?"

"Every day of my life." He flashed me a grin. "But she's worth every freakin' minute of it."

On my way out of the gym, Mike called me back. "I got the info you wanted. Are you sure you want to mess with this dude? He's got a rap sheet a "Lifer" would be proud of."

My stomach dropped. "I don't think we'll be dating any time soon."

"Man, Brandy, I don't feel good about this. Why do you need to get in touch with this scumbag, anyway?"

"I have a network marketing opportunity he may be interested in. C'mon, Mike. Just give me an address and we can put this conversation behind us. Oh, and if you could email me a copy of his rap sheet, I'd appreciate it."

"Anything else?" he said, only I don't think the offer was all that sincere, because he was talking through his teeth.

"No, that should do it."

"Henry Michael Lyons," Mike read aloud. "Last known address is 3700 North Camac Street. Look, be careful. He's been busted on everything from weapons charges to voluntary manslaughter. And he's slicker than a greased pig. A lot of the major charges don't end up sticking. Witnesses tend to disappear."

"I'll be careful, Mike. Thanks."

Okay, so now what? Do I come clean with Little Red? Tell him I'm a reporter and that he's my number one suspect in the case of the missing teenage hooker...Maybe I could get away with that if I was Geraldo Rivera. Oh well, I'll think up a plan on the fly. I work better under pressure anyway.

I got out my map book and checked the address. Then I took out my phone. If I was descending into Hell, I wanted someone who knew his way around to be my tour guide.

"Alphonso?" I said when he picked up. "It's Brandy. Are you busy?"

Chapter Ten

He told me to meet him outside of Ming's Pool Hall, located in one of the more dicey neighborhoods on Kensington Avenue. "Don't get out of the car. Keep your doors and windows locked. Call me when you get here and if you happen to catch anybody on the street in the middle of a business transaction, don't make eye contact!"

"Isn't there like a *Starbucks* we could meet at or something?"

"Let me tell you how this works, Sweetcakes. The person askin' the favor ain't allowed to be picky."

"Oh, *fine*. I'll be there in twenty minutes."

Alphonso was like the badass older cousin you'd see every once in a while at family functions. The kid you'd sneak off with for a smoke or a ride on his motorcycle. The one who'd take you to the edge of trouble but wouldn't let you fall off the cliff and risk the wrath of your mother, or in his case, Nick.

Hanging out with Alphonso I felt protected (due, in part, to the nine-millimeter Glock he packed into the waistband of his pants) and a little bit badass cool by association. That self-delusion was quickly dispelled the

167

moment I pulled up in front of the pool hall in my parents' hand-me-down burgundy Le Sabre.

Alphonso stepped out of the doorway and approached the car, leaning in through the passenger seat window. "Get out," he said. "We'll take my car."

"I can drive, no problem," I told him, unlocking the door.

He peered at me over his designer shades. "It is to me."

"What? My car's not good enough for you?"

He didn't bother to answer. Instead, he walked around to the driver's side and pulled open the door and waited for me to climb out.

"I don't want to leave it here," I said, looking around at a car parked on the other side of the street. It no longer had a back window...or a front one either...or any tires. "It might get stolen."

"Trust me, it won't."

I would have been insulted except that I was secretly hoping it *would* get stolen.

"You're a car snob," I said, climbing into his charcoal grey H3 Alpha Hummer. I ran my hand over the customized leather interior. Jeez, what do you do for Nick that you can afford a set of wheels like this?"

Alphonso grinned. "This and that."

I settled back into the seat. "So, speaking of Nick—"

"Were we?" He started the engine and pulled onto the road. Lines of mid-day traffic parted like the Red Sea to accommodate him.

"I'm pretty sure we were. Listen, is it my imagination or does Nick seem a little different to you since he's gotten back from..."

I waited for him to supply the location. He didn't.

"So what do you think?" I prodded. "Has he been acting different?"

Alphonso gave me a long look. It started to make me nervous.

"I like you, Sweetcakes, so I'm gonna give it to you straight. I work for Santiago and I consider him a friend. But I'm not under any illusions about the guy and you shouldn't be either."

"Well, what the hell does that mean? Can't anybody just answer a question without being so damn cryptic...hey, did my uncle put you up to this?" Frankie wasn't exactly president of the Nicholas Santiago Fan Club. At least not where it involved me.

Alphonso laughed, showing even, white teeth. "Don't get me wrong. Santiago's a great guy. But if you think you're going to get close to him, you'd better think again. The man trusts nobody. Not with the details of his life, anyway. And even if I knew what was up, I wouldn't be talkin' to you about it. I like my job and I value living, know what I mean?"

I thought back to the guy whose leg Nick broke, just because he wasn't paying attention. I knew what he meant.

We drove along in silence for a while, entering neighborhoods I'd only visited on accident or a dare. There were bars on every storefront and apartment building window. Even the church on the corner looked like it would rather do its soul-saving by email.

We passed a strip joint. Girls of varying ages, sizes and color stood on the curb or in the doorway, wilting from the heat and calling out half-hearted enticements. "Live sex acts!" shouted one girl, garnering no attention whatsoever. "Totally air conditioned!" shouted another and three men bolted inside.

"So have you given any thought to what you're gonna say if Little Red is home?" Alphonso asked, slowing the car.

"I'm still thinking about that."

"Well, you'd better think fast. We're here." He pulled alongside the curb of an ugly four-story '60's style apartment building and parked.

"I was hoping you'd just beat the truth out of him," I said.

"Works for me."

"I was just joking," I told him. *Sort've.*

Alphonso opened his car door and swung one long leg onto the sidewalk.

"You coming?"

I looked down at my lap and nodded, only the rest of me stayed rooted to the seat.

Alphonso stuck his foot back in the Hummer, closed the door and leaned back against the seat, eyes closed. I couldn't tell if he was relaxed or disgusted.

"I'm not scared, if that's what you're thinking," I lied. "I just realized that I may not have totally thought things through."

"I'll bet that's a first," Alphonso said, not bothering to open his eyes.

"Okay, so maybe I am scared. And maybe I should have planned a little better, but at least I realized the error of my ways before I totally stepped in it. I consider this a personal triumph."

"My little girl's growing up," he said, grinning.

"Shut uh–Ooh! Look. There he is!"

I ducked down in my seat as a familiar, pasty-faced figure in shades and a cowboy hat appeared from around the back of the apartment building and climbed into a black Escalade with tinted windows. The car looked incongruous amid the general decay of neighborhood.

Without bothering to stop for oncoming traffic, Little Red peeled out from the curb, leaving a trail of arrogance along with the skid marks. The hatred I felt for the man was visceral.

"Well, I guess that's that."

Alphonso raised his eyebrows over the rim of his shades. "Not necessarily. Come on."

He climbed out of the Hummer and started walking toward the front of the building. I unbuckled the seat belt and jumped out of the car, scrambling to catch up to him.

"Alphonso, you saw him leave. Why are we still here?"

He stopped and looked down at me, hitching up his baggy pants in the process. I could see the tip of the Glock protruding from the back of his underwear like some hip, urban accessory.

"You can tell a lot about a person by his environment," he told me.

We walked up the cement sidewalk, heating wafting off it like a stovetop griddle. At the front entrance there was a glass double door that led into a dilapidated lobby. I peered inside. Two old guys were sitting opposite each other in matching, torn Naugahyde chairs. A small, scarred table sat between them, with a chess set resting on top. They didn't so much as blink as Alphonso extracted a small, pointed instrument from his back pocket and proceeded to jimmy open the door.

171

We stepped inside and headed for the stairs, not trusting the look of the elevator.

"What'd you say the apartment number was?"

"Three-twelve."

There was the distinct smell of urine in the stairwell, mixed with someone's attempt to bleach it away. I held my breath and began the climb.

Little Red's apartment was located at the far end of a long hallway. We passed some kids playing outside of one of the apartments. There were two boys, around eight or so, and a little girl. She couldn't have been more than three, but she already wore the scowl of the defeated.

As we reached Little Red's door, Alphonso walked past it to the very end of the hallway. There was an exit sign above a door. He took a quick peek inside and closed it again. I was pretty sure I knew what he was up to, but I still feigned surprise when he retraced his steps and took out his trade tool again. I guess at heart I'm a "bad girl" who just wants to *look* like a good one.

"Alphonso, I really appreciate your willingness to help me, but Breaking and Entering is still a felony, even if the guy who lives here is more 'rat' than actual person."

"No worries, Sweetcakes. We're just gonna take a little look-see." He gave a cursory knock, waited a half a beat and then popped open the door like the seasoned professional he was.

Blackout curtains shielded the living room from prying eyes. Alphonso did a quick scan of the living room and kitchenette, looked out the window for signs of Little Red's return and turned on a lamp.

My heart skipped a couple of beats as I contemplated running out the front door and forgetting the whole thing.

After a minute I shrugged it off and began snooping around the pimp pad.

"I'm in a real den of iniquity," I marveled aloud. "Y'know, it's a little disappointing."

"Well what'd you expect? Leopard skin furniture and furry dice hanging off the mirror?"

"Yeah, something like that. This is just your run of the mill boring-guy-with-bad-taste apartment."

"If it makes you feel any better, he probably has another crib somewhere else. This dive is strictly for business so he can stay close to his girls."

The living room was furnished with a standard issue plaid couch and a matching chair, two end tables and a couple of ugly lamps with shades that hadn't seen a dust cloth since the turn of the century. A dirty mattress was laid out where a coffee table might previously have been.

"What's with the mattress?" I asked.

"The way these guys operate, they cruise around looking for cold, tired, hungry kids and they offer them a place to stay, a meal. Make them feel wanted. This place may not be the Ritz, but to a newbie on the streets, it beats sleeping in a dumpster."

I stepped around the mattress and into the first of two bedrooms.

The room was empty, except for two more mattresses that had been laid out side by side on the floor. They were sheetless and disturbingly filthy. An empty syringe lay at the foot of one of them. There was a body in the other.

I clamped my hand over my mouth and spun out of there, fast, bumping smack into Alphonso's chest.

"There's someone in there," I stammered.

Alphonso whipped out the Glock and, motioning me behind him, we ventured back into the room.

173

It was a kid, about seventeen or so, with long, greasy hair and the beginnings of a mustache.

He was naked from the waist up, the track marks on his arms advertising his drug of choice. He was either asleep or dead.

Alphonso shoved his gun back into his waistband and bent over the boy, checking for a pulse. He shook him, gently at first, then a little harder, eliciting a muffled moan.

"He's okay," Alphonso pronounced.

I began to move toward him but Alphonso stopped me.

"You can't fix him, Brandy. Let him sleep it off."

Reluctantly, I followed him down the hall to the other bedroom.

The door was bolted shut, but he had us inside in less than a minute. This room was decidedly more upscale with a real, king-sized bed, clean sheets and a flat screen TV. I opened up the side table. There was a pipe, a bag of weed, some breath mints and a book of matches with the name of a local breakfast eatery.

I spied the top half of a phone bill peeking out of a wastebasket on the other side of the bed. I picked it up and pocketed it.

"Ooh, you're crossing all sorts of lines, stealing the guy's mail," Alphonso said, impressed. "I think that's a federal crime."

"Yeah, well, a little B & E, a little mail pilfering—I like to mix it up. Besides, he already threw it away, so I'm actually just recycling his trash."

"I like you, Alexander. You're alright."

"I like you, too, Alphonso."

Our little love-fest was cut short by the sound of retching coming out of the other bedroom.

"I'll go check on the kid," he told me. "You finish up in here. We don't want to overstay our welcome."

Remembering what Harmony had told me about the acid, I shuddered. No, we certainly did not.

I opened the door to the walk-in closet. There must've been dozens of cowboy shirts and an equal number of slacks, all hung neatly in a color-coordinated row. *Talk about anal.* I kicked at a pile of dirty laundry and checked his pants pockets. All that yielded me was a card for an abortion clinic with the words "Fawn—9:30" written on it. I pocketed that too.

Next I checked under the bed. I had to admit, Little Red's housekeeping skills were far superior to mine, at least in regard to his personal space. There wasn't a shred of dust under there, let alone anything remotely resembling a clue as to Star's whereabouts. He was either great at covering his tracks or he really *wasn't* involved in Star's disappearance, a thought that was doubly disappointing, seeing as he was just about the only suspect I had.

I stood up and began heading out of the room, when a major attack of the creeps overtook me. It was quiet. Too quiet, and in that split second I knew something was horribly wrong.

Fumbling around for my pepper spray, I resisted the urge to call out to Alphonso and instead crawled on all four's to the doorway.

I stood up slowly and strained to hear something besides the erratic pounding of my own heart. From where I stood I couldn't see anyone, but soon Alphonso's voice echoed through the hall. Only it wasn't the smooth baritone I was used to. It was high pitched and whiney, like a kid pleading with his dad to let him keep his

175

skateboard after he'd left it in the driveway once too often. I couldn't make out his words but he sounded none too happy.

Slowly I crept down the hallway, the can of pepper spray held tightly in my hand. As I got to the end, I peered around the corner and sucked in a breath as Little Red stood, back to me, with a micro uzi trained directly at Alphonso's head.

Chapter Eleven

My legs were shaking so hard I could barely support myself. I ducked back around the corner and weighed my options, briefly entertaining the possibility of sneaking out the front door while Little Red was otherwise occupied. But I knew if the roles had been reversed Alphonso wouldn't ditch me. At least I *think* I knew that.

Alphonso stood stock still, hands in the air. If he had seen me he gave no indication of it.

I propelled myself forward and could hear him clearly now.

"Aw man, I'm just lookin' for my bitch. I heard she come sniffin' around here lookin' to hook up wit'chu, know what I mean? I didn't take nuthin'. Just come for what's mine. You know what I'm talkin' about, man. Can't let a ho dis you like that. Gonna bust a cap in her fat ass when I catch up with that bitch." He began to sway, ever so slightly, which seemed to unnerve Little Red.

"Stand still you crazy son of a bitch," he barked, which only made Alphonso rock harder.

Beyond them lay the kid, curled into a fetal position and rolling around in his own vomit. The whole tableau was like something out of a Quentin Tarantino movie, only without the fun background music.

177

I took a deep breath. Alphonso couldn't afford for me to be paralyzed with fear. Clutching the pepper spray, I began inching up behind little Red. I was *beyond* thought. I was *beyond* fear. I was on a mission.

As Alphonso kept up his steady stream of crazy talk, I took the cold, metal tube of pepper spray and jammed it into the back of Little Red's head.

"Drop the gun, ass-wipe, or I'll blow your fucking brains out," I growled, giving it my best "Joe Pesci in *Goodfellas*" impression.

He froze and I pressed harder. "Drop the fucking gun," I repeated. "Slowly."

Little Red lowered his arm slowly and let the uzi fall to the floor. Alphonso stepped forward, and in one fluid motion, kicked the gun out of the way, brought his arm into a perfect arc and pounded his fist into the pimp's face.

Then he watched with utter satisfaction as Little Red crumpled to the floor, a steady torrent of blood streaming from his nose. He was out cold.

"Come on, Sweetcakes, time to go home."

Now that the adrenalin rush was over, every day activities such as walking and breathing seemed really complicated. "Um, okay, just give me a sec."

I leaned against the door jam, my eyes resting on the boy. "What do we do about the kid?" I asked. "We can't just leave him here."

"It'll cause more problems for him if we don't. I'm sorry, Brandy," he shrugged. "It's just the way it is."

Tears of frustration welled up in me. "C'mon," he said, again, more gently.

"Just a minute. There's something I have to do."

I turned and marched back into Little Red's closet and rearranged all his meticulously color-coded shirts and pants, creating fashion-wear havoc. Satisfied with my small victory, I walked out the apartment door.

We didn't talk much on the ride home. Alphonso slipped in a CD, something dark and sultry, and I leaned back against the headrest and thought about what I would have done if Little Red had called my bluff. The truth is I had no friggin' idea.

As a nod to my two months in therapy, I gave myself a moment to "feel the pain" and then I shrugged it off. I figured if I was going to hang out with the big boys, I needed to learn how to shake off these near-death experiences like Alphonso does. *"No biggie," that's my new motto.*

"So, Alphonso," I told him, "I guess everything's cool, huh?"

He cut me a look. *"Have you been sniffing glue?* That was some scary shit we got dealt back there. But I'm impressed with you, Sweetcakes, you really had my back. You could've just snuck out and left me there."

"The thought never crossed my mind."

Alphonso dropped me off back at my car. Thankfully, it was still there, just minus the hubcaps, which (actually helped to modernize the look of it a little.)

"You gonna be okay?" he asked as I dug the car keys out of my bag.

"Me? Pfft. I'm fine. Listen, thanks for coming with me today. Except for the almost getting killed part, I had a really nice time."

Alphonso let out a belly laugh. "You always look on the bright side, don't ya, Sweetcakes?"

179

"I try." I climbed into the Le Sabre and locked the doors, giving Alphonso two thumbs up as I drove away. I made it a block and a half away before I pulled over to the curb and tossed my cookies. Then I drove the rest of the way home.

"Come on, Franny, push!"

"Yeah," Janine chimed in. "Don't be lazy. Pop that sucker out of there. I've got a date in an hour."

"You go, girl," Carla added, only half paying attention. She was painting her toenails.

"Screw all of you's," Fran yelled, but she was laughing.

We were all stretched out on the rug in Fran's living room, practicing for the "blessed event." We dimmed the lights and turned on a soothing c.d. that simulated the sound of rushing waters, but then we had to turn it off because everyone kept getting up to pee.

I'd arrived at Fran's house a little after six to take her to La Maze class, only she wouldn't get in the car.

"They're showing "The Miracle of Birth" tonight, she said by way of explanation.

"Isn't that the film they made us watch in 11th grade, where the woman is screaming in agony while her husband stands off to the side holding a bucket of ice chips?" *I had nightmares for weeks and refused to let Bobby touch me for at least a month after suffering through that movie.*

"Yeah, I'm hating Eddie enough as it is, right now."

"Why's that?"

Fran looked down at her mountainous baby-belly.

"He did this to me."

"The bastard."

We took a pass on the film and called Janine and Carla to come over, instead.

180

"Okay, Fran," I told her. I was taking my role as coach very seriously. "One more push should do it. Janine, man the camera. Carla, get ready to catch the baby. Little DiAngelo hyphen Bonaduce is on her way!"

Franny wiggled her hips and something black and shiny rolled out from between her legs. Carla held it high in the air, Lion king style.

"Congratulations, Mom, you've just given birth to a healthy, nine pound bowling ball."

"She looks just like her father," Carla cooed.

"Wow. Giving birth really works up an appetite," Janine said. "Let's order in some pizza."

"Can't," Fran said, frowning. "The grease gives me heartburn."

"Mexican?" I suggested.

She shook her head. "Gas."

"Sushi?" asked Carla. Franny made a face.

"What's wrong with sushi?"

"Too salty. Makes me retain water."

This baby couldn't come soon enough. It was really putting a crimp in our style.

"Oh, I forgot to tell you," Fran said, later, as we chowed down on frozen yogurt bars. (Nutritious *and* delicious—at least that's what it said on the package. They lied.) "DiCarlo called here earlier, looking for you. He said he'd tried your cell phone but you didn't pick up."

I'd turned off my phone when Alphonso and I were at Little Red's. (Through trial and error I have found that when engaged in covert activity, if you want it to remain covert it is best not to inadvertently announce your presence through a phone call from your mother.)

"Did he say what he wanted?"

"No, but he sounded really uptight."

"Uptight *worried* or uptight *mad?*"

"I'd say a little of both."

Uh oh. Bobby must've found out about me breaking into Little Red's apartment. What if Red filed a police report and Bobby's calling to warn me that I'm about to be arrested!

Okay, so the likelihood of a pimp voluntarily inviting the cops into his drug infested home with a teenage prostitute lying half dead in the back room to report that someone had been—what?—mean to him?—was slim to none. But I got a knot in my stomach anyway. I decided I'd call him back when I got home.

Turns out it wasn't necessary. He was sitting on my porch waiting for me when I pulled up in front of my house two hours later. I've known DiCarlo practically my whole life, and his moods generally fell into three categories: happy, pissed off or horny.

I tried to read the look on his face, but it was a new one on me.

I started up the path and caught Mrs. Gentile peering through her curtains from an upstairs window. *Jeez, does that old biddy ever sleep?* I gave her a little finger wave and she poked her head back inside.

Bobby stood as I approached.

"Yo," I said. "What's up?"

His face was tense in the moonlight. "I need to talk to you."

"Who's watching Sofia?" I unlocked the door and turned off the alarm.

"I had to work late so Eddie's mom stayed over," he said, following me into the living room.

Adrian ran downstairs to greet me, leaving a trail of torn up fluff in his wake. He was carrying the remains of my favorite stuffed bear, now minus one eye and most of his insides. It looked like he'd had liposuction.

"Bad dog," I shouted.

"Jesus, Brandy, it's not the dog's fault. You probably left it around where you knew he could get it."

"Whoa, back up there, cowboy. First of all, I did not!" *Okay, I probably did, but that was between me and my dog.* "And secondly, I may have made a tactical error today, but Alphonso and I handled it just fine and nobody got hurt— well, except for the pimp, but he deserved it, so you don't need to lecture me about being responsible!" I was yelling really loud, figuring a strong offense was the best defense.

Bobby stared at me like I'd grown another head. "What the hell are you talking about?"

"You mean you don't—oh, um, *nothing*. Bobby, what's goin' on? You're pacing around like a girl waiting for her prom date to arrive. If you've got something to tell me, just say it."

Bobby sat down on the couch, pulling me down next to him. He studied my face as if it held the secrets to the universe. Frankly, he was scaring the crap out of me.

"Bran," he said, quietly, "I heard something today and I just need you to tell me the truth. Whatever it is, we'll work it out together."

"Oh, for Christ's sake Bobby, will you just spill it?"

"Are you pregnant with my baby?"

"What?" If I'd had water in my mouth it would have provided a *hilarious* sitcom moment. "Bobby, *no!* Don't you think if I was pregnant with your kid, you'd be the first to know about it…well, the *second*, anyway. I tell Fran everything first. But, no!" I repeated. "I'm *not* pregnant!"

He leaned back on the couch, his shoulders sagging with relief, and, I'd like to think, a smidgeon of

183

disappointment. "Oh. Okay. Well, I'd heard you were, and what with the timing and all, I thought it might be mine."

"Man, I've got to put a stop to this crazy rumor…if I deck Mindy Rebowitz, how much 'time' would I be looking at? Whatever, it'd be like totally worth it."

"Listen, now that we've got the whole 'rumor thing' straightened out, were you able to check with your friend at the airline?"

"Oh, yeah. The guy was on the flight. He flew out on the evening of the 15th and returned a week later. I even cross-referenced to make sure he didn't sneak back into town on another airline. So, is that good news or bad?"

"It's frustrating news. If Garner checks out, I'm back to square one. I'm just not sure I believe it. Listen, as long as you're here, would you mind going through the house with me? I've been remembering to turn on the alarm and all, but knowing Bunny is still out there—well, better safe than sorry," I shrugged. God, I hated sounding like such a wimp.

I followed him through the kitchen to the back door, then up the stairs to check the bedroom windows. Everything was secure. Now I felt silly for asking.

"Thanks a lot," I told him, heading downstairs again and over to the door.

I opened it, only Bobby put his hand on the knob and closed it again. Leaning up against the door, he folded his arms across his chest and cut me a smile. "Did you really think you were going to get off that easy? Let's start with who's Alphonso?"

"An old friend of Frankie's," I said, automatically. *Maybe a little misleading, but definitely not a lie.*

"Right," he said, in a tone that let me know he wasn't buying what I was trying to sell. "So what were you and your uncle's old buddy, Alphonso, doing hanging out with a pimp?"

"Y'know," I said, reaching behind him to grab a hold of the door knob, "some day I'm going to write my memoirs. If I tell you everything now you won't spring for the book." I gave the knob a good tug, knocking him slightly off-balance. I took the opportunity to open the door wide and push him over the threshold.

"This conversation isn't over, just postponed," he said, letting me win this round.

"Go home, Bobby. Wake up your little girl and tell her that you love her, and hold her and kiss her like there's no tomorrow."

He settled his smoky blue eyes on me as if seeing me for the first time tonight.

"Sometimes you blow me away," he said, hugging me to him. "G'night, Sweetheart."

Bobby walked a few paces, slowed and turned to me. "Just for the record, if you *had* been pregnant with my kid, I wouldn't have been disappointed."

I waited until he got in the car before I started bawling my eyes out.

"How's the story on the missing kid coming along, Alexander?"

I looked up from my cubbyhole of an office to find Eric standing over me, eating a Chinese Chicken salad. "Want some?" he offered.

"No, thanks. I just ate."...*A king sized Hershey bar, which wouldn't have been so bad, had I not had half a cup of Ben*

185

Shelly Fredman

and Jerry's chocolate fudge brownie to go with it...oh well, anything that tastes that good cannot possibly be bad for you.

"I've got some stuff to check out," I murmured, vaguely. I didn't want to admit to Eric that my investigation was going nowhere, lest he reassign me to the Strawberry Festival. The last thing I wanted was to parade around in 108-degree weather dressed as a giant fruit tart.

I'd started the day by perusing Little Red's phone bill. Most of the numbers were local, lots of fast-food joints and an abortion clinic. One number had a 405 area code. *Gracemont, Oklahoma.* It looked from his outgoing calls that he dialed it every day, although there were none coming in.

I Googled Gracemont. The town was so small they'd be hard pressed to find enough residents to play a regulation softball game. Impulsively, I picked up the phone and dialed.

It took eight rings before someone answered. "Hell-oow?"

I imagined that was how dead people sounded. Dead people who'd died when they were really, really old. "Oh, uh, hi. May I please speak to Henry?"

"Henry? Why, no, Honey. He's been gone since 1970."

Huh? Little Red couldn't have even been born then. "I mean Henry Michael Lyons?"

The old lady chuckled. It was a scary sound. "Oh, *Henry Michael.* I thought you was talking about my late husband, Henry *David.* I'm Henry Michael's great grandmaw. He don't live here, Honey. He lives in Philadelphia. He's a lawyer. He calls me every day."

"Wow. That's really nice. Well, good talking to you."

186

"When he calls me, I'll tell him you called. What's your name?"

"Mary," I told her and hung up.

The phone call depressed me. All I learned was that Little Red has a very nice widowed great grandma who loves him and thinks he's a lawyer. I suck at investigating.

I had a little better luck on the next phone call. I caught Nurse Morrison just coming off her lunch break.

"Linda, it's Brandy Alexander," I said, when she picked up. "I'm sorry to bother you at work."

"It's alright, I've still got a few minutes. What can I do for you?"

"Well, when we last talked, you had mentioned that you have a friend that works for the city coroner's office in Camden."

"That's right. My friend, Stacey."

"I was wondering if you think she'd be willing to talk to me. I'm doing a story on runaway and homeless youth and I was intrigued by her story about the girl who had given birth and then died of a drug overdose."

"Stacey took that really hard. Here. Let me get your number again. I'm sure she'd be willing to talk to you, but I'm not comfortable giving out her personal information without permission."

I gave her my contact info and she promised to get back to me. I leaned back in my chair and closed my eyes in an attempt to ward off a headache.

Maybe a little protein would help. I opened a drawer and took out a Reese's Peanut Butter Cup, thought better of it and put it back in the drawer. After the lunch I'd had, that would be excessive even by my standards.

As I contemplated eating an actual meal, the phone rang.

"Hey, sis."

"Yo, Paulie. What's up?" I could tell he was at the club by the tinkling of glasses in the background.

"Would you be interested in earning a little extra cash?" he asked.

"Always," I told him, thinking about the broken air conditioner and my non-existant household expense fund. "What do you have in mind? Ooh," I said, not waiting for an answer. "Do you need me to fill in for one of the servers? Because I've been practicing at home carrying plates on my arm and I'm getting really good at it, and besides, you don't have to worry about me spilling soup on anyone like that one unfortunate time, because first of all that was just a fluke—I mean what are the odds of it happening again and besides it's July. Who would order soup in July? Nobody. It's too damn hot!"

Paul gave a low whistle. "So, like how much sugar have you had today?"

"Not much. Hardly any."

"Uh huh. Man, it must be exhausting being you."

"It's a full time job, that's for sure. So what do you need me to do?"

"I've got our old band booked for the club in two weeks, but Kenny was dating Gloria, their new lead singer, and, well, let's just say it didn't work out, so he wants to know if you'd be willing to fill in until—"

"Until they can find a female singer in the Greater Lehigh Valley that Kenny *hasn't* slept with and pissed off to the point of no return?"

Paul laughed. "Yeah."

"Sure," I said. "Be happy to."

Just as I was packing up to go home, Nurse Morrison called me back with her friend's number. I put in a call, leaving a message on her voice mail. I didn't know exactly what I was looking for but felt certain she could help me tie things together. I was deep in thought when my phone rang. It was Crystal.

"I'm bored," she said by way of greeting.

"Hang on a minute, I've got Brad Pitt on the other line. Brad, Crystal says she's bored. Can you go entertain her for a while?"

"Ha, ha,very funny. First off, he's not my type. He's too old. And second, how much longer do I have to stay here? I want to get back to my life."

As in sleeping on the curb and eating every meal out of a trash can?

"Are they treating you okay?" I asked instead.

"Yeah. Everybody's really nice. It's just—"

"I know, kiddo. It's hard being at the mercy of other people. Even when they're being kind. Hey, would you be up for a visit tonight?"

"*Really?* I mean, if you want to, I guess that would be okay with me. Could Nick come too?"

"I'll ask him," I said, matching her nonchalance. In reality, I was so grateful for an excuse to call him I could have done back flips.

I disconnected from Crystal and punched in Nick's number, but mid-ring I began to panic.

It's Friday night. What if he has a date? And now by calling him he'll know I'm free and he'll think I'm a big loser. He'll be all, "I'm sorry, my socially deficient friend. We popular people have a tradition of going out on Friday night, in my case, with the opposite sex, for an evening of fine dining followed by fornication."

Okay, chances are he wouldn't say that. Nobody in their right mind would. Still, I thought about hanging up, but then there he was on the line and he sounded genuinely happy to hear from me.

"Hey, Darlin'. I was just about to call you. Sal phoned and said Crystal's getting a little restless. He thinks she could use a visit. Do you have plans for tonight?"

"Nothing I can't cancel. You know, if the kid needs me. How about you?"

"I've got some business to take care of later in the evening, but since it's out in that direction, I thought I'd stop in and visit with her for a while. How about if I swing by your place and you can follow me out there. The directions are a bit complicated."

"Sounds good. Give me an hour to walk the dog." *And find a killer outfit, get my hair highlighted… maybe a boob job…*

I decided against the breast augmentation and just went with a clean shirt and a push up bra. That's really all I had time for. Adrian was chomping at the bit to go for a walk.

At six o'clock at night, the temperature was still in the high 70's. A flash of lightening shot across the sky and the crack of distant thunder warned of a storm brewing. It served as a backdrop for a wave of anxiety that rose up unexpectedly and settled in the pit of my stomach. A feeling of dread, so strong that I had to run all the way home, cutting short Adrian's nightly cruise around the neighborhood.

I called my uncle Frankie, just to hear a friendly voice.

"What's up, hon?" He was still at the gym, in the middle of a workout, from what I could tell. He sounded pretty winded.

"Nothing. Just wanted to say hi."

He invited me for dinner next week and told me a story about a guy at the gym who posted highlights from his bachelor party on Youtube, and now his bride is asking for a divorce and custody of their pet boa constrictor. It made me laugh, but I still couldn't shake the feeling of unease.

There was a knock at the front door, which sent spasms of joy through Adrian's furry little body. He stood on his hind legs pawing at the door as if he sensed someone fabulous was about to enter his domain. I knew how he felt. Nick walked in and neither of us was disappointed.

He was wearing jeans and a short-sleeved button down linen shirt that showcased forearms that were lean and muscular. He was wearing his trademark silver wristband, and a silver cross hung from his ear. He reached out to kiss me hello and his shirtsleeve rode up his arm, revealing the Native American tribal symbol tattooed on his shoulder. He was the coolest person in the history of cool and, yet, the least affected by it. He just—*was*.

"Are you ready to go?" he asked.

"Um, yeah," I said, looking vaguely around the room. I picked up my bag and did a mental check for my pepper spray, rape whistle and the set of brass knuckles I got at a yard sale from my neighbor across the street who used to teach middle school.

Nick stopped me at the door. "What's wrong, Angel?"

"I feel like someone's watching me."

Chapter Twelve

Nick slid his hand around to the small of his back and withdrew a .38 caliber pistol from beneath his shirt. His face remained impassive, but I could feel the heightened energy radiating from his body.

"Do you think someone's in the house?" he asked quietly.

"No," I said, resting my hand on the arm that held the gun. "I'm sure no one broke in here."

Nick relaxed and slipped the pistol back into its holster. "Where were you when you began to feel like you were being watched?"

"Outside walking Adrian. It was just a little while ago. All of a sudden it felt like I wasn't alone--like I was being followed. I can't explain it," I ended, sounding like the Delusional Paranoids they make Lifetime movies about.

Nick opened the screen door and stood on the porch, his eyes roving up and down the block. "I don't see anyone, but you have good instincts, Angel. Don't discount them." He closed the door and locked it behind him. "The cops still haven't located Bunny yet. Could be she's keeping tabs on you, waiting to make her move."

I plopped down on the couch, allowing myself a moment of royal self-pity. "Well, that's just great. Christ, you'd think the police would've picked her up by now. I mean how hard can it be to find a 5'8" hulk with bright orange hair and a face like a bulldog?"

"You'd be surprised," Nick said mildly. He sat down next to me and put his arm around my shoulder and I leaned into him, drawing comfort from his nearness.

"I've got a few people looking for her as well. But homeless kids are very loyal to their street family, so if Bunny wants to disappear, they'll go to any length to make sure she *doesn't* get found."

"But that doesn't make any sense. She's—she's scary and abusive and—and—nuts!"

"She's also the alpha female. As sick as it sounds, Bunny provides leadership and stability for these kids. For all intents and purposes, she's their mother."

"Okay," I said. "Forget what she did to Heather and what she's threatening to do to me. She probably whacked that poor case worker just for *knowing* Star."

"You're not getting an argument from me, Darlin'. It's a sick world, I'll grant you that. But for most of these kids, it's business as usual."

"How did you end up living on the streets, Nick? And how did you get out?"

Nick shifted in his seat, a slight shadow crossing his face. "Let's stick to one subject at a time. Can you think of anyone else who may be interested in a little *payback*? Someone you may have managed to piss off recently?"

I could think of several, but I knew what he was driving at. "You've been talking to Alphonso, haven't you?" I sighed.

"He's been talking to me. You really impressed him. That's saying something. Alphonso doesn't impress easily."

"Yeah, well, I think I'm growing on him. Listen, maybe this feeling I had is just the product of an overactive imagination. It probably doesn't mean anything at all."

"You don't really believe that and neither do I."

Nick stood and put his hand into his pants pocket, extracting a set of keys. He took one off and handed it to me. "If at any time you feel unsafe here, I want you to go over to my place. I may not be back tonight, but the security over there is a little tighter than it is here."

"Wow. It must be pretty important business if you're not planning to come home tonight. What's her name?" *Oh, Holy Jesus! Please let Nick go retroactively deaf so that he didn't hear what just came out of my mouth. Jeez, this is awkward. But... wait! It doesn't have to be. I'll just take it back!*

"Um, I didn't really say that. So, ready to go?"

I grabbed my bag and strode purposefully toward the door. Suddenly, I felt Nick's arms around my waist, pulling me back against him.

Oh boy, here it comes, the lecture on jealousy, or at the very least, some good-natured ribbing. Well, it's not like I don't deserve it.

He turned me around and wrapped his arms around me, a smile playing about his lips that was so tender, so sincere it took my breath away.

"Just when I think there are no good surprises left in the world..." He looked deeply into my eyes and sighed. "You continually amaze me in the best possible ways." Then he lowered his head and kissed me.

Talk about good surprises.

Alphonso was waiting in Nick's car, a 1964 hunter green Jaguar XKE. He grinned when he saw me and flashed me a hand gesture, signifying our newly formed status as partners in crime. I waved back, glad to be part of the Brotherhood.

I slid behind the wheel of the Le Sabre and we both took off, driving a few blocks out of the way to make sure no one was following us. When it looked like we were clear, we turned the cars around and headed for the Walt Whitman Bridge. The safe house was located somewhere in the south end of Toms River, New Jersey, a quiet beach community to the north of Atlantic City.

It was about an hour's drive, give or take two for rush hour traffic. I entertained myself by thinking about Nick's kiss. It was soft and sweet and all too brief. If Janine were here she'd tell me that he's horribly conflicted.

"Nick doesn't want to lead you on, but the man can't help himself," she'd say. *"His feelings for you are too powerful. He can't resist your womanly charms, so he kisses you like a brother, but in his heart he wants more...much more."* Yeah. That's just what Janine would say...if she were living in a Jane Austen novel.

And then there was the way Nick deflected my question about his past. I'd asked him about it before and was always met with the same enigmatic response.

What is he trying so hard to forget? And why won't I leave it alone? Because the past has a way of propelling itself forward, and unless you're a really fast runner it ends up biting you in the ass.

I was lost in thought so I was surprised when, an hour and a half later, Nick turned down a narrow deserted road and pulled into the driveway of a sprawling one-story beach house. I followed him into the driveway and cut the engine. Climbing out of the car, I breathed deeply, allowing the pure ocean air to fill my lungs.

The house was situated directly on the beach. Slabs of slate were laid down on the sand to create a patchwork pathway. Beach grass grew wild along an old wooden fence. I looked up and saw a flock of seagulls flying overhead.

Alphonso opted to wait in the car, so Nick and I took the path around to the front of the building. Inside, Crystal stood in front of a wall-to-wall glass window. She spied us and ran to the door.

"Hi," she yelled, swinging the door wide open. "How do you like my new digs?"

Although it had only been a few days, Crystal looked different, and it took me a moment to figure out why. She was smiling. Gone was the haunted looked she'd sported since that first day at my uncle's gym. Standing before me was a kid who was well rested, well fed and, even if only temporarily, at peace.

As we entered the house, a yellow lab and her puppy galloped over to say hello. Nick knelt down and scratched the big one behind her ears. She collapsed onto the floor rolling over on her back in unabashed ecstasy.

"That's Dolly," Crystal told us, "and this little guy is Elwood. He won't leave me alone."

"In reality, it looked more like the other way around, but the puppy didn't seem to mind being the center of Crystal's attention.

An attractive young woman in her late twenties walked into the living room. "Hi, I'm Mandy. I sort've run things around here. You must be Brandy," she added, shaking my hand. "Crystal's told me a lot about you."

Nick stood up and Mandy made a little sucking noise in the back of her throat. "And *you* must be Nick," she gulped.

To her credit, she recovered quickly and even managed to acknowledge that I was still in the room. "It's really nice to meet you…I mean, both of you."

"Hey," Crystal interrupted, "Want to see my room?"

We followed her to the back of the house, Dolly and Elwood dutifully trotting after us.

The place was owned by a friend of Sal's and used, alternately, as a safe-house and an interim crash pad for kids with varying transitional needs. At the moment, Crystal was the only resident. The rest of the bedrooms were occupied by staff.

We returned to the living room and I grabbed a seat on the sofa.

"So," Crystal demanded, returning to form, "are you any closer to finding Star? Or even Bunny? I mean this place is nice and all, but you can't expect me to stay penned up here forever."

My first thought was, "Why, you ungrateful little shit," and was immediately ashamed of myself. The poor kid probably felt guilty for enjoying the safety and comfort of her temporary home when her best friend was MIA. *Note to self: Stop being such a judgmental bitch.*

"I imagine you're very frustrated right now," Nick stated. His simple affirmation of her feelings seemed to release some of the tension from her body.

"Crystal," I said, after a bit, "I know you believe you've told us everything you can think of regarding Star, but sometimes the most insignificant seeming thing can turn out to be really valuable. Can you remember any interaction that you might have had concerning Star that may have slipped your mind?"

Crystal was quiet for a minute, thinking. "I'll be right back," she finally announced and disappeared down the hall. She returned a minute later, holding a small brown paper bag.

"Star took most of her stuff with her whenever she went anywhere, because she couldn't trust it to be there when she got back. Everything she owned fit in a backpack anyway, so it was easy. Well, when she didn't come home, I grabbed what little was left and saved it for her. I just thought she'd be mad if it was gone."

She turned the bag upside down and a small pile of random items spilled onto the floor.

There was half a pack of matches, a pipe, two shiny stones and a motel business card. I picked up the card. "Lemon Tree Inn," I read aloud. "Is this where Star goes when she's working?"

Crystal glanced at the card and shook her head. "Little Red's girls stay close to home. This place is too far north. Do you think it could mean something?" she asked.

"I don't know, but I'd like to check it out. Do you mind if I take this stuff with me?"

Silently she handed me back the card. "I should have thought of this sooner," she said, her voice breaking. "What if it's too late?"

I was about to launch into a Tony Robbins style pep talk on the powers of positive thinking, when Nick locked eyes with Crystal, and I sat back, deferring to what I knew would be just the right words to soothe her.

To my surprise he remained silent and just listened while Crystal went through a litany of emotions. I took my cues from him and kept my mouth shut. It seemed to be just what she needed.

Afterwards, leaning up against my car, I asked him about it.

"How did you know to stay quiet when Crystal started blaming herself, Nick?"

"Crystal didn't want me to fix it for her, Darlin'. Anything I'd say to reassure her would have been a lie anyway and she knew it. What she needed was to vent her feelings and know that she was being heard."

He leaned in close and brushed a stray hair out of my face. "That was hard for you, wasn't it?" he added with a gentle smile. "It goes completely against your nature to see someone in pain and not actively try to help them."

"Yeah," I admitted. "It was." *But I'm learning that sometimes, less is more.*

Nick knew a shortcut through the back roads to I 95, where we would then part ways; me back to my house and the new Disney Channel movie, and Nick, to whatever business he had that required him to go armed.

The route was windy and in desperate need of repair, and I was having a hard time keeping up with Nick. My phone rang, and rather than take my hands off the wheel, I let it go to voicemail. I rolled up my window part way to keep the dust out of my lungs.

I hadn't seen many cars on the road, so it surprised me when a late model convertible, packed with a bunch of guys in their early twenties began weaving down the road. By the look of their shaved heads, they were either neo Nazis or young army recruits from nearby Fort Dix. I thought about pulling over to let them pass, but the road was wide enough to get by and I didn't want to lose Nick.

The convertible came up close behind me, and as I looked in my rear view mirror the driver tossed a beer can out of the car.

Oh great, I've got a drunken litterbug riding my butt.

Suddenly, he tromped on the gas, pulling his vehicle alongside mine. I slowed down to let him pass, when the passenger riding shotgun leaned out of the car holding

199

what, literally, appeared to be some sort of sawed off rifle. *Oh shit.*

Instinctively, I leaned on the horn, my body bracing itself for the worst. Something hit my side window and blood spattered everywhere. *Wow. He must've severed my spinal cord. I don't feel a thing.*

It took me a few seconds to realize the blood was actually red paint that had been fired from a paintball gun. The shooter had managed to hit just below the open window, spraying me and most of the front seat with what I hoped was a water-soluble pellet.

Their laughter rang in my ears as the driver sped away from me. Unfortunately, he hadn't counted on Nick witnessing the whole event.

He came up behind Nick and honked his horn in "boys will be boys" horseplay. Nick slowed down, seemingly, to let the convertible pass, only the minute he was in position, he rammed the back of the car in a perfect pit maneuver. The convertible spun out and came to a screeching halt.

I pulled my car over to the side of the road, stopping about twenty yards from the others. Four sets of arms and legs piled out of the convertible. They converged on the Jaguar, the driver screaming at the top of his drunken lungs.

"What the fuck, dude! You tryin' to kill us? We were just havin' some fun."

Nick climbed out of the car, his gaze fixed on the shooter. The remaining three formed a protective circle around their friend, hands raised in classic fight mode. "Come and get us, asshole," they taunted.

That was a mistake.

In a blink Nick was upon them, kicking out his leg and catching the guy nearest him under the chin. He fell to the ground, yelping in agony, half his jawbone poking through his skin. Without losing a step, Nick grabbed the shooter around the neck and began choking the life out of him.

In the time that I've known Nick, I've watched him snap a man's arm in half (for the best of reasons) and then calmly claim it's the price of doing business. I have seen him coolly dispatch someone, with a well-placed bullet right between the eyes, (again, not without provocation) and not even break a sweat. But in all that time, I'd never seen him lose control…until now.

I raced over to the Jaguar just as Alphonso emerged from the passenger seat. "Alphonso, do something! He's going to kill that guy."

"Don't move," Alphonso barked at the two men left standing. They didn't seem inclined to run to their friend's defense. In fact, they looked like they'd rather go home and forget the whole thing.

"Nick." Alphonso yelled, trying to pry his hands loose. "Slow down, man. She's okay. It's all cool."

"This bastard needs a lesson on how to treat a woman."

And with a sudden, gut wrenching clarity I knew I wasn't the woman he was thinking about.

I ran over to Nick and placed my hand on his arm. "Nick. *Please.* Let him go."

The fear in my eyes must've snapped him out of whatever alternate universe he'd drifted off to. He loosened his grip and the guy collapsed, gasping for air. His friends ran forward and grabbed him and took off running.

We watched them pile into the convertible and peel out, screaming obscenities at us from the safe confines of the car, their voices slowly fading as they turned a corner in the road.

"Are you okay?" Nick asked.

I nodded, afraid to verbalize the lie. The entire episode was over in a heartbeat, but the effects were chilling.

Alphonso cut me a look. He felt it too—an invisible current of energy that emanated from Santiago and threatened to choke us all. It was the unmitigated power of barely contained rage.

To Alphonso he said, "Change of plans. I'm sure Brandy won't mind you hitching a ride with her." Not waiting for an answer, he took off without a backward glance.

"What just happened?" I whispered, even though Nick was long gone.

Alphonso scratched his head. "Fuck if I know."

Even ultra cool Alphonso "I mind my own business" Jackson couldn't help but speculate on Nick's recent behavior.

"I've known Santiago for five years and I've never seen him lose it before. Something's been eating that guy ever since he got back from—" he stopped short, finishing out the sentence in a memo to himself. "Keep your big mouth shut, Jackson."

"Alphonso," I said, trying my best to sound therapeutic rather than nosy, "it's not good to keep things bottled up. You'll feel better if you get this off your chest. So, you were saying, since he got back from—"

Nick's right hand man raised his eyebrows at me. "I'm not sayin' nuthin'. And don't you go ridin' my ass for

202

information neither. If Nick wanted you to know he'd tell you up close and personal."

"But—"

"End of subject."

"*Oh, fine.* You probably don't know anything anyway," I said, hoping he'd take the bait.

Alphonso shot me a look that screamed "amateur." Then he folded his arms across his chest, slumped down in his seat and closed his eyes. And that really was the end of the subject. Half an hour later, I dropped him off at his car and headed home.

To look at Robert DiCarlo's living room, one would never guess it housed one of the most testosterone-driven males in the city. Every square foot of available space with dominated by the miniature world of a toddler.

"You sit here," Sofia directed in that adorably bossy way only a three year-old can get away with. (I know, I've tried.)

I'd been sitting on the couch with Janine and Carla, dissecting my latest encounter with Nick, while Bobby's daughter orchestrated an elaborate tea party with her stuffed animals. Growing tired of providing all the dialogue for her inanimate guests, she was now demanding human participation. When I'd agreed to babysit, I had no idea it would be so exhaustingly interactive.

Propelling myself off the couch I walked over to the tiny table and grabbed a handful of the cookies we'd made earlier with her Easy Bake Oven. Sofia had even graciously offered to let me lick the bowl. It was a real treat for me, as I still haven't forgiven my mom for giving away *my* Easy Bake Oven. (The fact that I was 22 at the time did not lessen the sting of the loss.)

Frankie glanced over at me and snickered. Sofia smiled and sidled over to him. My uncle had been flying under the radar, sitting in the corner watching the Phillies battle the Mets in New York. The Phils were leading in the ninth, but the Mets were up with two outs and bases loaded.

"You sit here too," she said, tugging at his sleeve.

"In a minute, Sweetheart," Frankie said, absently eyeing the television.

Sofia stood in front of him, her lower lip quivering like the proverbial bowl full of jelly.

Carla looked up from her Sudoku puzzle. "Frankie, she's just a baby. You're making her cry. You can watch baseball any time."

"But it's bases loaded," he grumbled.

I could totally see his point. It was, however, lost on Sofia, who began to sob, producing copious amounts of huge, heartbroken tears.

Frankie panicked. "Oh, no, Sweetheart, everything is okay. You don't have to cry." He got up and walked over to the tiny chair and sat down. He drew his knees to his chest, one butt cheek hanging off the side. At that exact moment, the Mets drove in three runs to win the game. Frankie let out a groan.

Sofia got up close and peered into my uncle's face. "You're too big to cry," she decided. "Only little girls can."

It was 10:30 p.m. but the kid refused to go to sleep.

"Her bed time is at 7:00," Bobby had informed me, looking sharp in khaki pants and a new polo shirt. He'd even shaved. I briefly entertained the thought of Tina reaping the benefits of such meticulous grooming and then went into denial mode instead. Life is much more pleasant when you pretend to have control over it.

"She may want you to read her a story and she'll probably fall asleep in the middle of it. Thanks again for watching her, Bran."

"No problem," I told him. She'd be asleep inside of an hour and then Carla, Frankie and Janine would be over to watch the Phillies game. Ah, the best laid plans…

"…and then Prince Nicholas said, 'I have banished all the bimbos from my kingdom. I love you, Princess Angel. Please be my bride.'"

"What's a bimbo?"

Sofia was curled up next to me on the couch, holding her blankie and playing with my hair. Carla, Frankie and Janine were gone and Bobby would be back soon and I still hadn't managed to get his little girl to go to sleep. I gave up any illusion of competence and let her run the show.

"A bimbo is another word for…dog." *Well, technically that's true. Some bimbos are real bitches.*

Sofa thought for a minute. "Why did Prince Nicholas make all the bimbos go away? Doesn't he like dogs?"

"He's allergic."

"You're silly."

I sighed. "I know."

Bobby found us passed out on the couch. "Yo," he said, gently shaking me awake.

I'd been in the middle of a dream about a lizard wearing a red bandana, singing the National Anthem at Citizens Bank Park. He got a standing ovation even though he'd forgotten most of the words. I think I mixed up the ball game with an old Geico commercial.

"Hey, how'd it go?" I asked, sitting up. I was sweating and my hair was stuck to the side of my face. I tried combing it with my fingers but Sofia had tangled it up pretty good in her effort to give me braids.

"It was okay."

I moved over to give him room on the couch. "Just okay?"

"Yeah, I don't think we're exactly made for each other." He didn't elaborate. Instead, he leaned over and kissed me on the mouth. He tasted faintly of beer and hot dogs.

"Relationships are hard, he said. "From now on I'm sticking to fighting crime and other manly endeavors. So how'd it go with you?" he added, picking cookie dough out of my hair.

"I think it went really well. We made cookies in her Easy Bake Oven and Sofia let me lick the bowl."

"Hey, remember when your mom gave yours away without even asking?"

"Yeah, don't do that with your kid, okay?"

I picked up my bag and grabbed a few more cookies and Bobby walked me to the door.

"Thanks again for tonight, Sweetheart. I owe you one."

"You don't owe me a thing. It was fun." I looked back over my shoulder to the little girl asleep on the couch. "You do good work, DiCarlo."

He followed my gaze and smiled and then his eyes settled on mine.

"Bran, do you ever wonder how things might've turned out if you and I had—"

"Yeah. Sometimes." A vague longing passed between us and then the moment was gone.

Bobby watched me as I walked down the block to my car and drove away.

Babysitting had actually turned out to be a good diversion for me. It helped take my mind off of Nick. I'd been obsessing over him since he'd left me on the back roads of Jersey. Whatever it was he was going through, I didn't want him to go through it alone.

As I pulled onto my block it seemed especially quiet. Only the chirping crickets gave voice to the night. Used to be in the summer, the neighbors would hang out on their porches, talking, playing pinochle and eating Mrs. Esposito's homemade biscotti while we kids rode our bikes up and down the block and hoped our parents didn't notice we were up way past our bedtimes.

If we were lucky, Ronnie Cap's dad would bring out his accordion, or Uncle Frankie would drop by for a visit and slip us sips of beer. It's funny. It's been seven years since I've been of legal drinking age in the state of Pennsylvania, but nothing ever tasted so good as mooching Budweiser off my uncle.

I flipped on the porch light and went inside.

It was after midnight and I was still wide-awake. The double espresso I'd had early in the day seemed like a good idea at the time, but now, not so much. I was restless and bored, and there was nothing good on TV so I decided to dress up the dog and take pictures to send to my friend, Michelle, in L.A.

Turns out Adrian wasn't as keen on the idea as I was. He sat at the kitchen table, gnawing the sequins off my Halloween costume from when I was a baby, a bright pink tutu with a matching crown. I'd found it in the basement along with some broken toys and a box of old report

207

cards. Curiosity got the better of me, and I opened one of the cards to read the comment.

"Brandy is an impulsive child who needs to practice patience and self control."

Hunh! Well, obviously the teacher had me mixed up with some other kid. That doesn't sound like me at all.

I took about three shots of Adrian in various humiliating poses before he called it quits and ran off to hide under the couch. As I didn't have the energy to coax him back out, I decided to make vegetable soup out of the broccoli I'd bought a couple of weeks ago in a fit of self improvement. In the middle of picking off the brown, mushy parts my phone rang.

Uh oh. Middle of the night phone calls rarely bode well. I picked it up and prayed it was a wrong number or a particularly enthusiastic telemarketer who wanted to get a jump on the day. I uttered a tentative hello.

"I'm going to get you, Bitch."

"Excuse me?" I figured maybe I'd heard it wrong and they'd really said, "I'm going to make you rich." Okay, chances were slim, but a girl can hope.

"When I'm through with you," the voice continued, "you're going to beg me to kill you."

"Um, Bunny? I think there's been a little misunderstanding. I didn't tell the police where to find you, if that's what you're thinking. I mean, we've barely met, and—who knows, had it been under different circumstances, we could've turned out to be really good friends."

I had no idea how idiotic I sounded. I was just stalling until I could find a way to call the police on my landline.

"Bunny? You still there?"

"I'm in your house…in fact, I'm right behind you."

Chapter Thirteen

Without thinking I whipped around, ready to take her on. There was no one there.

Of course not. I would have heard her. I put my phone to my ear. The sound of Bunny's laughter echoed in my brain and then the line went dead.

It took me a full minute to stop shaking. *She's just messing with me for now, but one of these days it's gonna be the real thing.* I took a deep breath and dialed 911.

My head was killing me, so while I waited for the police to arrive I ran upstairs to grab some aspirin from the bathroom cabinet. Rocky followed me in and hopped up onto the edge of the sink, craning her neck for a drink from the faucet.

"Hang on a second, Sweetie. Mommy's had a rough day."

I set my phone down on the toilet tank lid and then turned on the faucet with one hand, while reaching for the cabinet door with the other. It was stuck so I yanked hard. The door flew open with a loud creak sending Rocky into a frenzy. She leaped off the counter top, her tail grazing the toilet tank lid on her way out the door. I heard a splash and looked down to see my "brand new-should I buy it – no, it's too expensive – but I *really* want it" cell

209

phone sink like a rock to the bottom of the toilet bowl. *Unhhh!*

I plunged my hand into the water, hoping that the five-second rule about eating food off the floor also applied to submerged electronics. *If I take it out fast enough, it'll be like it never happened.*

I dried off the phone with the hair drier and pressed the "power" button. It was dead as a doornail. *Note to self: five-second rule does not apply with big-ticket items.*

Twenty minutes later I sat in my living room as Officer Joiner and her partner searched my house and premises on the off chance that Bunny really was lurking close by. Finding no evidence of a nocturnal intruder, they asked to take a look at my phone to check the number Bunny had called from.

"Um, there's a little problem with that," I said, and went on to explain about the toilet mishap. Officer Joiner pressed two thin lips together and pulled some latex gloves from her back pocket. "It was clean," I added.

She ignored me and bagged my new phone as evidence.

After the cops left my imagination went into overdrive, interpreting every normal household sound to be someone breaking into my home. I tried to tough it out until morning, but the longer I laid in bed the worse it got, until even the sound of my own heartbeat was cause for alarm.

"Nick said you could crash at his apartment if you felt unsafe at home," reminded a little voice in my head.

"Yes, but do you really need to, or are you just using it as an excuse to spend the night with him?" countered a second little voice.

"Oh, shut up," said the first little voice.

After that, the second little voice was quiet, so I packed up Rocky and Adrian and headed on over to Nick's.

I didn't want to just barge in on him, (admittedly, not out of respect for his privacy, but out of who I might find there with him) so I called before I left home. He didn't pick up and I debated not going at all, but my house was seriously creeping me out. I left a message telling him that I was on my way over, figuring if he *was* entertaining it would give him time to move the party elsewhere.

Nick's car was parked in the loading zone. All of a sudden this really shy feeling came over me and I wanted to turn around and go back home, only it was late and I was scared, so I forged ahead, balancing Rocky's carrier in one hand and Adrian's leash in the other.

The closer I got to his apartment the more trepidation I began to feel, and I started thinking this was a bad idea. "But he *invited* me," I repeated to myself like a mantra. All the same, when I reached his place I knocked really loud in case he'd forgotten.

One of Nick's neighbors, a large, hairy man in boxer shorts stuck his head out the door.

"Sorry," I said, and knocked one more time for good measure. Then I dug out the key and let myself in.

I turned on the lamp in the foyer and noticed a set of keys and Nick's .38 lying on the table. "Nick?" I called out, walking into the living room. There was no answer. I put the cat carrier down and let Adrian off the leash. He sniffed the air for a second and then trotted off to explore the rest of the rooms.

Even though I had Nick's permission, it still felt weird to be there without having touched base with him first. His house phone was on the coffee table, so I picked it up

211

and punched in his cell number, hoping to give him a head's up.

I could hear the phone ring in my ear, however, there was a louder, more distinct ring coming from the other side of the room as well. I walked over to the baby grand piano that sat in the corner overlooking Rittenhouse Square. Nick's cell phone was sitting on the keyboard.

Why would Nick leave the house without his cell phone?

While I was pondering this, Adrian slunk out of the bathroom looking guilty. "Bad dog," I said, figuring he must have done *something* to look so ashamed. I walked into the hallway and found a trail of unfurled toilet paper leading back to the bathroom. I followed the trail scooping it up along the way.

It was dark in there and unbearably hot and steamy. I felt around for the light switch and flipped it on.

"Douse the lights, would you Darlin'?"

"Holy Jesus," I gasped, stifling a scream.

Nick lay naked in his claw-foot tub, his body immersed in water. His left arm dangled over the side, the right, elbow bent and resting on the rim, held a crystal shot glass. A half-empty bottle of Patron Gold sat on the floor within easy reach. He lifted the glass to his lips and quickly downed the contents, then gently placed the glass next to the bottle.

His hair was damp and matted and clung to the tops of his bare shoulders. His legs were bent at the knee. His face held a mixture of quiet rage and crushing melancholy. He never looked more beautiful.

"The light?" he repeated.

"Oh. Sorry." I turned off the light and waited until my eyes got accustomed to the dark. "Listen, I didn't mean to intrude on you. I'd tried to call...something happened and I didn't want to stay in my house…I should probably go—"

"Come here," he said, his voice a low growl.

My heart pounding, I walked over and stood next to the tub, straining my eyes to make out his features.

"Kneel down."

It was a rough command and my stomach tightened. This was a side of Nick I'd never seen before. He was scaring me, and yet, I was *exactly* where I wanted to be.

I knelt down next to the tub, unsure of what to do and feeling increasingly uneasy. Nick leaned over the rim and took my arm, wrapping strong fingers around my wrist. Placing my hand on his chest, he slowly guided me down the length of his body.

Relaxing against the back of the tub again, he moved my arm lower and lower. The water was so hot it was as if he were trying to purge himself of all things unholy. I closed my eyes and flattened my hand against his stomach, feeling the hardness of his abs, the peach fuzz just below his belly button.

My own stomach rolled as he pushed my hand lower still and I held my breath and waited. My fingertips grazed something wonderful and then his hand tightened around my wrist and he guided me away from that bit of heaven to his right side and the jagged remains of an old wound.

"You asked me once how I got this scar," he said, absently rubbing the rough patch. "Do you still want to know?"

"Only if you want to tell me."

"It was a birthday present from my father on the day I turned twelve. He gave it to me right after I watched him kill my mother."

Shelly Fredman

Stunned beyond words, I felt the weight of unshed tears spring up behind my eyes.

Nick pushed himself into a sitting position and grabbed the bottle of tequila off the floor, taking a swig from it. I watched him as his throat closed around the fiery liquid.

"You should go, Angel."

"No! Nick, I'm not leaving you like this. You wouldn't leave me…"

His response was slow and deliberate. "I can't guarantee what will happen if you stay."

I laid my hand on his cheek and felt the raw energy pulsating throughout his body. "I'm staying."

Santiago rose out of the tub pulling me roughly to him. I could feel the anger flow like lava though his veins. "I don't want to hurt you," he said, his voice a guttural whisper.

I believed him. I knew, too, that he would.

I hesitated just long enough to feel the fear and then I put my arms around his neck, pressing myself into him, trying to convey in my touch what my words could not. *I will ride this out with you, Nick. No matter what.*

My tee shirt mingled with the dampness of his bare skin and clung to my chest. I peeled it off, no boundaries between us. He cupped my ass and hoisted me off the ground, setting me down on the ledge of the sink. With one hand, he unsnapped my jeans and pulled them down over my hips, letting them fall to the floor.

I could feel the strength in his arms as he parted my knees and wedged himself between my legs. I was under no illusions about the act that followed. I was merely a vessel for him to deposit his rage.

214

Afterwards, he held me close, my head resting on his chest. "Lo siento," he whispered into my hair. "I'm sorry."

I pulled out of his embrace, forcing him to look at me. "Do *not* be sorry, Nick. You don't have one damn thing to be sorry about. *I'm* not."

What happened was not about sex or love or even redemption. It was about trust. Unconditional and unyielding.

Wordlessly, he lifted me up and carried me to his bed.

The room was bathed in the soft glow of street lamps from the park across the way. Nick put me down on the bed and slid in next to me, turning over on his side to spoon me. He brushed his lips against my neck, sending chills down my spine and radiating frontward.

I wasn't quite sure where this was going, seeing as he'd just scored a home run, which brought me to a whole new set of worries about the dangers of unprotected sex and *how stupid could I be*, even with the "swept away by the heat of the moment" excuse factored in. But it was more altruistic in nature than for my own benefit, so that should count for something, right?

Nick tightened his arms around me. "Just so you know, Angel, this was a 'first' for me. I always use a condom and I get tested regularly. Still, it was a selfish thing to do and I'm sorry."

I did a quick calculation of my monthly cycle and decided to put my concerns on hold for a while. No use crying over spilt milk, so to speak.

"Um, you don't have to worry about me, either, Nick. I *almost* always use protection too (for the four times I've had sex in the past decade).

"Look," I added, rolling onto my back. I sat up, taking the covers with me. "There's something I want to say and I'm just going to say it before I lose my nerve. I know you've got that 'man of mystery' thing going on, and I'm not trying to screw with your M.O. But you're my friend and you're in trouble, and I may not be able to physically take down the bad guys, but I can listen. You need to tell me, Nick. You need to let me help you."

He was quiet for what seemed like a lifetime, but that's probably because I don't do well with waiting. Then he rolled onto his back, too, and I leaned my head against his chest, feeling the gentle vibrations of his voice as he began to speak.

"My mother met my father when she was seventeen years old. One day she was waiting tables at her parents' diner, just outside of New Orleans, when in he walked. My father was a very handsome man, fifteen years her senior. He was born and raised in Bogotá, Columbia and had just arrived in the states. He immediately struck up a conversation with her.

"My mother was beautiful and smart and infinitely kind. She was fluent in three languages, a straight A student and could have done anything she set her sites on. But she didn't have a lot of life experience and she fell for the wrong man.

"He abused her for as long as I can remember. And then one day—my birthday—it was all over."

A chill ripped through me as he continued in the same even tone, as if reciting something long rehearsed but never verbalized.

"He was drunk and he became enraged when he found out she'd taken her pay check and bought a bike for me instead of giving the money to him. He cut her with a broken whisky bottle, severing a main artery. When I tried to help her, he went after me. Then he left us both for dead and disappeared off the face of the earth. My neighbor found me bleeding to death in my front yard and called an ambulance. I made it, my mother didn't.

"My grandparents had both died a few years earlier and I had no other relatives, so I became a ward of the state. For the next couple of years I was shuttled back and forth between foster homes and Juvi Hall.

"When I was fourteen I ran away from a particularly sadistic situation and landed in New York City. That's where I met Sal. He was stealing a car and I asked him if he needed help. I had a knack for hot wiring."

"*Father Sal?* Really?" I blurted out.

Nick laughed softly, remembering. "Even back then he had a conscience. He brought the car back the next day with $3.62 pinned to the windshield for 'gas money' along with a note of apology. Sal's family took me in and saved my life. I lived with them off and on for two years. Sal was going through some rough times himself and found salvation in the Catholic Church."

"And you?" I asked.

Nick shrugged. "The only thought in my mind was to find my father and put a bullet in his head."

I lifted my chin and my eyes sought his in the dark. "Um, just out of curiosity, you didn't find him, did you?"

His voice dropped to a hoarse whisper. "As a matter of fact I did."

Oh shit! This wasn't going anywhere near as well as I'd hoped.

"Nick, are you saying—"

"I didn't kill him, if that's what you're asking." He hesitated, his breathing labored, as if the very words were a weight on his heart. "You need to know something, Angel. I *would* have killed him if I'd had the opportunity."

"What stopped you?"

217

"Someone beat me to it. After the attack on my mother and me he fled to South America—that's where he'd been living all these years—in a little village just north of Bogata. He was working for a small time drug lord.

"A couple of weeks ago I finally tracked him down—at least I thought I had. So I flew to Bogata with the sole intention of killing the man.

"I found his house and knocked on the door but he wasn't there. A neighbor told me he'd been busted on drug charges and was sitting in a local jail awaiting trial, so I headed over there to find him. If I had to post bail for the fucking bastard for the privilege of blowing his brains out, it would have been my pleasure."

"Nick, you said someone beat you to it. What did you mean by that?"

"When I got to the jailhouse I was informed my father had gotten into a fight with another inmate and the guy shanked him. Slit his throat for a pack of cigarettes. By the time the guards discovered him, he'd been dead for two days. I suppose I should be grateful that I didn't have to get my hands dirty, but all I really felt was—robbed."

"Man! I *so* get that!"

Unhhh! Why did I say that? For God's sake, the man just bared his tortured soul to me and how do I respond? Like I'd just discovered we both like chunky peanut butter!

"God, Nick. I'm sorry. What I meant was—"

"It's alright, Darlin'. I know what you meant. I'm glad you're here," he added, his voice growing faint.

"For as long as you want me," I said, but he didn't hear me. He had fallen asleep.

As soon as I knew Nick was down for the count, I crept out of bed and retrieved my underwear and tee shirt from the bathroom floor. My shirt was still damp but I slipped it over my head anyway and then I sat down on the toilet seat and cried my eyes out.

Adrian trotted into the bathroom, jumped up and licked my face. I believe he knows when I'm sad and it's his way of consoling me. John says he's just after the salt from my tears. John is such a cynic.

"We have to find a way to help Nick," I told Adrian, scratching him behind his ears. "He needs us, whether he knows it or not."

Adrian sat down and cocked his head, looking very confused. He was probably wondering if I was using the Royal "we" or if he was actually expected to do something.

I stood up and splashed some cold water on my face, brushed my teeth with my finger and ran a comb through my hair. That was about as glamorous as I was going to get, which was just as well since Nick was out cold. After that I followed Adrian into Nick's office where Rocky was camped out for the night.

The office doubled as a spare bedroom with a couch that opened up into a queen-sized sleeper. It was open and unmade, the sheets rolled into a ball at the bottom of the bed. I flipped on the light and found Rocky curled up on top of the covers, fast asleep.

Hmmm, Nick must've had some company. Maybe Alphonso had to flea bomb his apartment and needed a place to crash…or one of Nick's old army buddies was in town for the weekend…that is, assuming Nick was ever in the army, which is doubtful since he's not much of a joiner…well, whatever, I'm sure there's a totally plausible, non-threatening explanation there somewhere.

I picked up one of the pillows and breathed deeply and caught the unmistakable scent of Chanel No. 5. *Crap.*

Nick's clothes lay in a tangled heap on the floor next to the bed, killing any illusion that the owner of the Chanel had bunked there alone. I bent to pick up his shirt and something small and shiny rolled off the sleeve and under the couch frame. Crawling on my hands and knees, I felt around until I found what turned out to be the other half of the pair of diamond earrings Crystal had discovered in the bathroom. Whoever lost them was out about $1500 bucks. I drop kicked the earring back under the bed and went to sleep on the living room couch.

"Good morning, Darlin'."

I opened one eye and grunted a small, tight hello. I had only just fallen asleep, having spent the previous four hours tossing and turning, unable to shake the urge to wake Nick out of his drunken stupor and smack him upside the head for being too stupid to love me back.

He was fully dressed in a pair of old jeans and a loose black tee shirt, showered and shaved and, by the look of the revolver wedged into his shoulder holster, ready to tackle a new day. He didn't seem inclined to bring up the subject of his dad, and for once I kept my mouth shut.

I flopped over onto my back and sat up. "Be right back," I mumbled and dashed off to the bathroom. I threw on my jeans and my shoes, did another quick sweep of my teeth with some toothpaste and headed back into the living room.

Nick had moved into the kitchen. The smell of freshly ground espresso beans made me forget for a moment that I was mad at him. Well, technically, I was mad at myself. Nick never promised me a thing he didn't deliver on. *I* was the one asking him to do the impossible. The thing is I really thought I could handle it. Turns out, I was wrong.

Just hours before Nick had poured his heart out to me, and I thought that was something special. But now, his nonchalance reminded me I was just another woman who had spent the night.

I sat down at the counter and Nick placed a steaming cup of espresso in front of me.

"Why did you sleep on the couch last night?" His voice was light but his eye searched out the truth. I decided to be a sport and give it to him.

"I went looking for Rocky in your office and found more than I'd bargained for. FYI, your girlfriend's other earring is under the bed."

Ignoring the dig, he said, "You never did tell me why you came over."

I shrugged. "Not important."

"It is to me, Angel. Are you in trouble?"

"No more than usual," I told him, hopping off of the stool. Okay, so I was being a brat. *Well, tough.* I grabbed my bag off the floor in the living room and turned back to Nick. "I've got to get going. Busy day today."

"You're sure you're alright?"

"Absolutely. You?"

"Absolutely."

"We're all good, then." I yanked open the door, crossed the threshold and shut the door behind me, making for the perfect exit. Except for one thing.

I knocked on the door. Nick pulled it back open.

"I forgot my dog."

"And?"

I sighed. "And my cat. I'll...just...be getting them, then," I said, squeezing past him and heading back into the spare room. I returned a minute later, carting the cat carrier, with Adrian trailing behind me.

I got to the elevator, turned around and walked back down the hall again. I stood in front of his apartment for a beat and then I knocked. It didn't take him any time at all to open the door. Either he likes hanging out in his foyer or he was expecting me.

"I'm sorry I got mad at you. It was dumb."

Nick stared at me intently, a sad smile crossing his face. "Thank you for being here for me last night. For what it's worth, I'd trust you with my life."

"Just not with your love."

"I wish I had it to give, Angel."

"But you don't."

"It's going to cost me *how much* to replace my phone?" I'd been standing in line at the Phone Mart for over an hour, waiting my turn to speak to a customer service representative about my options. The sign above the door promised fast, friendly service, but so far, it had been slow and surly, which did nothing to improve my mood.

I'd left Nick's feeling incredibly frustrated and sad. It felt like we'd taken a giant step forward and then the rug had been pulled out from under me and I landed on my ass. In a vulnerable moment, Nick had finally opened up to me, but in the light of day, it was back to business as usual.

"Toodie, you've got to cut me a break here. I don't have that kind of money." Last month, Toodie Ventura, my former roommate/plumber, had given up the plumbing business to become a "phone technologist" which, in his words, was "way cooler than sloshing around in someone else's shit all day." I suspect the job change had more to do with the fact that he just wasn't a very good plumber. Still, Toodie is sweet and means really well.

He cast a sideways glance over at his manager and hunkered his tall, skinny body down close to mine. I rose up on tiptoes to hear him.

"I could swipe one for you," he whispered.

"What? Toodie, no!"

"It wouldn't be any trouble, Bran. Besides, I really owe ya one."

A couple of months back, I'd helped Toodie out of a jam. The last thing I wanted to do was put him back into one.

"It's really okay, Brandy. I'm probably going to get fired, anyway. I haven't sold a single phone since I started working here. Personally," he said, shaking his head, "I think it's the inferior quality of the product."

"Um, Toodie, do you tell all your customers that?"

"I believe honesty's the best policy. So," he said, missing the irony, "how about that five finger discount? You can't beat the price."

I ended up buying a way more expensive phone with features it would take me a lifetime to figure out how to use.

"You don't have to do this, Bran."

"No, really, Toodie, I've always wanted a phone that can tell me the temperature on Mars in Celsius."

On my way out of the store, I stopped by the manager's station. "That sales guy is good!" I said, pointing to Toodie. "From now on I'm coming here for all my cell phone needs." I knew I was just prolonging the inevitable, but I figured it might buy him another month of employment.

Just as I finished downloading the *Rocky* theme song as my ringtone, the phone rang.

"This is Stacey Nichols. I'd like to speak to Brandy Alexander, please."

"This is Brandy."

"Hi, Brandy. I'm Linda Morrison's friend. Linda said you wanted to get in touch with me."

"Stacey. Hi. Thanks for calling. Did Linda happen to mention why I wanted to speak to you?"

"She did. I remember that girl as if it were yesterday. I'd be happy to talk to you."

"Thank you. Listen, you're already doing a lot for me just by agreeing to meet, but I have one more favor to ask. I assume the M.E.'s office took pictures of the girl. I'm not asking to satisfy some morbid curiosity, but do you think you could get me a copy? I swear I won't divulge where it came from."

Stacey emitted a grim laugh. "Normally I'd say you're crazy and hang up, but I happen to know a little bit about you. When Linda said you wanted to talk to me I did my research. I'll see what I can do."

We met the following morning at a diner on Division Street. Stacey didn't want to meet at work and I was just as happy, as I hadn't had much to eat since the cookies at DiCarlo's, and that seemed like a million years ago.

While I waited for her to arrive, I ordered a BLT minus the bacon because I'm trying to collect some good karma, but then the lettuce grossed me out on account of it was soggy on the ends so that just left me with tomato and bread which wasn't very satisfying, so I treated myself to a black and white malted.

I liked Stacy the minute I met her. She's one of those old school, no-nonsense, heart-of-gold sort of people you immediately trust. Plus, she ordered French fries for breakfast, which legitimized my sandwich and malt as a perfectly respectable choice.

"That girl still haunts me," she told me, dipping a fry into a pool of ketchup. "I've worked for the coroner's office for over twenty years, and I've seen my share of tragic endings, but the young ones always tear my heart out."

"Did anyone ever find out who she was? I don't mean to imply that people weren't doing their jobs," I added. "It's just that my ex-boyfriend is a homicide detective, and I understand the realities of the job. There's only so much you can do with limited staff and funds."

"Far as I know, she's still listed as a Jane Doe," she said, digging in her pocketbook. "I was hoping you'd have better luck finding out who this kid was." She took out some photos and held them close to her chest. "They're not pretty," she said, handing them over to me. "I could lose my job if it ever got out I gave you those," she said, "but the truth is I never did feel right about that girl and I'm hoping you can make some sense of her death. I've always thought there was more to it than an accidental overdose. You ever have one of those gut feelings?"

"All the time," I told her, staring at the photos. I was having one at that very moment, but not the kind she meant. I told myself it was the malted.

Stacey had to get to work. I thanked her profusely and said I'd keep in touch.

"Brandy, if you don't mind my asking, why exactly are you interested in this kid? I mean you'd never even met her."

Flashing on Crystal's thin, pretty face, I said, "In a way, I feel like I have."

I needed to regroup, so I made a pit stop at the public library to partake of their air conditioning and to look over my notes and try to coordinate everything I knew, which, admittedly, wasn't much. The girl was young, white and had given birth just before she died. According to the autopsy report, her drug of choice was heroin. A quick call to Linda Morrison revealed the Jane Doe from Philly had also had a penchant for "horse."

The girl I found, this girl, the one from the agency that Cynthia Mott told me about, the girl Bobby found in the dumpster…could it just be a coincidence that all these young, white girls, some of whom were known hookers, had gotten pregnant and then died of a heroin overdose?

No, every fiber of my being told me. Which led me to a horrific conclusion. This had to be the work of a serial killer.

Chapter Fourteen

Some psychopath was out there killing off young, pregnant prostitutes and making it look like they'd overdosed! I was convinced I was right—for about a nanosecond before realizing my theory made no sense at all. According to the M.O. of most serial killers, if they're going to go to all the trouble of killing somebody or a group of somebodies they want credit for a job well done. Half the fun is striking fear in society's heart.

Then if killing for the sheer joy of it wasn't the answer, what was?

Ruling out crimes of passion, motives for committing murder generally fall into two main categories—revenge and profit. So, who might have a grudge against these young, prostitutes? A disgruntled wife? Maybe there was an entire group devoted to taking revenge on underage streetwalkers.

I got a sudden mental picture of a roving gang of hype stick-wielding suburbanites killing off the competition for their husbands' affections, and then I ruled that out as too ridiculous to consider.

Okay, so if the killer—or killers—were motivated by *greed*, how could they profit from murdering these girls? After all, they couldn't turn tricks if they were dead. The whole thing was like a Rubik's Cube that I just kept twisting and turning, knowing the solution was in there somewhere if I could just assemble the damn thing correctly.

They were young…they were white…they were Jane Doe's …they were pregnant. And no one knew what happened to their babies. Their babies! Oh my God! A light went on over my head like a big neon "Duh-uhh!" *The girls were a dime a dozen. The true hot commodity was their babies.*

Last year, WINN did a segment on adoption and how white middle class Americans had put off having babies for so long they were now turning to private adoption to complete their families. Since the number of white babies available for adoption has diminished over the years, there was a premium on them, so a lot of couples were being aced out of the market.

If someone came up with a relatively cheap way to supply white babies they'd stand to make a mint. And who better to exploit than a young, scared, teenage girl? In each case where the girl went full term, the police were unable to find the infant. It may have been assumed that the girls had left them with family before shooting themselves into oblivion. But since no one filed a missing person's report, it was almost impossible to trace.

The person or persons responsible for their deaths must have counted on the fact that these girls were "throwaways." Since no one cared about them, no one would miss them when they were gone.

In defense of the police department, it would have been a huge red flag if all the girls had been discovered at the same time or in the same location, but their deaths had been spread out over the course of two years, and the bodies were discovered in various major metropolitan areas. There was no reason to think the deaths were related or more than tragic, but routine overdoses. Until now.

My head was spinning with a million unanswered questions, but my immediate thought was to find out more about the girl from the Camden morgue. If I could find the link between her and the other girls, maybe I could locate Star. I sat down at one of the computers and started my search.

Fresh Start Homeless Youth Services was a drop in center located in the Camden borough of Lindenwold. I pulled up to an old commercial building on the corner of Amherst and Broadway and turned off the engine. Having spent the entire afternoon schlepping all over the city checking out agencies that dealt with homeless youth, I was hot, tired and cranky. Plus, my deodorant had quit working about two agencies back, but the pit bull in me wouldn't let me stop until I found what I was looking for.

I checked in at the reception desk and asked to speak to the director. A few minutes later a guy walked into the room and introduced himself. "My name is Matt," he said, extending his hand to me. I'm the program director." Matt was about thirty years old, dressed in jeans and a New York Rangers tee shirt. I like a man who isn't afraid to dress out of season. I smiled and introduced myself and the reason for my visit.

I really wasn't expecting much in the way of information. Based on the reception I'd gotten from the three thousand other agencies I'd visited, I knew the people who worked there were bound by law and moral fiber not to divulge any information about their clients. Not even the dead ones. I took out the picture that Stacey had supplied for me and handed it to him.

"Look," I told him. "I'm trying to help a street kid locate her best friend. She's scared that something really bad happened to her, and frankly, so am I. The trail's led me to this girl," I said, pointing to the photo. "Supposedly, she died of a self-inflicted overdose right after giving birth. But there are just too many coincidences between her death and the deaths of three other girls I've been tracking to chalk it up to an accident. I believe this kid was murdered. And if I'm right, she's not the only one."

Matt stared at the picture for several moments and I noticed a subconscious working of his jaw muscles as he handed it back to me. "Excuse me a minute, would you?"

He turned and walked into an office adjacent to the reception room. It had a big glass window and I watched him as he rummaged through a large file cabinet. While I waited for his return, I began reading the inspirational posters plastered on the wall. My favorite one was simply and elegantly stated. "The streets are not the end of the road."

Matt returned just as I finished testing my "Drug I.Q."

"You really believe she was murdered?" he asked, his eyes searching out mine.

I met his gaze. "That's what I'm trying to find out."

He rocked back on his heels and blew a small puff of air through his teeth. "I'm not saying I knew this girl, but if she had found her way to this facility, it would have been on the recommendation of her state case worker. Child Welfare's located on Horizon Avenue."

I thanked Matt and turned to leave, but he called me back.

"Listen, if you do find out what happened to her, let me know, okay? I, uh, you hate to see this happen to any kid, y'know?"

"Yeah," I nodded. "I know."

It was after five and Child Welfare was closed, so I had to put my visit on hold until the next day. Just as well, seeing as I was supposed to meet the Baby Shower Committee for dinner at Chickie's and Pete's and I was running late.

There was a humongous traffic jam on the Betsy Ross so I used the time to test out my new "hands-free" phone equipment. I put on the headset and shouted a command into the air. "Call John."

A very pleasant, mechanical voice spoke to me through the ear piece. "Did you say 'call Tom?'"

I don't even know a Tom. I tried again. "Call *John*."

"Call Shawn? If that's correct say yes."

"No! Call John! John!"

"I'm sorry. Did you say, 'Call Jomjom?'"

"Listen you dumb bitch. That's not even a name!"

Okay, calm down, Brandy. The nice computer-generated voice lady is just trying to do her job. I took a deep breath. "Call Tom."

"Did you say, "Call John?"

"Yes."

"Where are you?" John asked, as I listened to the sound of ice-cold beer being chugged in the background without me.

"I'm stuck on the bridge and my car is beginning to overheat. Order me some wings, will ya? I'll be there soon."

231

John dropped his voice to a whisper. "Hurry. You don't know the hell I've been through. Janine brought her grandmother along."

"The one who talks really loud or the one who chews with her mouth open?"

"The chewer. She was in the middle of telling a story when her partial fell out and landed in her soup tureen. She's spent the past ten minutes rooting through the seafood chowder for her teeth."

"Hang tough, Sweetie. I'll be there as soon as I can."

I disconnected and moved exactly three feet when traffic stalled out again. I turned off the air conditioner and opened the windows, letting in the fetid smell of 'summer in the city.' It didn't look like we were going anywhere any time soon, so I picked up the phone again and put in a call to Crystal.

I figured she must be feeling frustrated that I hadn't found Star yet, so I braced myself for a verbal harangue and she didn't disappoint.

"I thought you said you could find her," she sulked. "Haven't you been trying *at all?*"

I did a mental count to ten. "Look, I know it's hard to be dependent on other people, Crystal. That's not exactly my strong suit, either. But I'm trying the best I can. Maybe it's time we called in the cops," I added, mainly because I had nothing else to offer.

"No! They don't care about street kids. They'll only cause more trouble. I swear if you go to the cops—"

"*Alright.* Forget I said anything. Listen," I added, changing the subject before she said something at least one of us would regret. "Was there any chance that Star might have been pregnant?"

"Fuck, no! Star knows how to take care of herself. Besides, she told me she can't get pregnant."

"Um, no disrespect to Star, Crystal, but a lot of girls think they can't get pregnant—until they do. Look, I'm not trying to be nosey. I'm just trying to figure out something here."

"Star was raped when she was eleven," Crystal said softly. "She ended up with some kind of infection and now she can't have kids. She used to joke about having one less thing to worry about, but I know it bothered her. We'd talk sometimes, y'know?"

Abruptly, her voice hardened. "Why did you want to know if Star was pregnant, anyway? You've heard something, haven't you!"

"No," I said honestly. "Nothing about Star."

Damnit. If Star wasn't pregnant, maybe I was wrong about everything.

Traffic started moving again. "Crystal, I'll call you as soon as I know anything." I hung up before she could utter a response. I'm sure it would have been a good one.

By the time I reached Chickie's and Pete's, Janine and her grandmother had left. John was on his way out too, which just left me and Carla. I ordered a Rolling Rock to go with my wings and slumped into the booth across from her.

Carla tapped a lacquered nail on her glass of chardonnay and looked at me for a long moment. "What's wrong, hon?"

"Nothing. Long day." I tried to smile but it came out more like a grimace.

"Honey, that is not the face of a happy camper." She hesitated. "Is it Bobby?"

I shook my head. "Bobby and I are cool. At least for the moment. I don't know, Carla. I think work's got me down. Sometimes I think I'd be happier going back to interviewing local chefs on the best way to cook a holiday turkey. I'm in way over my head here."

"Anything I can do to help?" she asked kindly.

"I know you would if you could." I took a long swig of beer and dove into my wings, smearing habanera sauce all over my face. I didn't bother to wipe it off.

Carla cocked her head, her beehive sticking out like an antenna. "Boy, you really are in a funk. Are you sure it's just about the job? I mean, no offense, but you're always in over your head and it's never stopped you before. C'mon Honey, you know you can tell me anything."

I did know that. But this was something I was having a hard time admitting to myself, let alone anyone else. The truth is I'd left Nick's with an ache in my heart that only grew stronger with time. He'd made it totally clear that no matter what we'd shared, we'd never be more than friends. Only I wasn't ready for someone to tell me to let him go…no matter how well intentioned the advice.

I smiled a big ol' brave smile. "I'm fine, Carla. Really."

"Honey," Carla said, and I could tell she was looking right through me. "I understand a little about falling for the wrong person."

"Carla, I never said anything thing about—"

"You didn't have to. It's Nick, isn't it?"

I nodded miserably and waited for the lecture to begin.

Carla picked up her napkin and leaned across the table, dabbing the habanera sauce off my cheek. And then she surprised the crap out of me.

"When I first met your Uncle Frankie, he was just coming off of a three week bender. All my friends said I

234

was crazy to get involved with a guy like that. He wasn't exactly a saint, you know. And it wasn't like he was looking for a girlfriend, either. In fact, he did everything he could to discourage me."

I sat up, not sure where she was going with this. "So what made you hang in there? I'm really glad you did, by the way. You're the best thing that's ever happened to Frankie."

"Feel free to remind him of that early and often, hon."

I laughed and took another swig of beer.

"Bran, the point is your uncle's and my relationship was anything but smooth sailing and there were times when I almost gave up. Only, I knew in my heart that he was the guy for me."

"Are you saying I should fight for Nick?"

"Look, Honey, the last thing I want is to see you get hurt, and if you get involved with Santiago, it's pretty much a foregone conclusion. But that's what people said about Frankie. And I thank God every day I didn't listen to them."

"Carla, I'd hang in there forever if I thought I had a snowball's chance in hell with Nick. But the truth is he doesn't want me. Oh, jeez, I'm friggin' pathetic."

"No, you're not, Honey. You're one of the bravest, brightest people I know and if that man doesn't want you it's his loss. Now, look, I might not understand exactly what been going on between you two, but I do know you, kid. You don't love lightly and you don't trust easily. So if your heart is telling you he's the one, I say go for it. Just don't tell your uncle I said that," she added quickly. "He'd absolutely kill me."

I woke up to the sound of my cell ringing. It was my mom.

"Dolores Giancola called. She said she ran into you in line at the *Ac-a-me* the other day and you were eating a Milky Way bar. She said you hadn't even paid for it yet. *Really*, Brandy Renee, the way you eat is a disgrace."

"Oh, should I have used a fork?"

My wisecrack was met with a sound that can only be described as "harrumph," followed by, "Don't be funny. You know what I mean."

Note to self: Don't joke with mom. The woman has absolutely no sense of humor.

My "to do" list was full, so, after my mother ran through her litany of complaints (Florida is too humid, my father snores loud enough to wake the dead, and, my personal favorite, the "early bird specials" aren't all that special.) I hung up, dressed quickly, fed Rocky and Adrian and took the dog for a quick jog around the block. I only had to stop three times to catch my breath. Wow. My plan to get in shape was definitely beginning to pay off!

Driving back over the bridge, I got to Child Welfare just as it opened. An hour and a half later I was still waiting for the agency director to see me, because, as the receptionist suggested, oh, about three hundred times, I probably should have called first.

I was about to give up when the director's door opened and a grim faced man in his late fifties beckoned me forward. Waving me into his office, he offered me a seat.

"Isaac Johnson," he said, extending his hand in greeting. "Sorry to keep you waiting. How can I help you?"

"I understand how busy you are, Mr. Johnson, and I appreciate you agreeing to see me. I'll try to be as brief as possible." I took out the photo of the girl from the morgue and handed it to him. "I was told, in so many words, that this girl may have been a client of your agency."

"I'm sorry, Ms. Alexander—"

"Listen, I know what you're going to say. Just, please, hear me out." And once again I launched into my story. "I'm not asking you to divulge any state secrets. But I'm at my wit's end here. I just need to know if you recognize this kid. I know it was a long time ago, but someone must remember her."

"While I sympathize with you, there's really nothing I can tell you."

I don't know if it was the lack of sleep or the realization that bureaucratic bullshit was robbing this girl and all the others of finding their possible killer, but suddenly it was too much for me. Tears welled up in my eyes and I swiped them away with my sleeve. If Eric could see me now I'd be back on the puff piece trail in a heartbeat. Well, I didn't care. I'd *had it*.

"Yeah. Okay, thanks, for nothin', Mr. Johnson." I stood. "Y'know, I get it," I said, my voice breaking. "You're just doing your job. But in the mean time, there's a girl out there who maybe we *can* save, only by the time I stop getting the runaround she'll be just another statistic. Like *this* kid."

Isaac Johnson stared hard at me, probably trying to figure out whether to call the cops or the psych ward. I raised my hands in the international 'I surrender' sign. "I'm going. No need to walk me out."

Johnson reached behind me and closed the door. "Sit down. Please."

I sat down and waited.

"First of all, we have rules for a reason. Secondly, I've been in this business for over thirty years, and I can assure you it's not for the great pay."

"I'm sorry. I didn't mean to insult you."

He shook his hand, waving off my apology. "Her street name was Blondie. She was one of our hardcore cases, fully immersed in street life. There are so many, you lose track sometimes, but this one—I'd often wondered what happened to her."

He gave a small shrug. "Her case worker was a woman named Eleanor Grady.

"Is she here now? May I speak with her?"

"She doesn't work here any more."

"Do you have a number where I can reach her?"

"Look, I've told you more than I should already. I'm not at liberty to give out personal information on former employees."

I stood again. "Thank you for your time, Mr. Johnson."

He opened the door and walked me out, stopping short at one of the cubicles. He hesitated for a beat and then addressed the man seated at the desk. "Harris, this is Brandy Alexander. She's trying to get in touch with Eleanor Grady. Any idea what happened to her?"

"I haven't seen Eleanor since she quit last year. I think she moved to Philly. You know who might still be in touch with her is Kathleen. She's not in yet, but if you have a card, I'll pass it along to her."

"I'd really appreciate it," I told him, digging around in my bag for my wallet.

I only had one left and I'd wrapped some used gum in it so I told him I'd call back later to speak to Kathleen.

On the way out I stopped in front of a large framed photo that was hanging on the wall in the entry. In the picture, Isaac Johnson was accepting some kind of award. Office workers were lined up behind him, smiling in the background.

My eyes settled on a middle-aged woman standing to the left of Johnson. "I know her," I said. "She works at New Beginnings, a homeless youth agency in Philadelphia."

Isaac cast me an odd look. "I'm confused. If you already know how to get in touch with her, why would you need Kathleen to arrange it for you?"

"I'm sorry?"

"That's Eleanor Grady."

"Bobby! I've got to talk to you."

"I'll call you back. I'm in the middle of a crime scene."

"But it's important."

"More important than a double homicide?"

"Those people are already dead. It's not like they're going anywhere."

Bobby didn't answer. He just hung up. *Unhhh!*

I'd left Child Welfare with more questions than I'd started out with and drove back over the bridge again into Philly. On my way to the station I stopped at Staples and picked up a poster sized tablet and markers. Spreading the paper out on my office floor, I knelt down in front of it and began writing.

Eleanor Gray, AKA Ellen, is the caseworker in Lindenwold for a girl who mysteriously disappears. The girl is later found. She had been pregnant and apparently, died from a heroin overdose. Not long after, Eleanor moves to Philly and begins work at another agency. A few months after she begins working there, another girl disappears under suspiciously similar circumstances. That girl is subsequently found and her death has the same M.O.

Fast forward to a few weeks ago. Another girl, this time, suffering a miscarriage, is found. The miscarriage is caused by what is assumed to be a self-inflicted heroin overdose. Star disappears at around the same time. Then Star's caseworker, Olivia Bowen is murdered. Bowen worked at the same agency as Eleanor Grady.

Could it just be a weird set of coincidences that placed Grady in the wrong place at the wrong time or could she have orchestrated the deaths of these girls for profit? Did Bowen have information about Grady that Grady wanted suppressed? Is that why Bowen was killed?

But then what about the eyewitness who saw Bunny talking to Bowen just hours before she was killed? And what about Star? According to Crystal, Star was unable to have children. So if she wasn't pregnant, what possible use could she have been to Grady?

I started a new page marked "Star," and under that I wrote "Suspects" in big bold letters. I guess I was hoping that if I wrote big enough, the truth would miraculously appear on the page the way the Virgin Mary does sometimes on a tortilla or in a bleach stain on a pair of blue jeans.

"What are you doing on the floor?" I looked up to see Eric standing above me, dripping mayonnaise from a turkey sandwich onto my notes.

"Yo, Eric. Watch it."

"What's a Little Red?" he asked, bending down to get a closer look.

"Pimp. Charming guy. You'd like him." I sat back on my heels and stretched the kinks out of my neck.

"Alexander, need I remind you that I'm the guy who signs your pay checks? You could show me a little more respect."

"Eric, you do not sign my paycheck. But as long as you're here, I could use someone to bounce some ideas off of."

"Bounce away," he said through a mouthful of turkey.

"Okay, remember that girl I told you about? The one who'd gone missing?"

"Yeah. How close are you to finding her?"

"I'm not sure." I said, pointing to the chart paper. "It's become a lot more complicated since the last time we talked." I filled him in as best I could within the five minutes Eric's attention span was good for.

"So in other words," he said when I was finished, "you've got one real crime—Olivia Bowen's murder. The girls who died could all turn out to be eerie coincidences and Star—" he shrugged. "She may have taken off on her own."

"Yeah." I conceded. "But I don't think so. There are a lot of people out there who would be happy to see that kid dead. For starters, there's her pimp. She was threatening to leave him. And then there's this client of hers. He was the last known person to be seen with her. Maybe she was blackmailing him. Threatening to tell his wife. Except that his alibi appears to check out.

"Then there's this psycho bitch named Bunny. She hated Star. She not too fond of me either, but that's a whole nuther story. The thing is, I keep trying to put my efforts into finding Star, but all this other stuff keeps cropping up and I can't help but think it's all interrelated somehow."

"You'll figure it out," he said, polishing off his sandwich. "In the mean time, how'd you like a permanent gig as Godfrey the Traffic Dog? You got a stack of fan mail last week after you filled in for Kevin."

"Really?"

"Yeah. Okay, it was mostly from this one really old guy out in Langhorne who thought your portrayal had nuance. I'm not really sure what nuance is, but apparently Kevin doesn't have any."

"Um, let me sleep on this, okay, Eric?"

"Sure. Get back to me."

I spent the better part of the afternoon checking out Eleanor Grady on the Internet, but that was a dead end. No Facebook page, nothing on Classmates.com, no blogs about her political views, the latest novel she'd read or the status of her dog's hysterectomy. The woman simply did not exist in cyberspace.

Next, I called Cynthia Mott, only her receptionist said she was on vacation. It was just as well, seeing as I really didn't know how receptive she'd be to my theory that her employee was a modern-day Jack the Ripper stalking pregnant prostitutes for profit.

The more I thought about it though, the more sense it made. Eleanor Grady had access to the girl's files, so she'd be able to target the pregnant ones. Only it was doubtful that she worked alone. Did she have a partner within the child welfare system, and if so, how widespread was the corruption? The thought gave me a stomachache.

I put in another call to Bobby, but he didn't pick up, so I took that as a sign from God that there really wasn't any need to trouble DiCarlo with my speculations. It's not that he wouldn't take me seriously. I just wanted to be sure I knew what I was talking about before I asked him to put one more thing on his already overloaded plate.

I got out my James Garner "Things to Do" list and ran my eyes over it. *Talk to owner of garage Garner uses to see if anyone made a copy of his car key. Well, if I'm going to ask the guy if he employs car stealing, joy riding kidnappers, I should probably do it face to face. Okay, what's next? Check out motel Garner supposedly took Star to on the afternoon of the day she disappeared.*

I got out the matches Crystal found in Star's backpack and Googled the location for the Lemon Tree Motel. It was in the same general direction as the garage. Grabbing my pocketbook I headed out.

I'd parked my car on the street in order to avoid the creepy new attendant Management had hired to patrol the parking garage. Last week I'd caught him peeling off bumper stickers he'd found personally offensive and replacing them with "Jesus Loves You" decals. And while I'm all for Jesus loving me, I thought that was really nervy.

The car had been baking in the sun all day and it was steaming hot inside. I unlocked the door and hopped in. Turning on the engine I adjusted the mirror and blasted the air conditioning. As I pulled away from the curb I remembered I'd left my laptop sitting on my desk, so I drove up in front of the building and got out, leaving the engine on to cool off the car. I figured it would be safe, since the Le Sabre was older than half of the city's population, which really cut down on its desirability factor.

Out of breath, I grabbed my laptop and took the stairs two at a time back down to the lobby. My car was still there, proof positive that I couldn't give it away if I tried.

I climbed back in and was about to put the car in gear when I was struck with the putrefying odor of massively sweaty gym clothes. I did an automatic armpit check. *Nope. Not me. Wow. Something must've crawled into the air conditioning duct and died.*

I checked the rear view mirror and jumped a mile as two beady eyes, surrounded by a halo of wiry, copper-colored hair stared back at me.

"Surprise."

Chapter Fifteen

I screamed and tried to scramble out of the car, but she snaked her arm around my throat and slammed me back against the seat. My hands flew up to wrench her tattooed arm away. Bunny held fast, digging into my skin with grimy fingernails.

Grabbing the steering wheel, I searched frantically for the horn. She raised her other arm, and I glimpsed the tip of a knife, its reflection gleaming in the mirror. She pressed the blade against the base of my skull, drawing blood, and I cried out in pain.

"Shut the fuck up and drive," she snapped, releasing her arm from around my neck.

As I was not in a position to argue I drove.

Hands shaking, I pulled away from the curb and started off down the street, my eyes darting about in search of a police cruiser, cop on horseback, *meter maid, anyone* who even remotely resembled an authority figure. I drove slowly, as one erratic move could send the knife plunging into my flesh.

From deep within my pocketbook my cell phone rang. Bunny made a grab for it, checking the readout.

"If that's John, could you tell him I'm indisposed and ask him to walk the dog for me?"

She answered by rolling down the window and tossing the phone out.

"Bunny," I said, gauging my words carefully, "I get why you're mad at me, but I swear I didn't rat you out to the cops. I could help you if you let me. I don't believe you killed that woman."

"What makes you so sure?" she asked, spewing rancid breath all over the back of my neck.

Maybe it was just my optimistic nature that preferred to think of Bunny as a misunderstood youth rather than a murdering psychopath.

Bunny leaned in close to the side of my head. "I've got some friends waiting for us," she said, her mouth practically sucking the wax out of my ear. "You brought the cops down on us. You fucked with my family and now you're going to pay for it, bitch. How's it feel driving to your own funeral?"

"Not that great. Look," I said, sweat trickling down my side, "could we just pull over and talk about this?"

"If you don't keep your fucking mouth shut I'm going to cut your fucking tongue out."

"Jeez, Bunny, you could've just said no." *Oh fuckin' A. Why am I baiting her like this? Why can't I develop a nervous tick instead of running at the mouth in tense situations?*

In the rear view mirror I caught a police cruiser coming up behind us. My heart rate tripled and I prayed they'd zoom up next to us, but they hung back, allowing a Smart Car to wedge in between us. *Stupid Smart Car.*

"Make a right at the corner," Bunny ordered.

My panic deepened. She was taking me farther away from the cops and the city. I had to stay on main thoroughfares if there was any chance of getting out alive.

246

The light was turning yellow so I slowed down to stop. "Keep going," she screamed. "Make the goddamn turn!"

Oh shit! I'm damned if I do and damned if I don't. So I did.

The corner was clear, so I wrenched the wheel to the right, grabbed a hold of the door handle and bailed out.

My shoulder hit the ground and I rolled a few feet into the intersection. The car kept going up onto the curb and slammed into the light pole. I laid in the street in stunned silence, blood oozing from the side of my head.

Bunny emerged from the car and stumbled down the street. I forced myself to my feet and hobbled after her. A crowd started to gather as the cops pulled up to block off the intersection.

"Stop her," I yelled as she began picking up steam. "She's getting away!"

I lunged at her back, catching her around the middle and we landed hard on the sidewalk, Bunny rolling on top of me from sheer momentum. I extended my arms and felt a searing pain in my left shoulder as I shoved her off me. She made a grab for my throat and I twisted out of reach, balled up my fist and delivered the sweetest right cross you'd ever want to see, hitting her dead center in the nose. Bunny was down for the count.

I felt a pair of strong arms lift me off her, but before I could utter a word of thanks, pain shot down the length of my left arm as my hands were wrenched behind my back and cuffed.

"You have the right to remain silent."

"Oh for Christ's sake," I yelled, twisting around to confront my captor. "She's a fugitive! She's wanted for questioning in the Olivia Bowen murder case. You guys should be thanking me, not *cuffing* me!"

Two more cop cars arrived on the scene, followed by a fire truck and an ambulance.

A guy in shorts and a wife beater undershirt stood on the corner, staring at me and nudging his friend. "Yo. It's that chick from TV. You know the one that wrestles alligators and shit. Yo! How *you* doin'?"

Oh my God. I'm in the middle of being arrested and this guy's flirting with me!

"Great! And thanks for watching WINN!"

Bunny was starting to stir. Blood gushed from her nose. It looked broken. Good. A paramedic was bent over her, checking her vital signs. She pushed him away shouting a few choice words about his sexual preferences and then spat at the officer crouched down beside her. He looked like he wanted to give her a swift kick. To his credit, he didn't.

"Please," I told the cop. "Just call your precinct. I'm telling you the truth here."

He left me sitting on the curb, handcuffed and humiliated while he went to confer with his buddies.

My head was pounding and the back of my neck stung as if someone had poured acid on it. When I'd bailed out of the car, the knife scraped the surface of my skin. I was lucky she hadn't sliced my head off.

The cop came back in a few minutes and he was a lot nicer the second time around. "I'm sorry, for the misunderstanding, Ms. Alexander," he said, uncuffing me. "We'd appreciate it if you could come with us down to the station and make a statement."

"No problem," I said, standing up. And in the next instant I was on my way back down to the pavement.

I woke up in the E.R. There was a huge knot on the side of my head where I'd hit the sidewalk, so I was sure I was hallucinating when I opened my eyes and saw Nick staring back at me. I blinked and he was still there.

Gaah! How long has he been watching me sleep? Was I drooling? I need a comb! I need a toothbrush! I looked down at my clothes, torn and bloodied from my dive from the car. *I need a fashion makeover!*

"Um, hi."

"Hello, Angel."

"How did you know I was here?"

"The hospital called me. Seems I'm your ICE number on your cell phone."

"Oh," I said, turning beet red. "I mixed you up with a *different* Nick. My 'In Case of Emergency' was supposed to be Nick San—ford—stein. We went to high school together. Great in a clutch! Voted most likely to succeed!" *Oh God, Brandy, just stop talking!*

Nick cut me a smile. "I could call this Nick San—ford—stein for you, if you'd rather."

"No, no. Stick around. I mean as long as you're here. So, how did I end up here, anyway? The last thing I remember is punching Bunny's face in. Did the cops arrest her?" I asked in a sudden panic. "I need to get out of here." I tried to swing my legs over the side of the bed but a wave of dizziness forced me back down again.

"Hold on there, Darlin.' You've been out cold for a while."

A nurse came in and checked my vitals. Actually, three nurses came in where none were needed, which led me to believe *I* was not the big attraction. "Glad to see you back among the living," she said, but her eyes were on Nick. "Your room is just about ready."

"My room? Oh, but I can't stay! I've got to find a runaway girl, help the police catch a killer, plan a baby shower for over three-hundred guests plus take my dog for a walk, he has to go potty. *I'm very busy!*"

"I'm sure you are, but you're going to be here for the next twenty-three hours so that we can observe you."

"But I'm *fine*, really—except I *am* feeling a little low on energy, so if you have a Hershey Bar handy, I'd really appreciate it."

The curtain was pulled back and in walked the cop who'd tried to arrest me followed by DiCarlo. He didn't look too happy to see Nick there. Actually, he wasn't looking too thrilled to see me, either.

I sat up and rubbed the back of my neck. Someone had stuck a bandage on the cut and it was starting to itch. Bobby gave a cursory nod to Nick and walked over to the bed.

"This is official business," he said, the little pulse in his temple working overtime. "Are you up to answering a few questions?"

No 'hey, how are ya?' Boy, he was really mad at me.

"I'm fine, thanks for asking."

"Sorry," he mumbled.

"Listen, Angel," Nick said. "It looks like you're in good hands, so I'm going to go." He leaned over the other side of the bed and kissed the top of my forehead. Bobby's temple looked like it was going to pop an aneurism. "You're welcome to borrow the truck for as long as you need it," Nick added.

"Thank you. I, um—"

"Take care," he said and then he was gone.

The abruptness of his departure was like a punch in the gut. I'd thought that getting Nick to open up about his past would bring us closer, but I could feel him drifting farther and farther away. Well, maybe it was the concussion talking, but I was damn sick of this "Lone Wolf" bit. Whether he could admit it or not, Nicholas Santiago needed me. And I wasn't about to give up on convincing him of that. *Not by a long shot.*

"Now," I said, turning my full attention to DiCarlo, "to quote an old boyfriend, 'What crawled up your butt?'"

The officer he came in with made a valiant effort to suppress a smirk but failed. Bobby shot him a death ray.

"I'm, uh, just gonna go get some coffee," the cop said, making a beeline out of the cubicle.

I could tell Bobby was trying to refrain from going off on me—at least while the nurses were still in the room. He lowered his voice to just above a whisper. "You wanna tell me what you were doing paling around with a prime suspect in the murder case I'm working on?"

"Unhhh! This was *not* my fault! And frankly, I'm sick of people jumping to conclusions about me all the time!"

He was quiet for a minute. "So, what happened?" he asked, finally, rubbing his hands over tired eyes. I instantly felt bad for yelling at him.

Wrestling with the pain in my head and arm, I took a deep breath and told him everything.

"So far, Bunny's not talking," he said when I was through. "Code of the streets and all that. Plus, she's nuts. It may take a while to get her to open up. Listen, I'm sorry about before," he added. "I just worry about you, y'know?"

"I know. I worry about me too, sometimes. But I swear, Bobby, I've been so much better lately. Working out," I cited, "asking for help, looking before leaping. I'd just like some credit for it."

"Understood," he said, with a small, dimpled grin. "Listen, I've got to get back to the station. I'll keep you posted on what's happening with Bunny, and if you can think of anything else, give me a call. I'll check in on you later," he said, turning to go.

"But what about Eleanor Grady?" I called to his retreating back. "I really think you should look into her."

Bobby glanced back over his shoulder. "Get some rest!"

"When you said you wanted to take me out to lunch, I thought you had something a little more upscale in mind." Uncle Frankie took a giant bite of his hoagie and leaned back in the cab of Nick's truck, giving me the once-over.

"What? You don't like your sandwich? I ordered it just the way you like it. Extra everything."

He didn't say anything while he chewed and swallowed. Frankie takes eating very seriously. It's almost a sporting event for him. Finally, he said, "So why are we sitting in Nick Santiago's truck spying on people from across the street?"

I raised my good arm and took a sip of soda. My other arm was in a sling, pretty banged up but, thank God for small favors, not broken. "Okay, the truth is, we're sort've on a stakeout."

"Yeah?" he asked, his interest piqued.

"Yeah. I'm waiting for someone to come out of the building, *but waiting is soooo boring.* I just wanted some company."

"Who are you stalking?" Frankie asked, taking a swallow of Dr. Pepper. For a guy who works in a gym, he sure doesn't eat that great.

"I'm not stalking. I'm investigating. Her name is Eleanor Grady. At least that's the name she's going by. I

252

think she's involved somehow with the disappearance of some teenage prostitutes."

"Does this have anything to do with that hell on wheels you had me babysit the other day?"

I laughed and soda went up my nose. "Crystal's a piece of cake compared to some of the characters I've met lately. But, yeah, it does. I called Grady this morning on the pretext of needing some information about an article I'm supposedly writing and tried to get her to talk to me, but she blew me off. Said she had to meet her family for her daughter's birthday lunch. I want to see if she was just trying to avoid me. Ooh, ooh, here she comes. Duck!"

I slouched way down in my seat and tugged on Frankie's arm to do likewise.

"I don't have to duck. She's never even seen me."

"Oh. Right. What's she doing?"

"She's climbing into a tan Volvo."

I scooched up a little in my seat and grabbed the wheel with my good arm, my eyes barely peeking over the dashboard.

"Whoa! You're not drivin' like that. Here, move over." Frankie opened the passenger seat door and hopped out, trading places with me. Then he eased into the flow of traffic, tucking in behind a catering van.

Grady was heading toward Center City. We kept a steady pace for about two miles and then lost her at a traffic light.

"Damnit. All that waiting for nothing," I sulked.

"Yo! Have a little faith in your uncle, here. I'll catch up to her." Frankie gunned it and did a classic gutter snipe, almost taking out a caddy.

"I see her," I shouted, two blocks later. "She's pulling up to the curb in front of Dunkin' Donuts."

Frankie hung a u-ie and parked on the other side of the street, next to a fire hydrant.

I dug around in my bag and took out a pair of binoculars, training my eyes on Eleanor Grady as she walked toward the restaurant on the corner. "She's headed for Henry's Bar & Grill," I announced. "I'll be right back."

"I'll be right here," Frankie replied, settling in with the rest of his hoagie.

I sneaked down to the corner and crouched behind a sandwich board advertising the opening of *Thai Manicure Salon*. Glancing down at my nails, I started thinking maybe it would be a nice change of pace from my bitten down nubs to get some acrylic glue-ons, when a kid on a skateboard barreled past me, knocking me on my ass. I banged my head against the sandwich board, and it toppled over with a clatter. *Way to be discreet, Brandy.*

I hauled it back up and reached for the binoculars in time to see two familiar figures rounding the corner on the other side of the street and heading directly toward Eleanor Grady.

Oh my God, it's James Garner and his kid! What the hell are they doing here? And suddenly it hit me. *Eleanor Grady, champion of downtrodden youth, is married to that teen-stalking pervert!*

Caitlin Garner sprinted on ahead of her father, heading straight for Grady. "Mom!" she called out, throwing her arms around her. Eleanor returned the hug, clearly delighted to see her.

Garner caught up with his wife and daughter draping a proprietary arm around their shoulders. Eleanor shrank away, visibly disgusted, and then tried to cover by dropping her purse. However, the moment did not go unnoticed by Caitlin. For a split second she seemed ready to burst into tears, and then she forced a smile upon her lips and led the way into the restaurant.

Woah! Grady looked about ready to kill James. Maybe she knows about her husband's secret life with Star. And if so, would that be strong enough motivation to get rid of her?

"Did you get what you were looking for?" Frankie asked as I climbed back into the truck.

"Yeah, I did." *And maybe a whole lot more.*

I was spread out on the living room couch doing yet another internet search on the Grady Bunch, when my *new* new cell phone rang. (As Toodie wasn't working at the Phone Mart anymore—his boss fired him for leaving on a lunch break and forgetting to come back—twice— I went for the cheapest phone I could find this time.)

Before I could say hello Franny launched into it. "Brandy, this baby is like an albatross around my neck. I can't do anything fun anymore!"

"Fran, you're not supposed to have these feelings until *after* the baby's born. That's why they call it *post partum*." I typed in "property search" on Google and hit "Enter."

"I want a beer," she whined. "I want to get back to the gym."

"I think the pregnancy has affected your memory. You never went to the gym."

"I know. But the point is I could have if I wanted to. Now I'm so fat my ass cheeks won't fit on the stationary bike. Will you come over tonight? Eddie's going to his mother's to retile her bathroom and I don't want to be alone. I think my hormones may be a little out of whack."

"Maybe just a little. Sure, I'll come. I'll bring over some Near Beer and we'll get wild. How's that?"

"I love you, Bran," she sniffled, going off on another hormonal bender.

"Love you too. I'll be there soon."

An hour and one rather humiliating phone call later my research paid off. I hadn't been able to stop thinking about Eleanor Grady and my theory that she was kidnapping pregnant girls and selling their babies. And now that I found out she was married to Garner, the more plausible the idea seemed. What a family of weirdos. Jeez, their poor kid!

But if my theory was correct, where did they put the girls once they took them? I figured it might be a bit awkward taking a young pregnant ho out of your car, bound and gagged in the middle of suburbia, and storing them in your guest room. *Which meant they probably had another property somewhere a little more private.* Only who did I know that could get me that kind of information? After a minute I thought of someone who could help me.

"Crap," I sighed. Then I picked up the phone and called Tina Delvechione.

Tina's grandfather owns T&A Realty (swear to God, you can't make shit like that up) named after his grandchildren, Tina and Adam. Tina works there part time while going to school to get her doctorate in Philosophy. Big deal. It's not like being a *real* doctor or anything.

"What's in it for me?" Tina asked when I explained why I was calling.

"What do you mean?"

"I mean," she said, snapping her ever present sugarless gum, "I'm doing you a favor, so what do I get out of it?"

Sheesh. I might want to sell my house some day. You'd think she'd be nicer to a potential client.

"Tina, it's really important that I get this information, so why don't you just tell me what you want?"

It was quiet on the other end of the line and I thought she'd hung up. Then, "I want you to talk nice about me to DiCarlo."

"What? I'm sorry, but I don't have any influence over Bobby."

Tina popped her gum a couple of times, real annoying-like. "Brandy, let's cut's the bull. Bobby DiCarlo practically worships you. And I think you had plenty to do with him not asking me out again."

Jeez, she makes it sound like I go around bad mouthing her every chance I get. I don't…that much…anymore.

"Fine. I'll tell Bobby you're swell. Now can you look up that information for me?"

"And get him to agree to go out with me again."

"Anything else?" I sighed.

"Nope. That should do it. Now, what were the names you wanted me to look up again?"

I hate having things hanging over my head, especially unpleasant things, so while I waited for Tina to call me back, I called Bobby.

"Tina's not as horrible as I might have made her out to be," I told him when he picked up the phone. Okay, so maybe it wasn't the most rousing endorsement, but it was the best I could do given the fact that she was forcing me into it.

"What brought this on?" DiCarlo asked, and I could hear the bemusement in his voice.

"Well, I was thinking you should probably go out with her again. Just once more should do it…um, what I meant was everybody deserves a second chance."

Bobby snorted. "Who are you and what have you done with Brandy?"

My call waiting beeped. It was Tina. "Okay, so we're good then with Tina, right? You're gonna ask her out again."

"Do you ever get tired of being Boss of the Universe?"

"I assume that's a rhetorical question. Gotta go." I clicked off of Bobby and clicked onto Tina. "Any luck?" I asked.

"You first."

"Okay, I spoke to Bobby and you're all set. He said he'll call you."

"When?"

"Tonight."

I was the tiniest bit concerned that God would get me for the big fat lies I'd told, but I hoped it would be mitigated by the fact that it was for a good cause.

"There's a property on Boonsboro Road in Haycock Township," she said. "The name on the title is J.E. Garner."

"Haycock Township?" I repeated, my heart skipping a couple of beats. "Isn't that in Quakertown?"

"Yeah. It's about twenty miles northwest of New Hope. The house number is 608."

"Thanks," I told her, typing in Map Quest on my computer. "If there's anything I can do for you—"

"I thought you already did."

"Um, right."

I hung up and called Bobby back. "Look, could you *please* call Tina? I sort've told her you would."

"And why would that be?" DiCarlo asked. "On second thought, don't tell me. I'm in a good mood and I want to stay that way."

"What's the occasion?" I looked over the directions for Boonsboro Road and hit print.

"I got a lead on the Olivia Bowen case."

"Ooh! What?"

Bobby laughed out loud. It made me feel good, even if it was at my expense. "I'll be happy to share that information with you, Sweetheart, the minute you graduate from the Police Academy. In the mean time, my other line's going. Later," he said and hung up.

How rude is that?!

"Fran, I just don't know if naming your kid after a dead rock star is a decision you should make in the state you're in right now."

"What's wrong with Kurt Cobain Junior?"

"Unless Kurt Cobain fathered this baby—a lot! Besides, you guys don't know for sure it's a boy, right? And anyway, just a couple of weeks ago you swore you were having a girl."

"It's going to be a boy," she said with her typical conviction. "Eddie's mother went to mass twice last weekend to pray for a grandson. She's still not over me keeping my maiden name and this is her revenge."

We were parked on the couch in Franny's living room, like a couple of beached whales, watching season one of *Sex and the City* and eating some fried mozzarella that I'd picked up from DiVinci's on my way over.

I had decided to wait until the next day to check out the address Tina had given me. I really didn't want to go alone so close on the heels of my encounter with Bunny,

259

but who could I ask to go with me? Bobby didn't have the time to cater to my hunches and besides, I'd look like an idiot if it all turned out to be a bunch of nothing.

"Wish I could go with you," Fran said, looking down at her feet. They were swollen to twice their normal size. "I haven't been to New Hope in ages. We could stop by Peddler's Village on the way home and check out the craft stores."

"Yeah, that's what I was thinking. A little espionage, a little quilt shopping."

Fran hoisted herself off the sofa and waddled off to the kitchen.

I was still hungry, so I followed her and opened the refrigerator, hoping to score some leftovers. All I could find was a jar of pickles and a gallon of Neapolitan ice cream. I took out the ice cream and scooped some into a cup. Well, just the chocolate.

Placing the carton back in the freezer, I turned to look at Fran. She was leaning against the sink, hands on her stomach, her face contorted like she'd just stepped on a bee.

"You don't look so good. Are you okay?"

"I think—ow!" *I think I'm in labor.*"

"Maybe it's just gas. You ate a lot of fried mozzarella."

"Yeah, maybe," she said, looking doubtful.

We went back into the living room and sat down. Ten minutes later she let out another howl.

"Time to call Eddie," I decided.

Franny held up her index finger, taking a deep, cleansing breath. I counted to thirty and she breathed out. "Don't call Eddie yet. He'll only panic. It may just be a false alarm. Besides, even if it is the real thing, the

260

contractions are coming ten minutes apart, so according to my La Maze instructor I've got plenty of time. The hospital will send me home if I show up there too soon."

"Okay," I said, feigning nonchalance. "So you want to watch another episode of *Sex and the City?*"

"Nah, let's go to the store and pick up some more ice cream. We're all out of chocolate."

Franny had another contraction in front of the frozen food section. "Sonuvabitch!" she yelled, clutching a pint of Ben & Jerry's.

"I feel the same way about them," said a woman passing by. "Always tempting us with their delicious flavors!"

"Fran," I said, trying to remain calm-assertive the way Cesar Milan taught me on *The Dog Whisperer.* "I checked the time and your last contraction was only five minutes ago. Why take a chance? Call Eddie and tell him you're on the way to the hospital so he can meet us there."

"I'm not leaving without my ice cream."

The look in her eye told me that Franny had already 'left the building' and in her place stood a crazy woman.

"Okay, go get in the car and I'll meet you there. And call Eddie," I yelled to her retreating back.

The checkout counters were jammed, so I hopped in line behind a guy with about six months worth of groceries and waited for him to tell me to go ahead of him. He didn't.

"Um, excuse me, but I'm in a terrible rush. Would you mind if I went first?" I held up the ice cream to show it wouldn't take any time at all.

He totally ignored me and stared straight ahead, only when he got up to the cashier he asked her if someone could run back to Produce for him and see if there were any honeydews left.

"Listen," I said, trying to cut in front of him, "all's I've got is this one little pint of ice cream, and my girlfriend wants it bad. She's about to give birth so I'm just gonna go ahead, okay?"

"As a matter of fact, it's not okay," he growled, blocking my way. "I was here first."

"Well, that's just too damn bad." I pushed ahead of him, threw five bucks on the counter and sprinted out of the store, not waiting for change. He followed me out, yelling about how that's what's wrong with young people today.

I reached Nick's truck and found Franny sitting in the back seat, her face pressed against the headrest. She was sweating buckets and swearing to beat the band.

"Did you call Eddie?" I climbed into the front seat and started the engine.

"I didn't bring my phone with me," she croaked. "Did you get my ice cream?"

"Here," I said, passing it back to her. "Try not to get it on the seat. I don't want to ruin the cushions."

"Uh, Bran, I think it's a little late for that."

"What do you mean?" I turned all the way around in the seat and found Fran sitting in a giant puddle, her skirt hiked up around her hips. "Holy crap, Franny! Why'd you pee in the truck?"

"I didn't! My water broke. Bran, I think the baby's coming!"

"I thought you said we had plenty of time!"

"Well, obviously I was wrong!"

I turned off the engine, whipped out my cell phone and dialed 911. "Hang in there, Franny. They'll be here in a few minutes."

"Tell that to the baby! He wants out NOW!"

Chapter Sixteen

I ripped open the back door and slid in next to Franny, helping her into a semi-sitting position. She grabbed my hand and squeezed so hard I was sure I felt a bone crack. The contractions were coming one on top of the next now, giving her no time to rest in between.

Fran's eyes were wide with fear. "It's gonna be okay, right?" she asked, her voice thick with pain.

Of all the life and death situations I'd found myself in over the last several months, this was, by far, the scariest. "Piece of cake," I told her. "The ambulance is pulling up as we speak. In the mean time, how about taking some of those deep, cleansing breaths we practiced in class?"

"Fuck the cleansing breaths, Bran!" she screamed, tears pouring down her cheeks. "It hurts like a mutha! I need to get this thing out of me!"

The guy from the Acme was still standing in front of the truck, waiting to give me another lesson in supermarket etiquette.

I opened the door and yelled out to him. "Yo, buddy, c'mere."

Warily, he walked around to the side of the truck and almost fainted at the sight of Franny, skirt up, knees bent, about to pass a basketball through the eye of a needle.

"Woah! You weren't kiddin'!" he marveled, staring at Fran.

"Hey! Eyes up here. Put your hands on her back to support her," I commanded. "And don't let go. Fran, I'm gonna need you to push now."

Franny bore down on the seat cushion and pushed. A moment later the top of the skull appeared. "Fran, I see the baby!"

"Oh, Mother of God!" Franny roared and sank back against the door.

"Come on, DiAngelo. Don't stop now. You're almost there."

"I can't!" she wailed. "I'm too tired!"

"Franny, *please,* just a couple more pushes and you're home free."

"Listen," she huffed, bearing down again, "I've got to ask you something."

"I'm a little busy here, Honey. Can it wait?"

"No busier than *I* am! Look," she said, her breath ragged, "I know we asked Eddie's sister to be the baby's godmother, but I've changed my mind. I want you to be the godmother."

"Me?" I yelled, instinctively forming a cradle with my hands. "Are you nuts? I had a half a box of Good N' Plenty and a can of olives for dinner last night. How can you trust me to raise your kid when I can't even feed myself?"

The head crowned and then a pair of shoulders came into view. Franny cursed and gave one last push, and a second later the baby shot out of her like a greased pig right into my waiting arms. I was shaking so hard I thought I was going to drop her.

"We did it!" yelled the guy whose name, ironically, turned out to be Eddie.

Franny held out her arms and I placed the baby carefully on her stomach. "Bran," she said, gazing down at her new baby daughter, "I trust you more than anyone on the face of the planet, and nobody would love and protect her the way that you would. So will you please consent to being Christina Brandy Bonaduce's godmother?"

"Christina *Brandy?*" I repeated, my eyes filling up.

Fran nodded.

"Wow."

"Bee-yood-ee-ful," said Supermarket Eddie, putting an arm around each of us. "Jus' bee-yood-ee-ful."

And then we were crying. All four of us.

Twelve people gathered around Franny's hospital bed, all talking at once. Squeezed into the mix of friends and relatives was a camera guy and a reporter from a local news show who'd gotten a tip about Christina's unusual entrance into the world. The din was enough to alert the floor nurse. She stormed into the room like a housemother in a college dorm.

"You can't all be in here now," she announced, slipping past Eddie's mom to check on Fran's vitals. "Some of you will have to wait outside."

We all stopped and looked at her. Nobody budged.

"Well?" she said.

Mr. DiAngelo's mother nodded happily at her. She'd just arrived from Italy and didn't speak a word of English. "Sono una bisnonna!" she shouted, pointing, first to herself and then to the baby. "Non e bella?"

"Non e bella?" we all repeated, grinning like idiots.

The nurse opened her mouth to say something and closed it again probably figuring it wasn't worth touching off an international incident.

After she left, I told Fran I had to go. "I've got to let Adrian out before he uses the palm tree for a urinal again. I love you and I'll see you tomorrow."

Franny's mother held my hand all the way down the hall. "Brandy, Honey," she said, patting my arm. That was the first time she'd ever referred to me by a term of endearment that didn't start with, "God bless her, but..." Mrs. DiAngelo stared at me so intently I started thinking I had a huge zit on the tip of my nose. "My daughter made an excellent choice, asking you to be Christina's godmother," she said, finally. "Welcome to the family." And for the second time that day, a DiAngelo made me cry.

Before I went home I swung by a car wash and got the interior of the truck shampooed. Thank God I found a place close by.

As I stepped into my living room, Adrian dove between my legs doing the "Happy Dance." I ran to let him out the back door. Outside, neighborhood kids were letting off fireworks, a preview of what was to come on the Fourth.

The phone rang and I went back inside to answer it. It was Bobby. He was working and just heard the news.

"Franny asked me to be the godmother," I said, trying not to sound too braggy and not succeeding.

"Yeah? Eddie asked me to be the godfather. I think we should get married. You know, for the sake of our godchild."

"You do understand how this works, right? She's ours in name only—and at Christmas and birthdays—oh yeah, and if I were you, I'd start saving for her college fund. We're responsible for that too."

"No kidding?"

"Look in the Godparents' Handbook. It's all there. Oh, hey, I'm getting another call. Can I call you back?"

"I'll talk to you tomorrow, Sweetheart. I'm beat."

I clicked onto the next phone call, my stomach flipping over in the process. It was Nick. The last time I'd seen him was when he'd visited me in the hospital, and that was just because he thought I was dying. He'd even arranged for Alphonso to deliver the truck to me instead of bringing it over himself. Was he avoiding me because he didn't want to get attached or was he really that indifferent?

I didn't have time to do an in depth analysis with the dog and cat because Nick broke in with some news.

"Crystal ran away from the safe house, Angel. She left some time this afternoon."

"*But why?* Nick, I thought she was happy there."

"Maybe too happy. It's tough on a kid like Crystal to enjoy perks her friends don't have. Sal said she'd been talking about going back on the streets to look for Star. She must've made good on her word."

Crystal set out to do the job I should have done. I let her down.

"I have to go find her," I told him. I grabbed my keys and headed toward the door.

"Slow down, there, Darlin'. As much as you want to protect her, Crystal isn't ready to come back. She'll contact you when the time's right for her."

The feeling of helplessness was overwhelming. "Thanks for letting me know, Nick."

"Brandy, call me if you hear from her."

"I will."

I was about to say goodbye when I heard a familiar voice in the background. "Oh, hey, is Alphonso there with you?"

"Yes, he is."

"Great. Could I speak to him a minute?"

I thought I detected a split second of hesitation in Nick's voice, which, ever hopeful, I immediately interpreted as jealousy caused by his unexpressed, yet deep and abiding love for me.

"Sure," he said. "Hey, Jackson. Phone."

"She wants to talk to me? What about?"

"She didn't say."

Alphonso got on the line. "Whaddup, Sweetcakes?"

"A reconnaissance mission, if you're interested."

"I'm interested," he laughed. "My life is *dull*. I need you to kick it up a little. So what's the gig?"

"There's a property out in Quakertown I want to check out. I thought since we had so much fun the last time…"

"What do you mean by 'check out'?"

"Um, well, maybe a little more than check out. I think some really bad stuff may be going on in this place and—"

"In other words, you need muscle and a tool kit. I'm in."

"Really? Uh, listen, I'm a little short on cash, so…"

"Don't worry about it," he said his voice sobering, "I'm happy to go with you."

"Thanks. Tomorrow night okay?"

"Hang on," he said. "Nick, you got anything goin' for me tomorrow night? We're all good," he said, getting back on the line.

"Great. I'll call you tomorrow."

After I hung up, I sat down on the couch and hauled my feet up onto the coffee table, allowing the tensions of the day to seep slowly out of me. Rocky crawled out from under the dining room table and climbed into my lap, butting her furry head against my hand for me to pet her.

"You must be wondering why I didn't ask Nick to go with me to Quakertown," I said, knowing full well she couldn't care less about my "man" problems. "Well, here's the thing. I don't know why. So if you have any ideas, feel free to chime in." She must have needed some time to think it over, because she didn't say anything.

When Rocky had had enough petting, she bit me and wandered off leaving me free to concentrate on the humongous knot in my stomach left by the news that Crystal had run away. I mean I really couldn't blame Crystal. Star was her family, and I was no closer to finding her or uncovering the truth about what happened to those young prostitutes than I was when I started out. Everything *had* to be connected, like a double-sided jigsaw puzzle where all the pieces lock together to make two different but thematically related pictures. Only how?

It was after midnight but I couldn't sleep, so I got up and tried to fix the air conditioner, (and it broke some more,) scrubbed the grease stains off of all my tee shirts and made a list of the ten essential things all babies should know so that I could teach little Chrissy and be the best godmother in the history of Godmotherdom.

I was about to restring my old guitar when the phone rang. I picked it up, making the sign of the cross to ward off bad news.

"Brandy, it's Crystal." Her voice was small and scared and tired and it broke my heart.

Keeping the fear out of my own voice I said, "Crystal, Nick told me you left Father Sal's safe house. Where are you now?"

"It's not important. I just called to let you know that I'm okay, because I thought you might be—y'know—worried."

"I'm glad you called. I mean I know you can take care of yourself and all, but—listen, maybe you should come over here for a while so we can talk. I could pick you up."

"Look," she said, her voice growing ever softer. "I appreciate what you've been trying to do for me and Star, but this is something I have to take care of myself."

"I get the feeling I'm missing something here."

Crystal cleared her throat. I could tell she'd been crying. "Little Red's spreading it around that he killed Star for trying to leave him."

Oh, fuck.

"Do you believe him?"

"Yeah," she said a little too calmly. "I do."

My stomach dropped. "Listen, he's probably just lying to bolster his street cred, but if what he says turns out to be true, you owe it to Star to see him punished. We've got to tell the police."

"No cops. We take care of our own, Brandy. That's just how it is." Her voice flattened. "Little Red killed Star, and now I'm going to kill him."

"Crystal, no!" I screamed, but she'd already hung up.

Frantically, I began to punch in 911 and then abruptly stopped. What was I going to tell them? I had absolutely nothing substantial to report and I'd only waste valuable time trying to convince them that this kid was in real danger. I called Nick instead. He understood Crystal in ways I never would.

"Try not to panic, Angel," he said, his voice washing over me like a warm bath. "We'll find her. I'll pick you up in a few minutes."

It felt like a lifetime.

I paced the living room, trying to talk myself out of the nauseating panic that was beginning to envelop me, but all that loomed before me were the worst-case scenarios.

What if Crystal does find Little Red? If she goes after him, he'll kill her. And on the off chance that she gets the drop on him, she'll be looking at Murder One. Okay, calm down! After all, what are the chances of Crystal finding this creep before we find her? Nick can probably track her down through the GPS system on her phone. And besides, she doesn't have a weapon, right? I mean, even if she's got a knife, she'd have to get pretty close to do him in. It's not like she's got a gun or anything...oh crap. The gun! Why didn't I see it when I cleaned out the planter after Adrian peed in it?

I raced over to the planter and began rooting around, only, the gun wasn't there. *Crystal must have taken it with her the day she moved to Sal's place. Great. A scared, hotheaded kid with a vendetta and a gun running around loose in the city.*

I opened the front door and spied Nick's car heading down the block, so I grabbed my bag and ran out to meet him. He pulled up in front of the curb and hopped out. "Let's take the truck, Darlin'," he said. "It's less conspicuous."

Nick popped the lock with his spare key and opened the passenger's side for me. "Unless you'd rather drive?"

"No. Please. You drive," I told him, relieved to give up control.

His eyes searched mine. "What's wrong?"

272

"She's got a gun."

We drove in silence to Little Red's apartment. If Nick was concerned about the possible outcome of our evening, he didn't show it. I, on the other hand, was about to pee my pants. I guess I didn't hide it very well, because he cut me a crooked smile and squeezed my knee. "Let's try a little music," he said, and popped in a CD. It was opera, which I always feel compelled to pretend to like because it shows I've got culture, but really, I find it kinda irritating. I like something I can sing to.

When we got to Broad and Erie, I directed him to make a left and then a quick right. We were on Little Red's block now. The street was deserted. Even the rats didn't want to be out after midnight in this neighborhood.

"It's that gray abomination on the left," I said.

Nick slowed to a stop in front of the building, leaving the engine running.

I looked carefully up and down both sides of the street. "The last time I was here I saw Little Red get into a black Escalade. It was parked out front, but I think there's parking behind the building."

Nick pulled into the driveway and drove around to the back. There was a carport with numbered spaces. I looked for 312, Little Red's apartment. The space was empty.

"Now what?" I said, on the verge of tears.

"Wait here," Nick instructed, cutting the engine. "I'm going to check out the apartment, just to make sure he's not in there with Crystal."

"I'm coming with you." I began unhooking my seat belt, but he put his hand on mine to stop me.

"I need you to stay here in case Little Red comes back. You can call to warn me."

He climbed out before I could protest and hit the lock on the door. To tell the truth I was grateful not to have to set foot in that place again. I watched him disappear around the front of the building.

About ten minutes went by and I started to get nervous, so I gave Nick a call. He didn't answer. I took out my pepper spray, slipped my keys between my fingers and took off to find him.

Rounding the corner I stopped short and flung myself back against the wall. My heart banged against my chest as I spied Little Red out on the street, his cowboy hat casting a bizarre shadow beneath the lamplight. Crystal stood opposite him pointing a gun directly at his crotch.

I grabbed my phone from my pocket and punched in Nick's number again, breathing a sigh of relief when he finally answered. My eyes glued to the scene enfolding in front of me, I whispered a hurried plea for him to get there stat.

"Stay put," he ordered his voice tense.

"I—oh shit!" Little Red knocked the gun out of Crystal's hand and it skittered across the asphalt, landing at my feet. Oblivious to me, he grabbed Crystal and twisted her arm behind her back. As she struggled against him, he pulled a semi-automatic out of his back pocket and pistol-whipped her about the face and head.

I scooped up Crystal's gun and sprinted over to them. "Leave her alone you fucking asshole," I yelled, and prayed I wouldn't actually have to use it.

With a savage swipe he knocked Crystal to the ground, worked the pistol slide, chambering a round, and leveled his gun at my heart. It was him or me. Without hesitation I pulled the trigger. Nothing happened. *Crap.*

Little Red threw back his head and howled with derisive laughter. "You dumb bitch, you don't have any bullets." *Fuck. I guess I overestimated a fourteen-year-old kid's familiarity with firearms.* Little Red leveled the gun toward me again, and in that instant Crystal crawled onto her knees and slammed into him.

It caught him off balance, giving me a nanosecond to roll out of the way. The gun went off and Crystal screamed. I turned to see Nick stagger forward. He dropped to the ground and I watched in horror as blood spurted from his upper torso.

As I raced over to help Nick, Little Red turned the gun on him. Grabbing Santiago's .38 off the ground I fired, hitting Little Red in the thigh. He reeled back on impact and then lunged for me.

Nick surged forward and lashed out with his leg, connecting with Little Red's arm. The bone shattered with a sickening crunch. Little Red dropped the gun and crumpled onto the pavement.

Shaking like a poodle on the Fourth of July, I knelt down next to Nick. His shirt was soaked with blood and his breathing labored.

"It looks worse than it really is, Angel," Nick reassured me. "Just a flesh wound."

"Shouldn't I be saying those comforting words to you?"

"Take care of Crystal. She's going to need you."

Crystal limped over to Little Red as he lay upon the pavement. Her face was battered, huge welts forming on her lips and cheeks. She hovered above him, watching him writhe in pain. And then she lifted her foot and kicked him senseless.

She was still kicking him when the cops arrived. I would have suggested she stop, but a part of me was enjoying it.

At 6:00 a.m. I dragged myself up the steps to my house, fumbled the key into the lock and walked inside. Adrian was waiting for me in the entryway holding something furry in his mouth. It was either a sock or a dead rodent, but seeing as I'd spent the last four and a half hours at the police station I was too tired to care which.

One of Little Red's neighbors had called the cops, thinking the gunshots she'd heard were punk kids setting off fireworks. When they'd arrived at the scene they called for backup. Within minutes the street was filled with patrol cars and emergency vehicles. Little Red was bundled into one of the ambulances and Nick into the other.

I climbed aboard with him searching his eyes anxiously. "That's more than a flesh wound, Nick." I overheard the medic say another quarter inch and the bullet would've struck an artery. "Swear to me you're going to be alright."

He smiled, but I could tell it was an effort. "Easy stuff, Darlin'. I told you once I'd never lie to you. I never have and I won't start now. I'm going to be just fine."

I leaned down and kissed him on the mouth, tasting the salt from my tears as they rolled down my cheeks. Then I climbed out of the ambulance and into the waiting patrol car.

Crystal was already sitting inside. She was petrified. I could tell by the way she was swearing at the officer sitting up front. He tried to explain to her she wasn't being arrested, there were just a few details they had to clear up. The cops had questioned us thoroughly at the scene and had pretty much determined we'd acted out of self-defense, but there was still the matter of an underage runaway toting a gun around. The police frown on that.

I called Father Sal and he met us at the station. Crystal gave me one of those looks I've come to recognize as her "Why are you getting up in my business?" face.

"You may be in a lot of trouble, Crystal," I quietly explained. "You could use a friend like Sal right now."

Sal spoke at length with one of the officers and then they walked over to the bench where Crystal was waiting in sullen silence.

"Crystal, Officer Janowitz has agreed to let me take you back to the safe house," Sal told her. "If that's okay with you, we can get out of here."

"I don't need a babysitter," Crystal bristled. "I can take care of myself."

Officer Janowitz blew out an impatient breath. "Let me put it to you this way. It's either the priest or Juvi. Your choice."

Before Crystal had a chance to protest further I pulled her aside. "Look, Crystal, the cops are stuck between a rock and a hard place. I know you see them as the enemy, but this guy's trying to cut you a break here. He can't just let you go. You're underage. He's giving you a good out. Take it."

"Okay," she relented, her voice a tad less belligerent.

"What happens now?" I asked as Sal drove me back to Nick's truck.

"According to Janowitz, Little Red will be booked on attempted murder charges. As for the story about Star, who knows? The cops will do their best to check it out, but without a body, it's hard to prove."

277

I glanced over my shoulder to the back seat. Crystal was curled up in a ball asleep.

"Are they going to charge Crystal? I mean she pulled a gun on Little Red."

"Funny thing," Sal shrugged, a slight smile crossing his face. "They searched the area extensively and no gun was found. So now it's just a pimp's word for it and I don't think the cops are inclined to believe him."

Note to self: Add Officer Janowitz to my Christmas list.

I slept fitfully, waking every few hours to call the hospital to check on Nick. When it got late enough, I phoned my parents and Paulie to fill them in so they wouldn't hear about it secondhand and freak out. I also promised an 'exclusive' to my television station as soon as I could speak in coherent sentences again.

In between, I dreamed, or, more specifically, I nightmared. My conscious mind couldn't stop thinking about shooting Little Red and it spilled over into my subconscious. In a million years I wouldn't have thought myself capable of doing that kind of bodily harm to someone no matter how despicable they might be. But when push came to shove, it was a no brainer.

Still, I couldn't help but think how Henry Michael's great "grandmaw" would feel had I actually killed him. Thank God I didn't have to find out.

By noon I had given up on trying to sleep. My bedroom was stifling hot and the dog needed to go out. I threw on some clothes, brushed my teeth and clamped Adrian's leash on him.

It was 90 degrees and muggy outside. Mrs. Gentile was standing on her little patch of lawn, putting the finishing touches on a miniature Revolutionary War scene.

I think it was supposed to be "The Father of our Country" crossing the Delaware, but it was hard to tell. A bearded George Washington was riding on a donkey, which led me to believe she'd used parts of her Nativity display from Christmas.

"Nice display, Mrs. Gentile," I said, thinking how much fun Adrian would have peeing on it.

I waited a beat for the inevitably bitter response. "Thank you!"

I am a terrible person!

When I got back from our walk, I called the hospital again. Nick was sleeping but the nurse assured me he was doing fine. I showered and changed into a clean tee shirt and fresh jeans, made a quick batch of Slicen'bake cookies because, as my mother says, "You should never visit anyone empty-handed," and took off for the hospital.

The cookies got a little burnt, so on the way up in the elevator I tried a couple to make sure they were edible. They tasted pretty good to me. I rewrapped the rest and walked down the hall to Nick's room.

I knocked softly and peeked into the room, expecting to find him asleep. He was awake and sitting in a chair, dressed in black sweat pants and a pajama top, open in front. A bandage wrapped around his chest was the only telltale sign that something traumatic had occurred less than twelve hours before. Otherwise he looked the picture of health. *And he had company.*

With her long, silken black hair, supermodel build and Eurasian knockout looks, I recognized her immediately. I'd met her several months back at Nick's apartment when I'd inadvertently intruded on their date. Her name was Alana and she was a royal bitch on wheels.

I tried to retreat before Nick saw me standing there like a dork in my *Princess Bride* tee shirt holding a plate of burnt, pseudo-homemade cookies, but he spotted me and called out my name.

I could pretend I didn't hear him and if he asks about it later, just deny it was me. He's probably hopped up on painkillers anyway and won't remember a thing.

"Brandy," he said again. "Come on in. I was hoping you'd stop by. Alana, you remember Brandy, don't you?"

"Of course, and you brought Nicky cookies. Wasn't that sweet? I wish I didn't care how I looked and just enjoyed food the way you so obviously do." She gave me a full watt smile.

"Nice to see you again, Alana. Oh, dear, you've got food stuck in your teeth. How embarrassing for you."

Score!

The corners of Nick's mouth twitched slightly as he fought to suppress a smile. It made me love him even more.

"Alana, thanks for dropping off those papers for me. I'll look them over and get them back to your office."

She bent to kiss him and I noted with some satisfaction that she kept her lips pressed together. "Take care, Nicholas. Call me." Funny, she didn't say goodbye to me.

Nick hoisted himself out of the chair and stretched out on the bed leaving room for me to sit down. "Talk to me, Brandy Alexander," he said. "How are you doing?"

"Me? I'm not the one who got shot. I'm fine."

Nick stared deep into my eyes. "I know you, Angel. You shot a man. That can't have been easy for you."

"Please." I told him, turning away from his gaze. "That nut job didn't have a single redeeming quality."

280

"And yet, given half a chance, you would drag him kicking and screaming down the path of redemption. By the way, my source down at the precinct tells me Red is humming a distinctly different tune than the one he'd been spreading on the street. Swears up and down he doesn't know what happened to Star. He'd made up that story about killing her to keep his girls in line."

"Do you believe he just made it up?"

"Well, from what we know about the guy, he's more than capable of killing Star. But he's denying it now and without a body—" Nick trailed off.

"So once again we're back to square one."

My phone began to play *I'm a Yankee Doodle Dandy*. I'd downloaded the ring tone in honor of the Fourth of July, thinking it would be fun and patriotic. Janine says it just serves to emphasize my supreme geekiness, but Janine's wrong. It's cool!

I looked at the readout. It was Alphonso.

"We still on for tonight, Sweetcakes?" he asked.

"Definitely. Want me to pick you up?"

His laughter filled my ears.

"I take that as a 'no.' Okay, fine. You pick me up. I'll see you around nine. And—Alphonso?"

"Yeah?"

"Thanks."

"You and Alphonso going somewhere?" Nick inquired as I threw my phone back in my bag.

"Yeah, we're going to—" I stopped, mid-explanation. There was something in the studied casualness of his question that thrilled me beyond belief. And then it dawned on me. Nicholas Santiago was *jealous!*

"Um, we thought we'd hang out. Well," I said, milking the moment for all it was worth, "I'd better let you get some rest." He did look like he was starting to fade. "I could come back tomorrow—y'know, if you're bored or anything."

"I'm getting released this afternoon, but you're welcome to stop by the apartment." There was a slight hesitation and then, "Look, Darlin', whatever you and Alphonso have going on—just be careful, okay?"

"What do you mean?"

"I mean just be careful."

If I thought I was going to get him to reveal anything about his real feelings for me I was delusional.

"I'm always careful," I muttered, heading out the door. *Damnit.*

I thought I heard him snort softly as the door swung closed.

"John, I can't talk now. I'm working."

"Then why did you answer the phone if you can't talk? I hate when you do that. I got all excited thinking you were available."

I sighed. Alphonso, seated next to me, cut me a bored stare. We had been parked for half an hour on the side of the road, about a hundred yards from the property at 608 Boonsboro Road.

It was one of those typical old farmhouses you'd find in the area, with a stone wall out front that had fallen into disrepair. The house was set back and surrounded by trees, the nearest neighbor being about a quarter mile away.

It looked like it had been twenty years since any farming activity had taken place, and the forest was quickly reclaiming all the fields. There was a light on in the front room and a car sitting in the driveway: a dark green Saturn.

It looked familiar to me and I searched my memory bank for where I'd seen one just like it. Then it dawned on me. There had been a dark green Saturn sitting out in front of the Garners' house the day Janine and I went there to talk to James. *Could it belong to the Garners?*

"Okay, John," I said, "the truth is *nobody* looks good in Crocs, and yes, that could absolutely be a factor in Garrett not calling you back."

I didn't even think Alphonso was listening, but he let out a short, bark of a laugh.

"Who's with you?" John asked.

"Oh, that's—Holy cow! John, I'll call you back!"

Alphonso sat up in his seat and focused his eyes on the house. The light had gone out and the front door opened. James and Eleanor Garner appeared in the doorway. James turned to lock up the house while Eleanor headed for the car and climbed in. James joined her a moment later and they drove off down the road and out of sight.

Alphonso retrieved his Glock from beneath his seat and opened the glove compartment, extracting a .38. He held it out to me and a sick wave of fear rippled through my stomach.

"I can't, Alphonso. I know I'm being a wuss, but I'm just not ready."

"No problem." He stuck it back in the glove compartment and we climbed out of the car.

Alphonso silently signaled to me to follow him around to the back of the property. A couple of big trash containers were lined up against the house. I opened one and started sifting through the rubbish.

About halfway down the first can I found an empty plastic bottle with a picture of a baby on it. *Hunh! Those creeps don't even recycle. Figures.* I tried to read the words on the back of the container but it was too dark to see.

"Yo, Jackson, can you make out what it says?" I whispered tossing him the bottle.

Alphonso dug in his pocket and took out a small LED flashlight. "Says 'Vitafuel Prenatal Nutrition.'"

My heartbeat quickened. "This stuff is for pregnant women." There were two more identical, empty containers down near the bottom of the can, along with four empty gallon cartons of milk. *Milk. The perfect food for someone in the "family way."*

"Alphonso, we've got to get into the house."

Alphonso shined the flashlight on me. "You don't look so good."

I was so nervous I could barely speak. "Just get us in there."

The back door was tripled latched but Alphonso Jackson is a pro. Within minutes we were standing inside the kitchen. It wasn't exactly designer decorated. There was a table and some mismatched chairs, a standard issue refrigerator and an okra colored stove that would go perfect with shag carpeting. I looked around and found a pot soaking in the sink. The whole place stunk of oatmeal.

Alphonso led us through each room, carefully checking every nook and cranny, for what, I was afraid to even imagine. There was something strange about the house. It had all the right touches to give the appearance of an actual home, and yet, it lacked authenticity.

Alphonso felt it too. "This place is giving off some badass vibes. You can almost smell it."

"That's the oatmeal. But, yeah, I feel it too."

Standing in the living room, I spied a heating vent in the floor. "If there's a heating vent, there's a furnace," I said, "only we've cruised around the whole house and haven't run across it... which means it must be in the basement...but there're no steps leading to a cellar. That's weird."

"Let me go outside and see if I can spot a basement window or a door for a root cellar," Alphonso said. "I'll be right back."

There is something so wrong here, I thought, looking around the living room, *I can feel it.*

My eyes gravitated to the hallway runner. It looked brand new, a sharp contrast to the rest of the threadbare rugs in the house. *That's weird. Why would they let the place go to seed and then care about a stupid little rug?*

I walked over and picked up the runner kneeling down to inspect the hardwood floor beneath it. There was a small notch in the wood. I stuck my finger in it and pulled. A square piece of flooring rose up revealing a stairway leading down to the basement.

"Alphonso was just walking back into the living room. "C'mere," I yelled. "I found the entrance to the basement."

"Take it easy there, Sweetcakes. Someone went to a lot of trouble to hide this. It might be booby trapped. Let me go first."

"I appreciate the chivalry, but that's not fair. Why would you put yourself in danger like that?"

"Because Santiago would kill me if I let anything happen to you. This way I've got a fifty-fifty chance of survival."

My stomach flipped very pleasantly. Sometimes I get these feelings at the most inappropriate moments!

When Alphonso got to the bottom of the stairs he called up to me. "You're not going to believe this. Come on down."

Following the beam from his flashlight, I took the stairs two at a time and found myself in a small, furnished apartment. There was a living room, complete with couch, end tables, lamps and a television set. I turned on a light and saw a door to the left that led to a tiny bathroom. There was a closed door on the right.

Alphonso glanced at me, Glock in hand and ready for action. He nodded toward the closed door and walked over to it with me right behind him. He opened the door and took an immediate step back, blocking my view. "Oh fuck," he whispered, losing his characteristic cool. "Man, that's *sick*."

"What's in there?" I squeaked.

Shaking his head he stepped aside allowing me a full access. It took my brain a minute to fully process the scene before me; *two, pregnant, teenage girls sitting on twin beds, chained to a post like a pair of junkyard dogs. Oh my God.*

Chapter Seventeen

The terrified look they gave us was almost too much to bear. One of the girls started to cry. She couldn't have been more than eighteen, with large, dark, haggard eyes and a swollen belly. The other was younger and less visibly pregnant. She stared at us, her eyes full of distrust.

"Alphonso," I whispered, "put the gun down."

I approached the beds slowly, swallowing bile and outrage. "We're not going to hurt you," I said calmly. "We're here to help get you out of here, but we can't do it alone, and we have to make sure the people that did this to you pay for what they've done. So that means I have to call the police. Do you understand?"

They just stared at me as if I were speaking Klingon. I dug in my bag, took out my phone and called Bobby.

"Call the Haycock Township police and I'll meet you there as soon as I can," he said. "If you have any trouble, tell them to call me."

"Um, we sort've broke into the house. Think that'll be a problem?"

"Not when the cops get a load of what you found there."

"Oh, and, uh, hypothetically speaking, what would happen if they found one of us packing a concealed weapon without permission?"

"I didn't hear you ask this question, but if I were Alphonso I'd get my ass out of there real quick."

"Thanks, Bobby."

Fifteen minutes later I heard footsteps pounding above our heads.

"Down here," I yelled.

Light flooded the stairwell and five armed officers appeared, guns drawn. A female cop stayed with the girls and tried to soothe them while her partner worked on sawing off the chains. Two more cops inspected the basement apartment and the last one took my statement.

"The people you're looking for are James and Eleanor Garner. They own this property and they're the ones who kidnapped the girls," I said, giving him the Garners' address in Philly.

As I finished giving my statement, Bobby showed up and all the tension I'd been holding in came out in one big whoosh of tears. He put his arms around me and let me cry into his shirt.

"You did good, Sweetheart," he said, hugging me to him. "I think you may have just solved the Olivia Bowen homicide as well. We figured it had to be someone who knew her, but we couldn't come up with a motive. Bowen was probably on to them so they had to get rid of her."

As we walked outside, local news crews stormed the property. My first instinct should have been to call Eric to give WINN an "exclusive" on this "Breaking News," but it wasn't. I just wanted to right a wrong and go home.

And then I had an epiphany.

I suck at my job.

Might be time for a career change.

Bobby offered to give me a ride home. On the way, he got a call that the Garners had been picked up just as they'd pulled into their garage. They were in custody and on their way to the station.

"Bran, do you mind if we go directly there? I'll have Osbourne run you home." Jimmy Osbourne is a rookie cop Bobby's taken under his wing.

"Fine by me. The sooner you get there the sooner you get those sick-o's off the street permanently."

I was sitting in DiCarlo's office when I saw them being escorted into the interrogation room by two police officers. Their hands were cuffed behind their backs. Eleanor had giant mascara stains running down her cheeks. She had obviously been crying. James looked like he was on the verge of crapping his pants. A ripple of satisfaction flowed through me.

Bobby told me to stay in his office, and I would have, except that I was very thirsty and had to get a drink of water at the water fountain that, coincidentally, was located *right next to the interrogation room.*

Garner shuddered in recognition. "This must make your day," he spat at me.

"Umm, not yet." I balled up my fist and socked him in the gut as hard as I could. "But I'm getting there," I said as I watched him throw up all over his shoes.

I stuck out my hands for the cop to cuff me. "It was worth it," I told him.

He looked from me to Garner to his partner and back to Garner again. "Must be the flu. It's going around."

"Paulie, I'm telling you, I'm fine."

"Th-then why didn't you call me back? Here I am closin' up the bar and I look up at the TV and see Breaking News, and the next thing I know, my sister is p p-parading cross the screen in the middle of a crime scene—what the hell, Bran?"

I glanced over at the clock in my living room. 7:15 a.m. I'd been asleep for three hours. Great.

I wasn't in the mood to be alone last night, so I'd waited for Bobby while he went through his paces with the Garners, and then he drove me home.

"I'm gonna come in for a while, if that's okay," he'd told me.

"You don't need to stay with me, Bobby. I'm really alright."

"Yeah? Well maybe I'm not."

Rocky greeted DiCarlo with her customary devotion, rubbing against his legs as if he were a giant can of tuna. I went to the back door to let the dog out. When I came back in, Bobby was sitting on the couch, his blue jean clad legs stretched out, feet up on the coffee table. Rocky was tucked in behind him on the couch pillow, purring softly.

Bobby shifted over to make room for me and I cuddled in next to him, laying my head in his lap.

"You're something else, y'know that?" he said, stroking my hair.

"So I've been told," I sighed.

"Love you, Bran."

"Love you too."

I fell asleep right after that and woke up when Paul called. DiCarlo was gone. He'd taken off my All Stars and stuck a couch pillow under my head. On the coffee table he'd left a note, written on the back of an old

Safeway receipt. "Sweet Dreams." Mercifully, I hadn't dreamed at all.

"Paul, I'm really sorry. I must not have heard my phone ring." I took my phone out of my bag and checked for messages. There were six. Four from Paul and two from Nick.

"Paulie, I'll come by later to see you, okay? Don't be mad—and don't tell Mom."

"It would serve you right if I did," he told me, hanging up.

I retrieved the messages on my phone, blasting past Paul's to get to Nick's.

"Hello, Angel, Alphonso filled me in on what happened. Give me a call."

The next message was sent a few hours later. "Just checking in to make sure you're okay. Call me."

I thought I noted a touch of urgency in his voice and was just about to call him back when I heard a knock at the door. I stumbled over to open it, in all my "morning breath" and bed-head glory.

Nick stood on the steps, unshaven and sexy as all get out. His chest looked slightly broader than usual and I could see the outline of his bandages under his tee shirt. He gave me a wry smile. "Hello, Angel."

"Nick," I squeaked, equal parts delighted and mortified. "Um, come in. I was just—uh—I'll be right back."

I took the stairs two at a time, brushed my teeth, changed my shirt, applied some fresh deodorant and ran a comb through my hair. When I came back down he was sitting on the couch, petting the dog.

"I *just* heard your messages. I'm sorry I didn't call you back—shouldn't you be on bedrest?"

"I'm fine, Darlin', good as new. I wanted to make sure you were okay. You had quite a night."

"Yeah, it was pretty eventful. Listen, have you eaten breakfast yet? Since you came all this way, the least I can do is feed you."

Nick sat at the kitchen table while I scrambled around trying to find him something to eat. "Would you like eggs or pancakes? Cereal?"

"Whatever you usually have for breakfast is fine with me."

That would be marshmallows toasted on top of the stove. "How about French toast?" I said, taking a stale loaf of sourdough out of the refrigerator.

For once I didn't have much of an appetite, so I sat there with Nick while he ate his breakfast. I'd only burned it a little bit and anyway he didn't seem to notice.

Nick finished his plate and put down his fork. He eyed me for a minute and then said gently, "What's wrong, Angel?"

"Nothing."

He sat quietly and waited until I was uncomfortable enough to fill the void. "Okay, it's just that—look, I'm really grateful that we found those girls, but—"

"We still don't know what happened to Star," he finished for me.

"Yeah," I said, absently running my finger through the syrup that was left on his plate. "Crystal needs closure, one way or the other."

"So do you, Darlin'. Let's go over it again."

"Star wasn't like the others," I began. "She wasn't pregnant. She got involved through a random meeting."

"You said you suspected Garner's wife knew about the affair. She didn't go on the trip to Los Angeles with him.

292

What if she followed him on the day in question, found out who he was seeing and then went back later to grab Star?"

"Bobby said she had an alibi and plenty of witnesses to back her up for the time period in question. I guess she could have hired someone to take Star, but...Nick, if Eleanor did take Star, why would she be driving her around in a car that's so easily identifiable? I mean it has *vanity* plates. That's like saying, *Look at me, look at me.* Unless Eleanor wanted to set James up to get back at him—but why would she mess up a lucrative business just to get revenge on her husband?"

And in the next instant I answered my own question. "Oh my God. She *wouldn't*. Eleanor didn't kidnap Star. But I think I know who did!"

I ran into the living room and shoved my feet into my shoes. "I'm sure I'm right. I've gotta go."

"I'm coming with you. You can explain on the way."

"It all makes perfect sense when you think about it, Nick. It was their daughter, Caitlin. It had to be. Make a right here." We were headed for the Garner's house. I only prayed the kid was still there, not spirited away by some well-meaning relative.

"Everything points to her. Remember I told you about the day I'd seen them at the restaurant. She saw how her mother reacted when her dad put his arm around her. What if she knew why they were having trouble and she wanted to do something about it? You know how kids are. I can just imagine her thinking if she can just get rid of Star, her parents will be happy again."

"That's a big leap from her wishing her parents would stop fighting to kidnapping a real live girl."

"Yeah, but that's not all. Eleanor was at a dinner party the night Star got picked up. She has an airtight alibi. *Someone* took their car. Caitlin had access to it, plus, a kid would be far less likely to think about the ramifications of driving around with vanity plates. Look, her mother's out for the evening, there's the car…but she couldn't have done this alone. Besides being too physically small to pull off something like this, Harmony said she saw a guy driving. It must've been Caitlin's behemoth boyfriend, Ben.

"The more I think about this, the more sense it makes. And if my hunch is right, I have a good idea where they took Star. Pull over a sec."

Nick pulled to the curb and parked. "What's going on?"

"Ben lives at his parents' house. They have a sound studio in the back of their house. I'm assuming it's *soundproof*. When I was at the Garner's place I met Ben. He said his parents were in Europe and they'd be coming back in about a week. He's an artist, and he's been storing his paintings in the Garner's garage because he was storing something else in the studio while his parents were gone. Nick, I'll bet you anything they stashed Star in there."

"So where's this kid live?" he asked, starting up the car again.

"Damn! I don't know! I don't even know his last name…wait…he wrote his signature at the bottoms of his paintings. I closed my eyes. "Ben…Stein? Stiller? St— Stivac! Ben Stivac!" I whipped out my cell phone and punched in the number for Information.

Two minutes later we were back in business. The Stivacs lived about three blocks away from the Garners. Nick pulled across the street from the house and parked.

"Unhh!" I whined. "The studio isn't visible from the street. Why can't anything ever be easy?"

"Because if it was you wouldn't be interested." It was an offhand remark and scarily true.

"It's only a little after 9:00 a.m." I said, checking the time. "Let's hope Ben isn't an early riser."

We snuck around to the back of the house and spied a small structure, about fifteen by twenty square feet. It looked like a converted garage.

Nick checked around for an alarm system. Not finding one, he pulled some tools out of his back pocket and went to work on the lock.

"Wait," I said, putting my hand on his wrist. I was shaking so hard I could barely stay vertical.

Nick put his hands on my shoulders and gazed steadily into my eyes. "You've been through so much, Angel, I wish I could protect you from this one. But no matter what we find in there, just know that you tried harder for that kid than anyone has in her entire life. And you're not walking into this alone. I'm right here with you."

I nodded slowly, blinking back tears as Nick opened the door.

As our eyes adjusted to the dim lighting in the room, we heard a rustling noise followed by an unearthly bellow.

"Get me the fuck out of here!"

I jumped a mile. Seated cross-legged on a mattress in the corner of the room was a teenage girl with stringy brown hair. She looked like she hadn't bathed in weeks, which come to think of it, she hadn't.

"Star?"

She jumped to her feet, looking like she was getting ready to bolt, only she couldn't figure out how to get

295

around the two of us. "Who the hell are you?" she sneered instead.

I bit my lip hard to keep from bursting into relieved laughter. "We're friends of Crystal's and we came to get you out of here," I told her, replaying an eerily familiar scene.

And for what seemed like the umpteenth time, I took out my phone and called the police.

Late afternoon found an unlikely trio traveling eastbound on the Betsy Ross Bridge to Tom's River. Nick was driving. I was riding shotgun and our newest charge, Star, was in the back seat, hanging her head out the window, sucking in her newfound freedom. The nightmare was finally over.

Ben folded like a house of cards the minute the police showed up at his door. The story bore out the way I'd suspected. Caitlin had heard her parents arguing about the "teenage whore" James had gotten involved with. So she convinced Ben to help her save her parents' marriage by eliminating her mother's competition.

On the afternoon of the 15th, the kids followed James in Ben's car as he picked Star up on her corner and took her to the motel. That night, with her dad in another state and her mother at a party, Caitlin and Ben drove back to the neighborhood to look for Star. There was one hitch in their plans. Ben's car was overheating, so they decided to take SMILEY 1 instead.

They had never planned to hurt Star. They just wanted to scare her into breaking off contact with Caitlin's dad. But Star, in inimitable street kid fashion, stuck an attitude and things just spiraled from there.

Caitlin was picked up at her aunt's where she had been staying since her parents' arrest the night before. She, too, seemed to welcome the chance to unburden herself. I asked Bobby what he thought might happen to them.

"They're both under the age of eighteen, so my guess is after a psychiatric evaluation, they'll be given community service and remanded to the custody of their parents, or in Caitlin's case, her aunt. Star refuses to press charges, so there's not much of a case against them."

I turned around to Star, who was now flipping the bird to a guy in the next lane over. "Um, if you don't mind my asking, how come you didn't press charges against Caitlin and Ben? Don't you want to see them pay for what they did to you?"

Star shrugged. "I've had far worse done to me. Besides, they were okay, and at least I was getting fed."

The more likely reason was it was easier to let it go than to get caught up in the legal system. *Street tough to the bitter end.*

As we pulled up to Sal's beach haven, Elwood, the yellow lab puppy ran to greet us.

A minute later we were standing at the screen door, Nick and I in front, with Star tucked in behind us.

Crystal opened the screen to let us in. "Any word on Star?" she asked by way of greeting.

"Gee, I don't know," I said, as Star stepped out from behind us. "Why don't you ask her yourself?"

A stunned silence ensued, followed by teenaged screams of pure happiness.

Two hours later we said our goodbyes to Star and Crystal. Crystal walked me to the door.

Shelly Fredman

"Brandy, I don't really know how to thank you for what you did for me and Star, and um, for the rest of the girls. Nobody's ever fought for me like you did."

I cracked a lame joke to keep from crying. "Yeah, well, I had to do something with those boxing lessons I've been taking. Listen, promise me you'll keep in touch when you get to your grandma's. I'm really glad you called her."

"Yeah. Me too. I couldn't believe she said I could bring Star along." She laughed. "That old lady doesn't know what she's gotten herself into."

I reached out and gave her a hug. "Take care, Crystal."

She hugged me back, hesitated and hugged me again, hard. And then, for the first time she looked me straight in the eye. "Natasha," she said. "My name is Natasha."

"You don't look so good." I never thought I would utter those words to Nick, but the truth is he wasn't as recuperated as he'd led me to believe. The ride to Jersey had taken its toll on him.

Nick cut me a tired smile. "I'm fine, Darlin'. Just thinking about Caitlin and her family. I guess that old adage is true. The apple doesn't fall far from the tree."

"And sometimes, the apple falls in a whole 'nuther universe. Nick, you're nothing like your father. In case you haven't noticed, I'm a pretty good judge of character. I wouldn't waste my time on someone who wasn't worth it."

Nick took one hand off the wheel and draped his arm around my shoulder. "Have I ever told you how grateful I am to have you in my life?"

"No, but feel free to start any time." *Wow. I guess fending off a psycho pimp, a crazy-assed street mom and a murderous husband and wife team was a real confidence booster.*

It was almost seven by the time we got back into Philly. I'd called John earlier to see if he could feed and walk the dog for me. Adrian is nuts about his Uncle John.

"I'll head out right now," John told me. "Oh, and by the way, it wasn't the Crocs. Garrett had the flu. That's why I hadn't heard from him. We're going to Fairmount Park to watch the fireworks tonight."

The Fireworks. With all the other stuff going on, I somehow missed the fact that it was the Fourth of July. "Happy Independence Day, John," I told him. "Enjoy the light show."

"You know," Nick said after I disconnected with John, "the Art Museum puts on a pretty good fireworks display. You can actually see them from my living room window. If you're interested, that is."

He didn't have to ask me twice.

For as many times as I'd been over to Nick's place, I still got a thrill riding up in the elevator, waiting while he opened the door, and stepping through the threshold into his apartment.

We'd picked up Indian food and some wine along the way and I set it out on his coffee table while Nick changed the dressing on his bandage. When I was finished setting out the food, I poured myself a hefty glass of wine and wandered off to take a peek in the spare room.

"Don't do it," warned a sensible little voice in my head. "You know you'll only get upset if you find evidence that another woman has been in there."

"You're right," I said aloud. But it was like trying to stop myself from checking out an accident on the freeway. I know I'm gonna wish I hadn't, but I'm always compelled to look anyway.

To my relief, the sleeper couch had been put together and there were no obvious signs of recent visitors. I took a large gulp of wine and crept backwards out of the room, smack into Nick. "Looking for something in particular?" he asked, shooting me a wicked grin."

"Ooh!" I squeaked, turning around. "I was looking for the, uh—bathroom. No sense of direction and all that. Oh, here it is."

I went in and closed the door and then turned on the faucet in case he was listening. When I emerged a few minutes later, Nick was on the couch. He'd changed into pajama bottoms, not the "old man" kind my dad wears, or if they were, they sure looked better on Nick. They were dark blue plaid with a drawstring, and it took all my will power not to give it a yank. He wasn't wearing a shirt, his chest swathed in fresh bandages.

"How are you feeling?" I asked, sitting down next to him on the couch.

"Surprisingly good."

"But doesn't it hurt?"

"Only when I laugh."

"Are you hungry?" I asked, reaching for his plate.

Yes, Angel, hungry for you. "Not particularly." He poured himself a glass of wine and took a sip. "How about you?"

I shook my head. "Me neither. Listen, Nick, this might not be the best time to bring it up seeing as you just got shot and all and you're probably not in the mood anyway—and really, there's no pressure, but after

300

everything that's happened lately, I realized that life is just too damn short to waste worrying about if I'm ever going to be loved back by you, and the truth of the matter is I love you more than I ever thought humanly possible so that's good enough for me, and as long as I'm letting it all hang out I might as well tell you I'm feeling really horny, so if you don't kiss me right now I'm just gonna curl up and die—but like I said, no pressure."

Nick put his glass down on the coffee table. "Well," he sighed, "I certainly wouldn't want to be responsible for your demise, so it seems you've left me no choice." He leaned into me, cupping my face in his hands. "After all, a man's gotta do what a man's gotta do." *And man, did he ever!*

Nick gently nuzzled my neck with his mouth and teeth, slowly working his tongue around to my mouth. I invited him in and we played that way for a while, letting the anticipation build, enjoying the heat in our bellies. He licked behind my ear and down into the cleavage of my shirt, and then without missing a beat, his hands were under my shirt and before I could take my next breath my bra was unsnapped and he was massaging my nipples into hard peaks.

"Oh," I moaned and felt obliged, *excited* to return the favor. Reaching into his pajama bottoms, I felt him instantly spring to life. He was hard and warm to the touch. "Hmm," I smiled into his mouth. "You seem happy to see me."

"You have no idea," he whispered into my ear.

Gently I pushed him onto his back and lowered his pajama bottoms over his hips. And then I made him even happier.

"Oh my God, I can't believe I'm saying this," Nick groaned, after a few minutes, "but you need to stop." He pulled me up to a sitting position. "Darlin', I have a lot to make up to you after the last time we were together, and, frankly, if you keep doing what you're doing, I won't be fit for anything."

"But, Nick," I protested, "you're not in any shape— "

"Shh," he whispered. "It's non-negotiable. I'm going to make love *with* you."

So who was I to argue with a man on a mission?

I walked with him into the bedroom and waited while he pulled back the covers. "I'm sorry, Angel, under different circumstances I would have swept you off your feet…"

"Don't you know you already have?"

I kissed him and climbed into bed and waited for him to settle in next to me. Then I drew up the sheets and reached down to take off my underwear. Nick grabbed a condom, hurriedly putting it on. Then he reached for me but, once again, I pushed him onto his back.

I raised my leg and straddled him, taking him in my hand and slowly guiding him into me. When he was all the way inside, I began to move gently, steadily, careful not to injure him. He raised his head to kiss me deeply, caress my breasts and whisper those same words he said to me the first time we ever made love. *Me tocas mi alma.*

After a while I felt him begin to surge inside me. "Brandy," he said, his voice a guttural cry.

"Let yourself go," I whispered. I was right behind him.

I awoke to an empty bed and the sound of a female voice, shrill and demanding. I couldn't make out the words, but it seemed to be coming from the living room. I grabbed my clothes, threw them on and tiptoed down the hall.

Alana stood in the foyer, holding her diamond earrings and waving her arms around like a conductor who was really angry with the orchestra. Nick stood several feet away, wisely saying nothing. She saw me peek around the corner and she flipped out, resuming her rant with added vigor. Now I was able to hear every word, loud and clear.

"*You let her sleep in your room?* Well, that's just great. I've stayed at your apartment a dozen times and never once was I allowed into the *inner sanctum*. If I was lucky, you let me sleep in the office instead of sending me home in a cab after we fucked! What does she have that I don't, Nick? Why does *she* get to sleep with you? Do you love her, Nick? *Oh my God, that's it, isn't it?* You're *in love* with that—that…little…"

Femme fatale? Sex Goddess?

"Gidget?!"

Okay, I could have done without the Gidget crack, but *was* Nick in love with me? I held my breath and waited for him to deny it. Alana waited too, but there was no denial forthcoming.

Finally, she turned and walked stiff legged to the door. "Goodbye, Nicholas. Have a happy life."

When I was sure she was gone for good, I sauntered over to where Nick was standing. He had his eyes on the front door, more, I think, to avoid looking at me than for any great interest in the mahogany.

"So," I said, unable to keep the smile off my face, "you do love me."

"You know, Darlin'," he started, "these things are very complicated."

I positioned myself directly in front of him, arms akimbo. "No, they're not. Just admit it."

Nick gazed down at the floor for a minute, and then he raised his eyes to me, matching my smile with one of his own. "Yes, Brandy Alexander, I love you."

He reached for me and I wrapped my arms around him, leaving soft kisses on his cheeks, his eyes, his mouth.

"I guess there's really no fighting it, is there?" he murmured. "I love you, Angel. Me toca mi alma. *You touch my soul.*"

"I knew it all along," I whispered into his chest.

Epilogue

"Do you know how many times we've made love, and yet I've never seen you naked?"

"And you never will," I said, groping around in the dark for my underwear.

"Oh? Why's that?"

"Okay, I've never told anyone this before, but I've got three nipples."

"Really?" He thought about it for a minute. "I find that rather alluring."

"Thank you…I think."

Nick got out of bed and went to the bathroom. He returned a minute later and flipped on the bedroom light. He was holding a box I'd mistakenly left on the bathroom counter. I jumped off the bed and tried to grab it and a wave of nausea hit me like a ton of bricks.

"Early Response," he read off the label. "Something you want to tell me, Darlin'?"

Afterword

In this fourth installment in the Brandy Alexander mystery series you met Crystal, a young adolescent girl enmeshed in a violent street-subculture of drugs, prostitution, and exploitation. Angry and alone, she does the best she can to survive a nightmare world where she is little more than prey for pimps, older street kids, and unscrupulous adults. We can take comfort in the fact that Crystal, and this story, is fiction. Sadly, the world that Crystal inhabits is not.

The National Runaway Switchboard estimates that between 1.6 and 2.8 million youth run away each year. Many of these youth are short-term runaways acting out to call attention to a viable family in need of help. Far too many of them, however, are escaping abuse, neglect, or have simply been abandoned to fend for themselves. Out on the streets they find each other, forming a subculture that helps them to survive, but in a world to which no child…no *person*…should ever be subjected. All over the country…all over the world…children live in the culture Brandy stumbles upon, and the author has done her research well. This is, as I've said, a work of fiction…but the culture of the streets is accurately portrayed in the storyline.

For you, the story is over and I'm sure you're anxiously looking forward to Brandy's next adventure. But whether you live in an urban or rural area, not too far from you, right now, tonight, there is a Crystal, or some other adolescent girl or boy, for whom the story continues. And the closest thing they have to a Brandy in their life is a youth worker who, I promise you, is overworked and underpaid. They could both use your help. To learn what you can do, visit the InterNetwork for Youth at http://www.in4y.com and follow the Brandy Alexander fan link.

Thank you.

Jerry Fest
Author of Street Culture: An Epistemology of Street-dependent Youth

Breinigsville, PA USA
19 February 2010
232821BV00001B/1/P